FAMILY DIRT

L A David

© Copyright 2025 L.A. David

All Rights Reserved

Orange Dog Publishing values creativity and supports copyright. We encourage free speech and diverse voices. Thank you for supporting independent authors and their publications. You are encouraging others writers to take a chance and write. No part of this publication may be reproduced, stored in a retrieval system, or transmitted in any form or by any means, electronic, mechanical, photocopying, recording, scanning, or otherwise, except as expressly permitted by law, without the prior written permission of the Publisher, Orange Dog Publishing.

Library of Congress Cataloging-in-Publication Data

North Carolina: Orange Dog Publishing 2025

ISBN 9798992295863 (Hardcover)

ISBN 9798992295887 (Paperback)

ISBN 9798992295801 (ebook)

TO ALL MY FRIENDS

Thank you for listening to my stories over and over and never getting bored (or at least acting as though), you always told me I needed to write a book. This book is dedicated to all of you. I hope you read something that reminds you of my stories and the crazy times we had together. You are my family – not related by blood – thank you for believing in me.

TO THE PUBLIC LIBRARIES

Thank you for allowing a poor little girl to sit for hours reading books. As an adult, I realized you were my babysitter.

TO WEEKLY READER

Thank you for inserting your book order form, and allowing a girl with only $1 in her pocket, be able to purchase two books. I always thought I was important when my book order arrived and the teacher called my name. p.s. no one needs a cat poster

Contents

Dedication ii
1998 – Meet Me 1
1995 – Meet Anna 24
1998 – Buried Bodies 37
1998 – Rinse Repeat 51
1995 – Anna Is Missing 72
1998 – Finding Anna 94
1998 – Branches Emerge 107
1912 – Meet The Martin Family 123
1922 – Meet The Conti Family 144
1937 – One Woman's Mistake 158
1945 – Justice Is Not Fair 184
1952 – Martin Children 206
1954 – A Sons Mission 217
1956 – A Daughters Mission 237
1998 – My Broken Branch 249
1972 – Mission Completed 258
1998 – Trees Fall 265
2024 – My Tree Remains Strong 278

1998 – Meet Me

I am trying to capture a murderer, and my cell phone suddenly rings. I saw everyone take a glance at me. Yes, I forgot, I am not perfect. No way did I dare reach for it. I was in the middle of a murder simulation, and my team was sitting in the top spot of the competition. This afternoon's discussion was titled: Where Are The Tire Tracks? Or, in layman's terms, you need to find them because they are there. My hands were so sweaty that I doubted if I could even grasp my phone without it slipping through my fingers. It was so hot that I was having a difficult time paying attention and breathing simultaneously, hoping I would not pass out.

The simulation was a game of five teams, with three agents for each team. The instructors place a body (mannequin) face down in a semi-wooded area, and the teams map out how the perpetrator dumped the body and fled the scene. The team with the most correct answers recorded in the shortest time would win a prize. These simulations were designed for five days, and instructors would add new items daily. The game created interest among the agents and increased our skill levels. Since this was state-certified paid training, the prize was a free drink at a local bar or a $3 plastic trophy. But that was not the reason I wanted to win; I wanted to win because I was competitive in everything I did. I played sports most of my life, and underestimating me fueled the fire. I had a knack for winning these simulations, and this week would be no different. My team's expectations were always high because law enforcement officers knew how I played and wished they knew my strategy. They always needed to understand how I did it. You just had to think like a killer. Today, I was the killer.

I loved playing games since I was very young. The game of Clue[1] was my favorite, but I had to play as a player of one 99% of the time. Other seven-year-old girls found a Barbie more enjoyable than figuring out if it was Mr. Green with a lead pipe in the library. I will not lie, but the lead pipe was one of my favorite murder weapons. My mom thought it was bizarre that someone my age would ask for a game well above my age group. She soon realized I was a different type of child. Yes, I did have Barbie and also, Ken. I wanted Barbie for two reasons; she had a pink dune buggy and a big-ass camper. And no, I never allowed Ken to drive either of the two.

I would be the first kid in the neighborhood to search for a missing dog. Not only was it a game, but it was satisfying to see the owner's face when I returned with their pet. Since I was never allowed to have a dog (my mother hated animals), finding them gave me a feeling of worthiness. My mother did not instill that virtue in me and forgot many others. I had to earn those on my own time. Little did I realize that one day, it would not be a missing dog but a missing child.

I will always have the Anna Boyd case to remind me of how challenging and heartbreaking my job can be. That is the case that always gives me nightmares. I sensed that the Boyd case

---

[1] Clue, officially known as Cluedo, in North America, is a murder mystery game for three to six players.

was much like the game of Clue. One may have confidence that they chose the correct killer, only to find out they missed the obvious clues and pointed the finger at the wrong person. I still see a therapist due to Anna, even though the relationship with my mother primed me for PTSD[2] well before becoming a police officer.

It was mid-July, over 90 degrees, and only 1 p.m. I wouldn't say I liked summer, especially in the south. Atlanta was not one of my favorite places during this time of the year. I am not a fan of sweating, and it was not my choice to attend a training session this particular week in this city. But, like any job, I go where they assign me. All calls would have to wait. My phone vibrated more than once, and it was either my live-in partner, Syd, or her mother, Nancy, who most likely left me messages asking about the heat. They loved reminding me about the Southern heatwaves and used every opportunity to talk about it, knowing I was not born in the South.

My 65-year-old future mother-in-law was excited about everyone carrying a phone and that she could reach her daughter or myself when neither of us was home. Technology surprised her, and we had to explain how the Internet worked many times. I always answered when she called because, as a cop, I feared the worst. Someone died, or there was a medical emergency. Texting was out of the question because it was complex, pushing numbers repeatedly to get the one letter you needed. If you missed that letter, cycling through them again was complete madness. On the other hand, Syd would roll her eyes and say it was okay to let the call go to voicemail; her mother would not be offended. Nancy was more of a mother to me than my mother, so I always loved hearing from her.

---

[2] Post-traumatic stress disorder

I was an NCDOJ[3] officer, and I proudly wore that logo on my navy polo shirt, sewn in Tarheel blue over my left breast. The NCDOJ has twenty or so sworn law enforcement agents in North Carolina. We assist local, county, and state police departments when they request help. Agencies may become overwhelmed, or if a suspect committed a violent crime, they may need specific skills that our agents possess. I worked on cases ranging from missing persons to bodies found under suspicious circumstances. Cases could last from three days to three months. I am known for working hard and never giving up. I have a reputation for wanting the most burdensome investigations and never backed down once I received that phone call. These actions may not be advantageous and can backfire, so balancing on that thin line was continuous. And it was starting to take its toll.

I am one of the youngest agents, not even 40 yet. I am considered the top officer in my division. I learned to complete impeccable paperwork, which allows the state's attorney to file adequate charges and arrest suspects. I also had the art of salesmanship, where questioning possible suspects turned into the suspect admitting to the crime. When that happened, it was considered a good day. Understanding criminals and getting in their heads was not that difficult for me. Somedays, I questioned how close I was to being a criminal myself. I could see certain things when interviewing a suspect, like sitting in a dark room with a spotlight showing me where to place my focus. The blink of an eye, licking lips, looking away, fidgeting with clothes, all tales that told me I had a liar in front of me. I would take every opportunity to flaunt those insecurities and apply more pressure as the interview chugged on.

---

[3] North Carolina Department of Justice

That is why I would try to think like a killer. How would I commit the crime, hide the body, and what would I do after? I had extensive training with cadavers and was invited to many autopsies. I questioned the forensic examiners about anything remotely wrong with the body. They would shake their heads at some of my outlandish questions. My unique skill was assisting them with building a story on a body found lying in the environment for a considerable amount of time. The forensic examiners would joke that I missed my calling and that it was not too late for a second career. No, thank you, I love what I do.

Recently, I won Top Gun, posting the highest score in my team's yearly shooting range competition. Anytime I beat my supervisor, Paul, it gave me an extra bounce in my step. I only liked attention and being singled out for accolades if it was a competitive endeavor. The Boyd case showed my other side, the side that contained insecurities. News correspondents interviewed me on the Today Show and Morning America. That was three years ago, seemed like ten, and everyone reminded me how much younger I looked than my age. People would question my knowledge and my being young as the reason we had not brought Anna home. Age had nothing to do with it. Deep down, I knew the suspect or suspects had a relationship with Anna; it was not a stranger. There was insufficient evidence to get a warrant. If I was wrong, it could cost me my career and a lot of community hate. I never gave up hope that I would bring her home one day and we would tell her story. Since those days, I rarely spoke to the press. I had my connections and found ways to get them a story when it benefited us. But staying off the morning and evening news was my lifetime goal.

Even though I loved my job, seeing families and friends during their deepest and darkest pain was taking its toll. I had recently speculated if I should leave the field and turn to the academic side of the law sooner than expected. Captain Reynolds inquired via email about a position within the North Carolina State Police Academy. A vacancy would be happening later next year, and he has thoughts on how it may be a good fit for me. I have the credentials and experience, but leaving the field may be a sacrifice I am unwilling to take. Three years ago, the decision would have been easy after the Boyd case. But now, I feel comfortable in my skin with leading investigations, taking risks, and challenging local professionals to be more creative with their thought processes. I was the only woman in my division and liked being in the minority. I had not shared the email with Syd because once she read it, she would bake a cake, pop champagne, and host a party for me, all on the same day. She worries about my mental health and all the traveling that I do.

We have started laying out our ten-year plan, and Syd would like to venture toward local politics, and I wanted to support her. She was brilliant and was a master of computers and marketing via the Internet. She ran our Governor's web page two years ago, and when he was elected, he gave her credit for the win. Syd got a thank you during his acceptance speech, but so did thirty other people. Whenever I beat her in a game, she always had to say, "You may have won, but the Governor told me, thank you for his election win." She has an excellent eye for knowing what draws people towards online information and how to get them to take the bait with mouse clicks. Catchy music, colors, or dogs is her specialty. She claims people cannot ignore puppies. She had our Governor with his family and their three dogs plastered everywhere on social media. She will be finishing her PhD next year, and I would love to plan a significant trip for her out of the country, but I needed to figure out where to go. If I knew my family heritage, that could help point me to a possible continent. I did not have that luxury.

I finally returned to my air-conditioned hotel room, got out of my sweaty clothes, and jumped into a cold shower. I needed to meet my team at a local bar to get my winning drink, so I moved quicker than usual. After the shower, I grabbed my women's soccer shirt, shorts, and flip-flops. I checked my phone and had seven messages, but only two needed to be returned tonight—Syd and Nancy. Nancy first because I knew it would be quick, and she and her husband, Mack, would be heading to our house the following weekend. Nancy has a great sense of calmness due to her being a teacher for thirty years, corralling third graders. She was married to Mack for just as long; they had the best sense of humor of anyone I have ever met. Those two did not fit into the Birmingham, Alabama scene. They were two liberal teachers, a small blue dot in a very large red city. I have no relationship with my dad or very little of one, so Mack was a gift when I needed it the most. Plus, they raised a great daughter I was madly in love with. They were always open to our relationship from the word go. They were never offended that two women could love each other, much like a straight married couple.

Nancy was excited to hear from me and was checking in to see how my week was going. She asked if we needed anything before they arrived for their visit. She wanted to know about the weather and that she was bringing Syd's favorite home-cooked meal. Nancy prepared Syd's great-grandmother's spaghetti, which was also my favorite. She was storing it in special containers so we could freeze it and have it whenever our hearts desired. That was Syd's go-to meal when we needed a comfort meal. I would pick up garlic bread from the baker, grab some fresh Parmesan Reggiano, make a big salad, and we had one hell of a meal. We would chase it down with our favorite bottle of cheap white wine, a chef's kiss to end the night. I told her Syd would be happy to see them and the spaghetti. I finished the call to give Syd a quick hello before heading to the bar.

Calling Syd was always the highlight of my day, between telling her my work stories or her giving me a rundown on what happened in the neighborhood. I would call her McGruff the Crime Dog. She said it came with the perks of working from home. College was out, so no sports filled our days and nights. We lived in a divided community with three major colleges, which made it exciting, especially when neighbors were tailgating throughout the street. We would be listening to the games blasting through the speakers. Summers could be pretty dull for our community. We did miss our parties.

Syd and I met in college, have been together for eighteen years, and hope we are allowed to get married one day. I was a freshman at UNC[4] and went to a lecture hall to listen to a woman who wanted to be our next States Attorney General. I was not interested in politics, but I was passing by when I saw the crowd entering the hall and remembered seeing the flyer around campus. North Carolina never had a female Attorney General, so why not go and see if that woman might make history? Also, would they offer free food?

I sat down and took my notebook out of my backpack when I felt someone lean over my left shoulder and say, "Excuse me! Would you happen to have an extra pen that I could borrow?"

---

[4] University of North Carolina

The voice had a southern twang with a draw. I knew it was not a North Carolina accent; maybe Alabama? Soon, I realized that this could not be true. Why would someone from a Confederate State want to listen to a person running for a Democratic seat? I reached down in my bag, pulled out one of my favorite black-inked gel pens, and turned to my left to give it to the stranger with the mythical voice. My eyes locked onto Syd, and my breath left my body. This gorgeous woman was a few years older than me, with reddish brown hair and green eyes. Of course, she had a ponytail, glasses, and a light blue denim shirt.

She simply said, "Thank you." And like a fool, I stammered and replied, "You can keep it if it does the trick."

My reply horrified me, and I knew she thought I was a complete idiot. By the way, there was no evidence that her breath left her body when she first saw me.

At that moment, the lights dimmed, and the event started. All I could do was plot out how to meet the woman sitting behind me. I just wanted to slip into oblivion with that stupid ass remark I just made. I was timid and knew I would not talk to her, but in my head, I was very smooth when meeting women. My male friends would tell me this is a game they play in their heads daily. Betty Glover spoke for thirty minutes, explaining her political experience and what she could do for the state. I was not paying attention because I was working on my strategy to meet the woman holding my pen. After thirty minutes of speaking, Betty had the lights turned up and asked the audience if anyone wanted to ask her a question. And as fate would have it, that person holding my pen had a question for the speaker. Not only did I get Syd's name, her major, and her class year, but I also got the hand on my shoulder when she stood up and sat back down. Without her knowledge, I had set my plan in motion.

Syd answered on the second ring. "Hey baby, how is Atlanta? A little hot for you?" she said with a slight laugh. I could only think about Syd wearing one of her politically branded Tee-shirts, her favorite shorts, barefoot with recently pedicured toes, sitting on her distressed leather chair, legs draped over the side, with our two labs laying on the cool floor. The house would blow cold air with a 68-temperature setting on our thermostat. I knew she set it at 68 because I could not adjust it to 74.

"Atlanta is not playing nice, and I'm looking forward to coming home tomorrow."

"Did your team win, or did you allow someone else to take the prize this time."

I laughed, "You know better than that. How's the pups tonight?"

"Missing you, like their momma."

Our talk ranged from the latest episodes of our favorite series to the current political climate, vet appointments, weekend plans, and what we needed from the grocery store before her parents arrived. We said our goodnights since I needed to walk a few blocks to meet my team. Our group decided to work ten-hour days this week so we could have a half-day on Friday. It was always good news since I had about a six-hour drive from Atlanta to Chapel Hill.

Nancy and Mack would be coming into town the following weekend due to heading to Pennsylvania to visit Syd's aunt and uncle. Syd wanted to tag along, but she had a new client she needed to have face-to-face and collect a signature required on a contract. Syd working from home 90% of the time was excellent for me, given that my job had a lot of travel uncertainty. I would travel around North Carolina but would assist surrounding states when needed. I had been to Texas, Illinois, and West Virginia, and once, I was sent to North Dakota (wrong decision). I could plan accordingly just watching the news and wondering if I would receive a call. I also worked cold cases and had eight white notebooks that needed attention whenever I was at my home office. I had one purple notebook for Anna and wore that binder down much more than all the others.

The following day, I called Syd to say good morning, packed up, grabbed a muffin from the hotel breakfast bar, and my usual two cartons of chocolate milk. I finished up with the training session and started my drive northeast. I had a list of people to call, including my boss, a few friends, and my mother, Lynn. My boss was a great guy who had forty years of police work and was retiring the following year. Another reason that I was contemplating making a career move. Paul and I have been working together for the past five years, and he was my only boss in my current position. We had tremendous trust in each other, and Paul really liked Syd, which made my life less uncomfortable.

Paul explained that there was a potential case in South Carolina on a second body that was found by the state police, both in the same area, and there was a pattern linking them. He felt Jay would be next assigned if that department asked for assistance. I did not think Jay was ready for a potential serial killer investigation, but Jay was pretty sharp and didn't feel he would become unraveled getting the assignment. Paul wanted me to mentor Jay if he needed assistance with the case. Of course, I agreed. After making all my calls, I had no more excuses not to call my mother, the call I dreaded the most.

My mom picked up my call on the fifth ring, just as I was about to end the call. I always thought she answered after numerous rings because she was giving me the hope that she might not answer. I knew she had caller ID; there was no fooling my mom. We didn't have the best relationship; it always seemed strained, whether because she had me at a young age, didn't love my father, I was gay, she was adopted, or perhaps all of the above. She accepted me, but I always felt she disliked me for my "personal choice" of Syd, and yes, "personal choice" was her words, not mine.

I could hear her voice giving a slight sigh, "Where are you today?" It was never a hello or good afternoon- just right to the point. That's my mother.

"I am driving back from Atlanta after a training session."

"Did you learn anything new about finding the bad guys?"

My mom always used the term "bad guys." She was from the baby boom generation, so I am sure she picked this term up by watching Steve McQueen movies. We don't say bad guys anymore. We use the word "perp," which sounds smarter and much cooler.

"Yeah, it was pretty intense but well worth my time."

"That's good. I would like to know when you may be coming my way for a visit."

I thought that was strange since my mom never acted like she wanted to see me.

"I wouldn't mind if you brought my two granddogs with you."

My mom never allowed me to have a pet when I was growing up, but she would ask about Keaton and Ruth in every conversation. I also knew she loved the names since they were both named after two of my favorite women and hers. My mom was a die-hard Norma Rae type, where women must rise to the occasion, even if the opportunity never arose. She hoped she would see a woman in the White House one day. People probably think having such a strong woman as a mother would be exciting and pave the way for a better life for a daughter like me. My mom did not get that memo.

"I could look at my schedule and see if I have time to drive over, and you know, you are always welcome at our house. We would be glad to pay for your plane ticket."

She lived in the same house I reluctantly grew up in, right outside Columbus, Ohio. Lynn was 59 years old and became a nurse after two years of junior college. She started working on the cardiac floor when she turned 20 years old. Lynn was a nurse manager at the age of 28. She returned to college and earned her BSN[5] and Master's in Nursing Education, yet she still worked the floor as a nurse manager. I was born somewhere in between all of that and her failed marriage. She thought she loved John, and he did love her, but the two did

---

[5] Bachelor of Science in Nursing

not make a good pair. He left when I was three, and I rarely spent time with him. My dad had a drinking problem, and my mom would remind him of that every chance she got. I was their only child, so I grew up with no siblings to interact with. He now lives in Kentucky and texts during holidays or my birthday. He married again twice, unlike my mom, who never remarried. She doesn't even date. She works hard and spends time in her yard gardening, reading, and following current events through any political news she can find.

"Well, I was thinking about selling the house and wanted to start boxing things up, and you may want to look and see if anything has value before it ends up in a donation bin or the trash."

"What, why would you sell your home, and where will you live?"

I was so confused and did not understand why she suddenly wanted to sell a home she had lived in for over thirty years. It was the first and only home she ever bought and paid for.

"The market is good right now, and I was thinking of moving into a smaller home, preferably in a retirement community. They have new ones being built monthly, where everyone has to be over 60, and all have a one-story, open floor plan with a decent-sized yard. They have a pool and rec center. And it's rumored the developer will be including a community garden."

"Mom, you don't work out or go to a pool now."

"Maybe I would if one was close."

"You are 59 years old going on 45. Why would you want to live next to old people?"

" Emily, bite your tongue; they are not old."

"Mom, you are not retired and will work another ten years."

"I am not going to work another ten years." She had to know she was lying.

"I just think you need to see the full picture before jumping in and selling your home."

"I have given this much thought and started planning months ago, looking at different neighborhoods and watching the market."

That meant she had things boxed and pictures off the wall and had already met with a realtor. For a brief second, I wondered if my mom could be getting scammed and needed money.

One thing about my mom, she was very savvy. She was adopted by a couple when she was a baby and grew up with a father who was a school principal and a mother who stayed home and cared for her. They were a childless couple who could never have children. When they adopted Lynn (I have no clue if that was her real name), they were both over 40. I never got the opportunity to meet them since they both died before I was born. My mom, not even 21 years of age, had just accepted her first nursing job at a local hospital. Her nurse manager pulled her into her office to tell her there had been a car accident, and her parents were pronounced dead at the scene. Her adopted father, my grandfather, lost control while driving on black ice, crossed the center line, and struck a snow plow. They were out in the weather when they should have been home. My mom would continuously repeat that event when talking about her parents. I had no clue if the story was true, but I had no reason not to believe her. Ironically, they were returning from the local mall, buying a gift for my mother's birthday, which was the following week. She was an only child, and now she had no parents. They did not leave much, even though they were thrifty. My mom sold their home and put the money into a retirement fund. She kept a small amount to buy her first home and, eventually, her new car.

"Can I call you later next week after I check our schedules?"

"Sure, you know, Syd is welcome to come too."

I would always hold my breath when she said Syd's name. She never understood why someone chose to be gay. She eventually came around and appeared to like Syd, but deep down, I knew she felt Syd was the reason I was gay. My mom never wanted grandchildren and most likely didn't want to have children herself. I didn't fight it and felt I had Syd's parents who treated me like I was their daughter. This upset my mother. Two women loved her daughter more than she did. My mom was so petty that she would always spell Syd's name with a C, just to be indifferent. Due to that, I would never display her Christmas card with all the others we received. If Nancy were in town for the holidays, she would look at all the cards sent to us and ask if my mom sent a card, and I would reply that my mom doesn't do cards.

"Syd has been busy, but I will ask. I will call you in a few weeks, and we agree on dates I could drive over, spend some time with you, and visit the old neighborhood."

"Ok, that would be nice. The neighbors always ask about you after seeing you on television. That little girl was the talk of the town for a long time. Call me in a few days."

And the line went dead.

My mom never ended a phone call with the words love you, miss you, or anything else that would make me feel like she was my mom. But she was, and I still worried about her with her demanding job and living alone, sometimes like a hermit. She always found a way to make me feel worse after talking to her. And once again, she didn't ask about Syd or our home, but most of all, she found a way to bring up the Boyd case. Again, she was purposely getting under my skin because she could. I have always wanted to know what makes her tick, but I have no barometer. She was an only child, adopted, and I had no evidence of who her family was or how they lived. Syd and I would talk about this many times, usually over wine. It was the one thing that bothered me the most. Not having closure on our ancestors.

Arriving home was always a great feeling, and opening the door was where two big Labrador Retrievers were waiting to see me. Our town had just been hit with a small storm earlier that morning, and it was now a light rain and a few hints of thunder. Syd had opened the windows, and I could smell the rain throughout the house, one of my favorite scents. Listening to the slight sound of a thunderstorm made it even better. Syd was talking to a coworker when she heard me come in. She yelled at me to come to the office; she was on a call with someone who wanted to say hi.

" Emily!" I heard my name being yelled by a familiar voice through the speakerphone.

I let out a big laugh and knew Alice very well. She lived in Chicago, and whenever we would travel to the windy city, we would meet up and eat some great pizza.

"Hey Alice, how are the kids?" Alice had two boys, one ten and one thirteen, who were very active in hockey.

"Growing and keeping me busy. When are you two coming back to Chicago for a visit? The boys want to see their favorite aunts, Emily and Syd."

I looked at Syd, who had that pretty-please look on her face, and I was sure it was either due to one of the Chicago sports teams or deep-dish pizza.

"We could plan a long weekend getaway, maybe this Fall or Winter." Syd smiled, and I was sure she would want Blackhawk tickets. "We have a few things to plan for. I have my mom's 60th birthday to consider, and Syd's parents may be coming in during the holidays."

Then Alice said the curse words, "What are you getting your mom for her big 6-0?"

Syd busted out laughing, and we just looked at each other.

"Alice, we need to end this conversation because it will take me months to figure out what would make that woman happy. What do you get a woman that needs nothing?"

Alice laughed out loud because she already knew my mother was difficult to buy for and never celebrated birthdays, but if you missed calling her or sending a card, it would be a disaster.

We said goodbye to Alice, and Syd let out a laugh, "I can tell you spoke to Lynn today."

"I did, and she is thinking of selling the house."

"What! Lynn wants to move? Like actually move to another area?"

"Yeah, in a retirement area, a smaller home not yet built."

"Wow, I am just really shocked because I thought she would die in that house."

"So, did I. She asked if I would drive over and look at some of the things that I may have left at her house before they ended up in a donation bin."

"What would you still have there, old softball trophies?"

"Maybe, but I certainly am not worried about it. But you know what I am worried about? Getting a good pizza for dinner."

"Let me make a call, and we can load up the girls to pick it up."

For a change, the week was slow, but not for the nightmares that continued to haunt me. I would often wake up and realize after a few seconds that I was in a dream, but within minutes, I could no longer remember the dream. I knew it was about Anna but could not put the pieces back together. Ruth would wake me, laying her head on my mouth or giving me a lick on the face. Syd could sleep through a disco party, so her waking before me was always low odds. I did not have the heart to tell Syd that the dreams were back, even though they never really left. Three long years of having Anna visiting me created a loss of sleep and tremendous anxiety. This was why we got Ruth.

Syd felt the house had been without a dog for too long due to Lucca passing away. She thought we were both depressed with his passing, and she wanted me to get a bigger dog, a lab, to match my personality. Ruth matched Syd's much more than mine but attached herself to me as if we were made for each other. Then Keaton came, and she was the class clown and doofus of the family. Ruth, black, and Keaton, a fox red, made a stunning pair. Those two have been a great comfort to me. They brought normalcy to my life when work offered much stress and uncertainty.

I would have the same dream continuously or the same part of that dream. I used to keep a pen and paper beside my side of the bed to write down anything I remembered when I woke up in the middle of the night. My therapist told me this would help me put structure to my dreams. I had to eventually stop doing this because it was a sign to Syd that I was still having nightmares about Anna. The dreams would mainly consist of a young girl being lost in a very dark place, and she was calling my name over and over. I would get closer to her by listening to where her voice was coming from. When the voice could no longer be heard, it would be followed by a loud bang. It was not loud enough to startle me awake, but in my dream, I knew it was loud because I would cover my ears. I would yell Anna's name over and over even though I had never seen Anna other than in a school picture. Neither did I know her voice. Yet, these dreams were of her, and I knew that without being told. Some nights, I would get closer to the voice but always wake up before I found her. I would have less than a minute to capture my dream on paper, scribbling in the dark, hoping to decipher it later if I could make out my horrible handwriting.

The therapist tried to explain that these dreams would most likely continue because the case was still open, and deep down, I needed to solve it. I had the suspicion that it was one of Anna's family members. We did not have enough evidence to prove it. All had alibi's and confirmation of those. The district attorney did not want to charge anyone in case the wrong person might be prosecuted. Or it was the right person, and they were found not guilty and never charged again due to double jeopardy. West Virginia seems to move at a slower speed than most states. And the thought that someone would harm a little girl for no reason was unimaginable.

The weekend finally arrived, and we welcomed Nancy and Mack to our home. They have often stayed with us, and we always loved their visits. Since they would only be with us for one night, I went to the butcher and bought prime fillets. Nancy and Syd were responsible for the baked potatoes, side salads, and strawberry shortcakes. I sautéed some mushrooms and onions as well as asparagus on the grill. All of that, with a few bottles of our favorite cheap wine, beer for Mack, we believed we were eating a feast like no one else could compare to. We soon moved to our fire pit, sitting in a circle to catch up and talk about family. I explained that I would be taking a side trip to my mom's because she was possibly selling the house. Nancy was shocked and asked if my mom had met someone. After choking on my drink, I explained no, and it was due to the market and her wanting to downsize.

"Emily, isn't her home small to start with?" stated Mack.

"It is around 1800 square feet, but it is a two-story, and she is interested in a ranch-style home."

" Does she want to stay in the same area, or does she want to move closer to you?"

Again, we laughed.

"My mother still has not really accepted Syd and me, and you know that."

Nancy touched my arm and said, "I know, but we always hoped one day, as your mother got older, maybe she would see how happy you are."

"My mom never cared about my happiness, that will never change. She will soon be 60, and a side of me has just given up, hoping she would not resent me."

"Oh, that's right, your mom is hitting the big 60!"

"Yes, and the older she gets, the unhappier she is," said Syd.

I agreed with Syd and looked at Mack. In a playful voice, I said, "Too bad she had never met a man who could make her happy."

"That stud is all mine," Nancy laughed as she got up, walked over, and sat in his lap.

Mack looked at me, reached over, and grabbed my hand.

"Darling, maybe if you knew more about your mother and her kin, you would understand what makes her tick."

"That is true, but my mother never really wanted to find out about her biological parents or grandparents. She felt that it would make no difference, so why dwell on it."

"Wouldn't you like to know where your family came from or when they arrived in the States, and maybe why they had to put a child up for adoption?"

Syd agreed, smiling, and said, "I would love to know what country my future wife came from, and let's hope she has family in Australia! We need a nice long vacation." I made a mental note that Australia could make an excellent graduation gift. It would be fun to bring her family and enjoy kangaroos and the koalas. Then I realized the cost of a trip to Australia, and maybe I could tell Syd I am Canadian.

When everyone was asleep that night, Syd was snoring due to a shortcake coma, and her parents were fast asleep upstairs. I was the only one wide awake. I snuck out of the bedroom, leaving the door cracked so the two-night watchwomen could follow if they liked. I went to the office, pulled out the well-worn purple binder, and headed to the other side of our home. We built a screened-in porch that was as long as the side of the entire house. We put a hot tub and many plants in the room, with some nice outdoor furniture. It was like a tropical island when the ceiling fans were powered above. It was the best place to be in the entire home. Listening to the tree frogs never got old, and a neighborhood owl made sure I heard her voice. Syd loved the air conditioning, but I did not. I curled up on the sofa, put on my reading light draped around my neck, and opened the purple binder with the words A. Boyd on the spine. I started back down the rabbit hole, even though I knew better.

1995– Meet Anna

Anna was a fifth grader living in West Virginia with her brother, Jim Jr., who went by JR, and sister, Marigold, who were twins in the seventh grade. Her dad, Jim Sr., worked at a nonunion bottling company, and her mother, Daisy, worked at the grade school as an office clerk, the same school her children attended. Jim and Daisy have been married for over fifteen years and have lived in the same home since their wedding night. They got married in their late 20s; Daisy was an introvert, while Jim was a rebel, arrested for misdemeanors, shooting out windows with a pellet gun, and drinking while driving. They knew each other from high school, but only in passing. Jim saw Daisy at a local outdoor concert and invited her to sit with him and his friends. That night, Jim gave Daisy a kiss, and she thought she hit the lottery. It was Daisy's first kiss she had ever received, along with her first boyfriend crush, and all happened on the same night. What a lucky girl.

Jim lived with his parents and moved Daisy home on their wedding night. Jim's parents moved once the twins were born. Both parents are no longer alive; both died from cancer. Jim's grandparents once lived in a home on the back of the property, now a dilapidated structure, or ramshackle as they called it. The family called it "the shabby." The grandparents moved, when they became of ill health, to a state nursing home, where they later both passed. The Boyd's lived in Crab Orchard, West Virginia, a tiny community often ignored by government and state funding. The residents wanted it that way; less politics meant leaving them alone and letting them be free. If they only knew their local leaders were lining their pockets with much of that funding that was meant for them. Maybe they already knew that and didn't care. They consistently voted for the same politicians and never welcomed change. The local police force was a nightmare and offered little value to the community.

It was rural America, where homes or double-wide trailers were located about a quarter of a mile from each other. Residents lived in their homes forever, with new tenants rarely moving in or out (unless due to death). Jobs were scarce, and driving the ninety miles one way to the bottling company was too far for some to commute. They considered that the best-paying job for adults with a high school diploma or GED. It paid $5.10 per hour. The same job in a union shop would earn $9.32 per hour, with benefits. The kids who lived in Crab Orchard did not receive health or dental care. They would only seek emergency room trips if they were bleeding to death or had a broken bone that was sticking out of the skin. The bottling job beat working in a coal mine, and Jim Boyd was not a man who wanted to work too hard. He sat on his ass and watched the bottles move down an assembly line, reporting if a bottle was missing, broken, or fell to the floor. He was considered a quality inspector despite requiring no quality skills. He would never leave that job; it fit his attitude perfectly.

There was one grade school in town, while the high schoolers had to bus at least thirty to forty minutes north to a larger community. Many of the adults were unemployed, and spent their time, talking about each other. If there were not enough juicy stories being circulated, someone would start a new rumor. They were living in their 90's version of Peyton Place. It could be plucked out of its current state and set back into the 1950s.

I knew the story like the back of my hand. There was no reason to open the binder, but looking at the pictures taken of the Boyd property allowed me to find creative ways to look at each image differently. Anna was a shy kid just entering fifth grade. Her brother was the basketball team star the prior year as a sixth grader, and her sister was a popular cheerleader. Anna dreamed of following in her sister's footsteps and becoming a cheerleader. She was so excited when school started in August because cheerleader tryouts would be happening soon. The basketball season began in late October, and Anna had the dates circled on the family calendar posted on their refrigerator. Anna knew being a cheerleader would make her family proud because her parents never missed one of JR's games. Many weekends, the older Boyd children were allowed to have their friends come to their home to play or hang out. JR would take his friends outside, while Marigold would practice cheers with her friends. Anna was never allowed to be with the older children, so she became a loner and found happiness in books. She became an avid reader and spent time at the public library. Daisy would drop Anna off numerous times there while she ran errands.

The librarian knew Anna well and would give her suggestions on what books to check out. According to the librarian, Miss Graham, Anna loved to read about horses and dogs. She stated that Anna was a good child, intelligent, and had impeccable manners but was very shy. Miss Graham reported that Anna was usually unkempt, had wrinkled clothes, and sometimes had an unpleasant odor. She always had a purple ribbon in her hair, and the librarian staff wondered if the little girl only owned one ribbon, so she wore it repeatedly.

When Mrs. Boyd would come inside to get Anna, Miss Graham noticed she always looked disheveled. Her hair was a mess, and she acted jittery. She had never met Mr. Boyd but had heard around town that he was a drinker and abuser. Miss Graham reported that if she had ever seen a mark on Anna, she would have reported it immediately. She claimed she would have loved for Anna to come and stay with her because she thought the little girl was living in a bad family situation. She should have elaborated on what she meant by that comment but was not asked to.

Anna's parents treated her well, never worried about her, and probably wouldn't even notice if she wasn't home, other than being absent at the dinner table. She always did what she was told and was rarely in trouble. All three kids understood they had to listen to their parents, and the rumor was that their father would use a belt if not. If people around town were asked about Anna Boyd, they most likely would reply, "Oh, that little girl, she doesn't talk. I think there is something wrong with her."

I heard a noise, looked over, and saw Ruth staring at me. She came over, jumped on the sofa, and laid her big head on my thigh. I looked at her and said, "It will be okay; I know better." I could hear my whispered voice cracking, and I could not believe my words.

It was the second week of October, and Anna was excited about cheerleading tryouts. Fifth graders could not be on the team but could come to tryouts. If the coaches thought they were good enough, they would let them dress for games after mid-season. Mrs. Wilson was a stickler and never broke the rules when coaching the cheerleading team. If any fifth-grade girl made the team, it would be one girl or none.

It was a Wednesday, and Anna was supposed to sit and watch her sister's team tryouts in the school gym at 3:15 p.m. JR would be at his tryouts on the opposite end of the gym. All the boys made the team because they did not have that many boys who wanted to play basketball since they lived in football country. Daisy had to stay later than usual due to a monthly PTO meeting starting at 5 p.m. She had to prepare the meeting room and could leave before the event began. PTO would be an open invitation for a woman with three children who went to the same school where she worked. But Daisy knew better. Jim would be home shortly after 6 p.m., and she had to have dinner on the table. That was the rule, and all the children had to be present. Jim would remind Daisy that she needed to think of him since he was the one paying the bills, and she would never be able to care for herself without him. Daisy would get all the kids rounded up after their practices and get home as fast as possible. She put a roast and potatoes in the crockpot that morning so everything would be ready when she arrived home.

Around 2 p.m., Daisy was told the cheerleading tryouts for the 5th graders were canceled. The coach wanted to avoid the fifth-grade girls sitting and watching due to the number of kids in the gym. Daisy knew Anna would be heartbroken because she was so excited that morning, and that was all she could talk about on the way to school. Daisy called Anna to the office and explained why fifth graders would not be staying for cheerleading practice. Anna was upset but understood she could sit and watch tryouts the following afternoon. Anna did not want to stay until five since she could not sit in the gym. Nor did she want to sit in the office with her mother. She asked if she could stay in the library, but the library had to be closed due to the carpets getting cleaned that afternoon.

Anna wanted to go home and watch Barney, her favorite television show. Daisy knew the bus driver would drop her daughter off about a quarter of a mile from their home, and Anna had walked that route before, but never alone. Henry was the nearest neighbor, and he would walk with her to their home and onto his. Henry was in sixth grade and very dependable. Daisy knew Henry was in class that day because she saw him. This was a fatal error made by Daisy.

Anna proudly jumped on the bus and headed home around 3:10 p.m. The only problem was that Henry was not riding the bus that day. His mother was picking him up from school. Henry had a less-than-perfect vision and had worn glasses since the first grade. He had an eye checkup later that day. Had he been with Anna, the case would have been solved.

The bus driver, Allen Springer, dropped Anna off, told her to go right home, then made a three-point turn on Apple Blossom Lane and started back in the direction he came from

Pemberton Road. Springer recalled seeing Anna walking down the road towards her home when he looked in his rear-view mirror. There was no traffic or other cars seen during that time. Springer believed Anna was dropped off around 4:10 p.m. because they had to stop for a train; she was the day's last stop. Springer would soon change his story because he was nervous and did not know when he dropped her off or returned to the bus barn. A black man getting questioned by white police officers about a missing, little white girl would do that to someone. He would later be fired and would move from the area due to the speculation that followed with this case.

Luck would have it; basketball practice ended early. JR yelled over to his sister, Marigold, and told her to tell their mom he was getting a ride home with Wade, another basketball player. JR hated sprints; the coach always ended his practice with them. The coach did not on that day, so JR grabbed his jacket and headed out the door before the coach changed his mind. He turned to see Marigold's face, and she shot him a look that their mother would be mad. JR did not care; his mother knew there was not much she could do to him; he had his father's name. Something Jim Sr. liked to brag about quite often. JR was unaware that Wade's mom, Phyllis, had to stop at the local Piggly Wiggly to pick up a few items for dinner. This would add time to their trip home. The basketball coach, Mr. Mitok, believed he ended practice around 3:45 p.m. Phyllis reported it, more like 4 p.m., that she arrived at the gym to tell Wade to wait for her and that she would return to pick him up after she finished shopping. It was just a fluke that the practice ended early so Wade could go to the supermarket with her. Both Wade and JR ran to Phyllis's car in the parking lot to hitch a ride before she could leave the school grounds. The boys stayed in the car during the trip, and no one remembers seeing them, but they do remember Phyllis because she asked for chewing tobacco for her husband. They were out of his favorite brand, so the manager had to locate more in his office. JR was eventually dropped off at home around 4:45 p.m. at the end of his driveway.

Marigold met her mom in room 113 and told her that JR had gone home early. Daisy was happy because that meant her youngest child would not be home alone. They finished setting up the room together, and Daisy stated in her police interview that they left the school a few minutes before 5 p.m.

Daisy drove down their white rocked driveway to their home around 5:15 p.m. She went to the kitchen while Marigold went right to her room. She could smell the roast, which made her happy that dinner would not be a chore tonight. Daisy got busy setting the table and cleaning the green beans. Around 5:30 p.m., she started calling out for JR and Anna. She yelled through the house and heard no answer, so she went out the back door and started yelling their names.

Their property was around three acres, mostly wooded. The shabby was about a mile straight out the back door and a few yards east. The kids knew not to visit due to glass on the floors, a partial roof that had fallen in, and many different rodents living in the filth. The Boyd's kids heard the same stories, over and over, on how stepping on a rusty nail could kill them if they did not have their tetanus shot. Adults claimed the needle was over eight inches long and had to be given in the butt. That meant they would have to take their pants down in front of a nurse. Scare tactics by parents rarely worked with kids like JR, who still found a way to linger there without his parents knowing he made frequent visits. He would also take his friends there to show he was not scared. Kids made up stories that the place was haunted. The shabby took on a life of its own, and kids used it in their stories as a rite of passage. If a kid never got invited to the shabby, they were not popular enough to be asked.

The other side of their property had a barb-wired fence where the neighbors had three horses. The Boyd's were not friends with that family due to the color of their skin. Jim Sr. was very upset when they purchased the land and boarded horses so close to his property: the double whammy, black skin, and livestock. Anna was known to steal an apple and walk a quarter of a mile over to the horses even though she was not allowed to do so. Daisy would watch her daughter break the rules and walk the entire route there and back. Rocket was her favorite, and he was the lucky horse to get the apple. He was a beautiful chestnut-colored horse with a long, flowing blond mane and tail. The fence's top strand was electric, so Anna knew she could not cross that barrier. An inviting creek could be seen on their neighbor's property. Anna loved the water, and Daisy was always afraid that Anna could get hurt since she did not know how to swim. The creek was not deep, but the water could get chest-high on her little body if a major storm erupted. Daisy wanted Anna to have some freedom, and as long as she could see her, she felt Anna would be safe from harm.

After calling her children's names half a dozen times, with no kids in sight, Daisy went into the house and noticed nothing had been touched in the living room. The television remote and pillows were left the same way from the night before. She did not see Anna's backpack or shoes, almost as if she never arrived home. JR had his backpack on his bed, so she knew he had been home. He must have changed clothes and shoes because his school clothes were lying on his bed. It was getting closer to 6 p.m., so her husband would be dropped off soon at the end of their driveway. Daisy started to worry.

Jim Sr. came home a little after 6 p.m. Marigold and JR sat at the dining room table while Daisy prepared dinner in the kitchen. Jim wanted to know what the kids learned today at school, and history told them they had better have at least one thing to report, or they would go to bed hungry, with a sore ass. When Jim asked where Anna was, Marigold told her dad about cheerleading practice and how they will have new cheers this year.

"Anna's practice was canceled, so she rode the bus home after school. She may have gone to Henry's to play until I got home."

"Did you call his parents?"

"I tried but got no answer."

"Where were you two, after school, that you did not see your sister?"

JR said he got home late and went back to play on the rope swing.

Marigold said she rode home with her mother and went to her room to start homework.

Jim looked at JR, ignoring Marigold, and said, "You better not be using that ladder off that big hickory tree so you can go farther out, over that gully. If I go back there, I had better not find that old wooden ladder next to that tree. You know you are not supposed to be out there without someone with you. You could fall off that rope, and we would never find you!"

Jim looked at Daisy and said, "So, what will you do? Just hope she shows up."

Daisy said, "Where else would she go?"

The family ate dinner in silence. Jim started to get worried since it was around 6:30, and Anna was still missing. He would never admit she was not his favorite child because he always wanted boys and blamed Daisy for birthing two girls. Yet, he did not want anything bad to happen to his children.

"When she gets home, she is getting her ass whooped," said Jim.

Daisy pleased, "Please, Jim, let's not get mad. I will drive to Henry's house and ask if she came home off the bus."

"Well, get off your ass and go now. It ain't going to hurt you to miss a meal."

She put on her jacket since the sun had gone down and it was getting brisk. She got in the car and started backing down their driveway when she noticed Jim Sr. out in the back of the property, yelling Anna's name. Daisy knew she would not be in the back of the property because her youngest daughter was scared of her shadow. She would never go in the woods without her brother or sister. Daisy knew she needed to find Anna before her husband did, or he would beat her for wasting his night looking for her. He always took advantage of every opportunity to use his belt on the girls. She also wanted to check the horses because Anna loved them and may have gone into the pen to try and pet them. Highly unlikeable, but Daisy was getting scared. What if someone picked her and Henry up on the road? That may be why they are not answering their phone.

Daisy sped up the road and saw lights on in Henry's house. She banged on the door until someone answered and saw Henry coming to the door.

"Hi, Mrs. Boyd, nice to see you."

Henry's mom, Juanita, came to the door.

"Hi Daisy, is something wrong?"

Daisy stammered, shifted her feet, and looked down at Henry.

"Did you walk home from the bus with Anna today?"

Juanita chimed in, "He didn't ride the bus today. He had an eye appointment."

Daisy felt lightheaded like everything was spinning, and she put her hand out on the door to steady herself. The blood drained from her face.

She turned around and started heading for her car.

Juanita shouted out, "What's wrong?"

Daisy yelled, "Call the police and have them come to my house. Tell them my daughter is missing."

Henry screamed, "Mrs. Boyd, what do you mean Anna is missing? She was at school today."

When Daisy returned home, Jim sat on the couch, reading the newspaper. He wanted to know why Anna was not with her.

She told her husband what she learned and that the police would be arriving to help find her.

Jim wailed, "What did you say? You called the police without asking me?" His voice was angry, and Daisy knew he could not hit her with the police coming.

"We need to find our daughter!" she screamed back at him.

At that time, Jim called the children from their rooms.

"The police are coming, and I want you two to stay in your rooms. Do not speak to them if they speak to you. I am not going to have my kids interrogated like criminals."

Daisy said, "We need their help; we need to know if they saw anything."

"What could they say? They were not here with her; they know nothing, and I will not be embarrassed whenever I go to town."

The kids got sent to their room, and Daisy started crying.

Fifteen minutes later, two cops showed up: a local county officer named Larry Emery and a state trooper, Jerry Gray. Trooper Gray had been in the area talking to Emery about an accident on the interstate the day before, and it was by chance that he was in their town. Daisy hoped that was a good sign.

1998 – Buried Bodies

I felt Ruth start snoring as I flipped through the binder pages. It was 3:33 a.m., and I knew I had to stop and return to bed. I started getting sleepy, so I laid the binder down, stretched out with Ruthie, and fell asleep.

I woke up around 7 a.m. with someone staring at me. It was Nancy. She saw the binder and was holding my hand.

"Are you okay?"

"Good morning, and yes, I just needed to take another look."

"I am sure that little girl knows you are doing your best, and you will catch the bastard."

"Thank you, but what do you say? I put this notebook back, and you and I take the girls for a walk to the coffee shop?"

"Good deal because Mack and I must be on the road soon. Let's let those two sleep, get their coffee, and you and I can have some alone time."

"You read my mind."

I wondered if Nancy knew how much I loved her as a person, not just as a future mother-in-law.

We said goodbye to Mack and Nancy, started our Sunday afternoon yard work, listened to music, and talked about everything we wanted to do with our week. Within a few hours, my cell phone rang, and it was my boss. He wanted to let me know another body was found in South Carolina, and I was requested to travel down to the town and give the troopers a hand. I asked if Jay was having a difficult time or if they just needed more boots on the ground. Paul claimed that my expertise would help greatly but I need to allow Jay to run the investigation. I may need to stay a week or two, but Jay would stay longer if needed. Syd could hear my conversation, and we had already discussed the probability of me having to go. The plan was to drive down on Tuesday after a long weekend at home. The drive will be easy, just under three hours, south to a little town called Marion—a town of a few thousand and one apparent serial killer.

Jay met me at the local motel where he was staying, and now I have that same benefit: a low-budget room. It was 8:30 a.m., and we headed to a coffee shop to grab some caffeine. Jay had to explain not to expect breakfast because they only offer coffee. Who names a coffee shop, Grind and Dine, when they serve no breakfast? Jay also explained that they don't take credit cards, so he could spot me if I needed cash. He didn't understand that women were always prepared, and we were taught to carry money in case of emergencies. Today, coffee was that emergency. It seemed strange that a town this small would have a serial killer moving around amongst them, not being seen, which was a sign that this case might be more difficult than I thought.

We first visited the coroner so I could view the bodies. There were four, all white, with no hands, feet, or heads. Paul didn't tell me that tidbit. There were two men and two women, and guessing at the look of the torsos, I would say they ranged from 70 to 80 years of age. There was no cause of death since the bodies showed no trauma other than missing parts. I collected notes and asked the coroner basic questions about the community and past criminal behavior. He looked to be around 72 years of age and was a great historian. In a community with no crime, people leave their doors unlocked and garages open. Suspicious cars and strangers never pass through the area. He laughed and said that the motel probably hadn't seen a visitor all summer, and now they have two. I immediately started thinking of the movie *Psycho*.

The last unnatural death was the drowning of a 12-year-old playing in a local creek after a significant downpour. He dove in head first, striking his head on a large boulder, but was conscious and continued to play in the water. His friends claimed he seemed fine, rubbed his head, and just said it hurt. About ten minutes later, he was found lying face down in three feet of water. The community was shocked, and it took months for the family to accept that their son was dead and that no one was at fault except himself.

All the bodies were located in an open field off the main route that passed through town. The field was deep, almost two hundred yards wide one way by one mile wide the other. There were many old palmetto trees spread throughout the field. All bodies were buried, but by the naked eye, one would not know that detail. The person who placed the bodies took the grass and weeds off in a layer, dug the hole, and then, after refilling the hole, laid the grass or weeds back over the hole. A serial killer who takes the time to uncover, dig, and cover back up. A serial killer who takes the chance of dumping bodies off a route where they could be seen. Why would they take that much time and care? They would have to park and drag the bodies or drive back into the area. At night, they would need a light that anyone passing by would see. With a town this small, someone would notice strange lights or vehicle lights in the dark.

The town had no police, fire department, hospital, late-night restaurants, or bars. Meaning that not many were moving around at night. I asked Jay what his thoughts were. He motioned over to the area where orange plastic numbers were sitting in the grass, with yellow caution tape boxed around trees, the site of the burials. Three state troopers remained on site looking for more bodies due to such a large area that needed to be searched. We walked from location one to location four, and Jay described each body unearthed from the area. He read his notes verbatim and did a great job. And yes, it was hot.

It was my turn to ask the questions.

"Jay, I don't understand how the first body was found," pointing to marker number one in the distance.

"Funny story: a guy needed to let his dog out to pee while traveling through the area. The dog was on a 50-foot lead, so the guy, Mr. Bobbie Sever, took the dog for a walk into the field after parking his car off the road (pointing over my shoulder). About 50 yards in, the dog took a dump and then kicked his feet. Sever saw a huge divot fly off his dog's feet. Being a golfer, Sever thought it odd to have a large divot fly out of the ground. He went over to the hole his dog made, put his fingers in the hole, and pulled out more dirt, which was in a large clump the size of a softball. He then got a whiff of the air and knew right away it was a dead body."

"Ok, please tell me how he knew that?"

"Mr. Sever was an infantry soldier in Nam during the war."

"Did we get all the information to talk to him again?"

"Yes, and his story was pretty believable. He resides in Florida and was returning home after attending a recent antique car show."

"You know my next question," as I tilted my head and gave him that look.

Jay said, "How did we find the next body?"

I shook my head yes.

"The state police were called, and their trooper had a cadaver dog. When he arrived, he started walking the area, and the dog went to that spot (pointing over my other shoulder), sat down, and barked."

"Interesting that the state came in with some extra help."

"Yes, and they found the other two bodies within 24 hours. We called all the communities around us, and no one has found hands, feet, or heads. We put a bulletin out to the surrounding states."

Jay then asked the question, "Your thoughts?"

I sighed, then said, "This isn't a serial killer."

Jay gave me a surprised look and said, "Will we be placing a bet on this one?"

"Oh yes, and I think we should go big this time, maybe more than a cold drink?"

"I gotchya, let's do this."

Within two days, we found no additional bodies, but after the coroner completed all four examinations, he was perplexed and could find no injuries. The bodies appeared only to be missing parts. The victims did not have their hands, feet, or heads cut off while they were still alive. He could tell by the blood flow or lack of it. This means these people were already dead and then had all the cuts completed. The cuts were all clean, and it appears an electric saw was used, or the killer could have access to a bone saw. The heads were taken at the top of the neck, hands at the top of the wrists, and feet right at the top of the ankle. All cuts matched each other but appeared to happen at different times. He did not believe the four had cuts made on the same day because he could tell they died at various times. Their stomachs were all full; one female had a hip deformity, so he believed she used a wheelchair. The order of death was male, male, female, and lastly, female with hip distortion. The first male had been dead for over six months, and the last female, most likely only three weeks. He said he was guessing because he had never worked with bodies in this manner. The state was sending a top-notch forensic pathologist, Benita Jackson, from Texas, who would arrive later that afternoon. This crime was her expertise.

I had an idea, so I asked Jay to find Yellow Pages for the surrounding counties and meet me back in my motel room. Jay and I searched every telephone book and started internet searches for nursing homes. I purchased a $3 state map from the local gas station, taped it to the wall in my hotel room, and drew a perfect one-hundred-mile perimeter circle around where the bodies were found. My thought was that there was a nursing home that was keeping a secret. When a resident died, the coroner would not receive a call, and the bodies were removed without them being reported to authorities. It was a crazy thought, but the nursing home owner could continue collecting social security and pension checks as usual.

Jay thought I had lost my mind, but the story was believable. The four deceased would not have family or visitors, which could be a prerequisite on how the facility owners chose who got a room. Residents would die, be removed from the premises, and be buried, with no obituary placed in the local papers. The body parts could be placed in an incinerator, but then why wouldn't the suspect get rid of the entire body in the same manner? That told me the killer didn't know where one was located. I put that on my list as a possible avenue to investigate. I also put on my checklist to review state nursing licenses. Nursing homes would have at least one nurse and would also need a physician order for medications. That made the checklist as well. It was apparent why the hands, feet, and heads had been removed. It would make it challenging to identify the bodies if or when they were found. That would also give time for the killer to skip town before police closed in. The killer would have to find another way to dispose of the appendages, including deep water, wood chipper, buried in other locations, etc. I put wood chipper rental places on my list.

We contacted the state police officers working with us and explained our thoughts. We divided into three groups, leaving one state officer at the scene with the forensic pathologist, and headed out the following day with our lists of nursing homes. Jay and I took the furthest nursing homes on our map, about a two-hour drive west. We also did not want to stretch the state police since they lacked resources. We chose three nursing homes fifty miles apart, which would take most of our day to investigate their records. We started our drive to a tiny community located in Florence, SC. I had yet to learn if any of these smaller nursing homes were still in business, so it was a guess if this would be a waste of time.

Everything next was like a bad dream.

We pulled into a gravel parking lot facing the front door of a small reddish-brown, brick building. A side door was off the left wing of the building, with an adjoining sidewalk leading into the same parking lot, about 75 yards away. Jay and I had difficulty believing this was a nursing home and wondered if we had the correct address. The sign hanging out front was made of wood and was very weathered. I could barely distinguish the words Bellwood N.H. I assumed N.H. meant nursing home. I was starting to second guess myself and thought this would lead to a boondoggle.

I returned to my printouts and found the Bellwood Nursing Home, with an address of 502 W. Freemont St. The building had that same address printed in big white letters on the glass transom over the front door. We noticed one car in the parking lot, a new, very shiny, black Cadillac that was parked to the left on the other side of the sidewalk. The grounds could have looked better kept. The grass needed a cut, and I saw weeds against the exterior brick wall. How depressing for someone to be a resident here or visit a loved one. I wondered if this was a nursing home, a business that laundered drugs, or a betting parlor.

We were in Jay's unmarked white Tahoe, with no plate on the front bumper, wearing khakis, navy polo shirts with our badges worn around our necks. Our guns were visible on our waists, so people understood we were police officers. We asked for a state trooper to meet us for our safety and to deal with management at the nursing homes. We sat in the car, drinking our coffee, waiting on the trooper, who had called us and said she was only a few miles down the road. We could barely see through the glass double doors in front of the building and witnessed no movement, coming in or out. We saw a sign on the front glass that read, ALL VISITORS MUST SIGN IN. I found that strange because I could only imagine a few visitors and the administration had to inform them to sign in, telling me no one was at the front door to greet visitors. Jay and I talked trash about our college football teams since the season would start soon. He was a fan of Florida State, and I was a fan of UNC. Both in the Atlantic Coast Conference, so last season, we always had side bets, and I was happy that Paul finally hired someone who followed sports as much as I did.

Jay announced, "The trooper just turned the corner, and she's hung up at the stop sign with a farm tractor in front of her." He could see the squad car as he looked out the rear-view mirror. He shut the car off, which stopped the air conditioning, and we started to exit as the heat hit us all at once. I heard Jay groan, and I remembered laughing to myself. I think I mumbled something like, "Stop being so soft."

I don't know how something can happen so fast but play out in slow motion. I heard a noise, like a door being opened, with the hinges letting out a loud, long squeak. The sound made me turn to my left. Jay still had his car door open, sitting in the driver's seat, and he looked to his left after hearing the same loud noise. I was ready to ask if he heard the noise as I exited the car. I remember gravel being tossed around me, which was the trooper pulling up off to my right. We did not turn towards the trooper and must have taken for granted that it was her.

The trooper told me later that she could tell something was wrong because we were not looking at the front door of the building but instead were looking to our left. The trooper was putting her car in park when I heard Jay yell, "He's got a gun." Everything stopped for me at that moment. Who has a gun? Why would anyone need a gun? Does someone think we are trespassing? A hundred thoughts raced through my mind. My last thought was, *Am I going to die today?*

I saw an older white male, around 65 or so, aiming a long, black gun at us, and he was shooting as he walked down the sidewalk adjacent to the side door. I realized that the door he exited made a loud sound. The shooter was only about fifty yards from us, and I could see his gun recoil after each shot. He had a damn assault rifle. Jay ducked behind his door, pulled his gun, and then started firing somewhere above or to the side of his door. I grabbed my gun off my hip, staying between the car and my open door, and started firing just as quickly. The trooper had exited her squad car and went behind our vehicle when I heard a loud boom from whatever she was firing. For a second, I thought this man would not go down. Right then, he dropped to the ground, letting go of the gun. We all breathed, having no idea how many times we had hit him with lead.

The following two days, Jay and I had to give our statements, how we ended up in that situation, and, to our regrets, turned over our guns. We walked both our boss and the captain of the state police over and over again on our actions. They could not understand how we got that lucky in finding the actual serial killer on a hunch. We didn't know he was the person we were looking for, and we just returned fire. I thought maybe the suspect thought we were not law enforcement officers and we were there for other reasons, to cause harm to him or one of the residents. Or he may have had an active warrant and did not want to go to jail.

The shooter, Jack Cisco, had disposed of bodies for over a year. We just happened to find four of those bodies. There were two more bodies located later. When a resident died and had no family, Cisco would act as though they were still alive so he could cash in on their monthly checks. He would not be able to give a statement since he was dead, leaving many questions that had to be pieced together. The trooper had a shot that most likely killed him since she had used a shotgun with a deer slug and hit him in the head. Law enforcement has not found where he was dumping the feet, hands, and heads. The thought was that Cisco might have used the ocean as a dumping ground because the people interviewed claimed he had taken many trips to Myrtle Beach. Bellwood only had a few staff, and they were shocked when being told about the bodies. They contended that Cisco was a good guy and cared for the residents. By Saturday morning, I was driving home with a few weeks off due to the shooting. Syd was very sad for me and wanted me to come home. She was planning for some rest with a few days in the mountains if I felt up to it. I told her I wanted to go home and start considering our ten-year career plan. This one was close, and Cisco got off 12 rounds, mostly hitting the car or going over our heads. He only practiced with the long gun once, according to his friends. Had he practiced more, come out the front door, or I had not called for backup, the scenario could have ended differently. I needed time to articulate my life and how short it was. I was not ready for it to end quicker than expected.

Our agency has only been around for six years, and we are not in the habit of experiencing gun violence. We had only lost one officer, and he did not die in a volatile situation. The officer was 50 years old and came to the agency as one of the first officers to be hired. He had spent over twenty years with the Asheville police department before that. He was a great guy and very well-liked. He was assisting with a brush fire near Mount Mitchell, and they closed off some of the roads due to the thickness of the black smoke. An intoxicated driver came through the blocked lane and hit him as he was directing traffic. He died at the scene. He had five kids and had married the only woman he ever loved. The funeral was almost unbearable. Since we are a task force, we answer to the Governor, and I had a bad feeling that this shooting may cause anticipated heartburn for him. We were nonexistent on the state budget and wanted to keep it that way. Flying below the radar was our key to success.

I got lucky, and the media did not print our names in the paper concerning the shooting and all the events surrounding it. The journalist had a decent story and gave much history about Cisco, the nursing home he owned, and the community. Jay and I grabbed a copy of the story as we headed home in different directions for an extended vacation. My phone rang most of the trip home, and calls were from Syd, Nancy, Mack,

Syd's younger sister Alex, and brother Levi. My mother would not have known about the shooting, and I needed no excuse to call her. The family was checking in, asking if I needed anything, and just wanted to ensure that I knew they cared. Alex lived in Denver, and Levi was in San Francisco; both said we needed a family trip, and I agreed. It had been over a year since seeing them due to not heading our way for the holidays. Nancy and Mack traveled west to see them; which made me think we should host the family this year. All the calls made my trip go by quicker, and I appreciated it.

When I pulled into our driveway, Syd and our two labs sat on the front porch. I was so happy to be home and see my family. Syd hugged me and started crying, which also made me cry. Many emotions needed to get out from both of us. Syd was the one person that could do that to me. Syd grabbed my bag, and we went in for a nice, cool drink. She started unpacking my bag while I went to our screened-in porch to sit and close my eyes. A few minutes later, Syd came out carrying a bright yellow notebook.

I gave her a look, and she said, "Hear me out."

I knew that meant she had already done work on whatever it was, and I could see the spine on the notebook. It read Wolfe Family in the black, old-world font.

Syd explained that she had an idea, and I could take it or leave it. She thought about the conversation with her parents and started wondering about Lynn and her parents, and who their parents were. She told me that new software was being introduced that would allow us to begin building a family tree. With her computer skills and my investigation skills, she knew we could tell a pretty good story. Then she thought I could give it to my mother for her 60th birthday if we were successful. I found it interesting, and just learned that collecting ancestry information was possible. I took the binder and noticed Syd had already put separators in it and had started laying out how the data would be collected. There was no way I could say no. It was crucial to Syd, and I also wanted to know my heritage. She told me our plans for the night: drinks, a hot tub, a movie, and then some quiet time. I agreed to everything, but it was not in that order. Later that night, at about 2:13 a.m., Anna was back for a visit.

1998 – Rinse Repeat

I woke up from the dream, listened to the quietness, and realized I was in my own home. Syd was curled around me, and I heard her breathing, which always comforted me. One of the dogs was snoring, and I assumed it was Keaton since she had a loud snore, which was most likely why I was woken up. I knew I wanted to get up and write some things about the Boyd case before I forgot. I remembered walking the land the Boyd's owned, and I did not see anything unusual. I wanted to review the weather patterns from the week Anna went missing. I always felt I was not grasping all the details and could not understand how I could tell the investigators what color Cisco's shoes were and what side his hair was parted on. Yet, with Anna, I felt detail in my work was missing. In my notes, I would have guessed Jim Sr. as capable of hurting Anna, but not intentionally. He was not there when she went missing, so he was not on the suspect's list. It was a puzzle, but I was missing that last piece. I fell back to sleep, exhausted, and hoped I remembered the weather report, even though I had no idea why I wanted it.

The next few days were a whirlwind. I had to see my therapist early in the week. Paul wanted to talk with me and see how I was feeling. I was sure that was due to some HR policy, but he said it wasn't. He also told me I had to be released by a psychiatrist, and it could not be my therapist. Paul showed up early Tuesday morning and wanted a debriefing session with me. I knew he wanted to get everything out in the open without unanswered questions. Paul loved our dogs and always took time to play ball with them when visiting. This always made me love him more. He knew Syd well and asked her to listen to what he had to say. We went to our formal dining room, which we rarely used for eating but the best place to have a serious conversation. Syd brought iced tea for us and pulled her chair next to mine.

Paul opened his briefcase and pulled out a few manila folders. Paul was old school, and he sucked with computers. He also pulled out my .45 Ruger, which was placed in an evidence Ziploc bag, much like a sandwich bag a parent would pack in their kids' lunch bucket. He opened it, laid out my gun and magazine, and placed them on top of the bag. He told me he cleaned it himself. He also pulled out a box of ammo, hollow point, fifty rounds. Paul wanted me to return to the shooting range as quickly as possible, hopefully by next week. He had talked to many police officers after a shooting, and it was essential to understand that the gun would feel as comfortable in one's hand after using it to shoot a person versus a paper target. He looked at Syd and said it was important that this happened soon, and she replied with an affirmative nod. The same thing was told to me after I was shot years before, so I pretty much knew the routine.

Paul had the ballistic report that outlined where my shots traveled. Of the three, one hit Cisco in the left shoulder, one to the right wrist, and a shot glanced off his gun and hit him in the upper chest. Cisco shot an AR 15 with a capacity clip of 30. He also had a .45 Colt, which he carried in the back of his waistband between his shirt and belt. Paul stated that the shot that hit Cisco in the chest nicked his aorta, and that would have hindered him. The deer slug to the head happened immediately after the chest shot. "Your shot killed Cisco." I released a breath, and Syd squeezed my thigh. I had only been in one shooting before this, and I was the one that got shot.

Killing someone is never taken lightly, even if they are trying to kill you. It was out of necessity that Cisco was no longer living. Paul explained that Cisco most likely knew we were law enforcement officers. The state reviewed camera footage captured around town after the bodies were found, and Cisco was seen more than once traveling through town, stopping for gas or cold drinks at the nearest convenience store. When they outlined the date and times of his travel, he would have seen the officers at the burial site. They found packed bags at his home, and it appears he was looking to run. The day Cisco was shot was most likely his last at Bellwood.

Cisco was originally from Maryland and moved to South Carolina ten years prior. He was 67 years old and had a sketchy history. He had a high school diploma but claimed to have earned a bachelor's degree in business administration when he purchased Bellwood. He acquired all the proper paperwork to buy the building, and they could not find any link to explain why he would want to buy and manage a nursing home. Cisco had always been a scammer, with a history of operating a shoddy used car dealership, running illegal betting circles, cock fighting, and more. The man never had a job that didn't involve taking money from others. He soon realized that people dying in nursing homes could be part of a scam, especially if the deceased had no family or friends to report the death. Cisco would be picky about who got residency after interviewing them and reviewing their monthly income. Officials did a paper chase and discovered that over ten people had died in the past three years at that facility. They are in the process of locating those bodies, but they may never find them. Cisco lived in an older home in town and showed no signs of having a windfall of money coming in. He purchased the new Cadillac six months ago and told people he had started collecting retirement benefits to afford it. Neighbors reported that he would hand wash that car every other day in his driveway.

Officials located a building Cisco owned thirty miles out of town. That property included an old garage, most likely used for quick oil changes when first built. When the economy failed, it closed and just sat vacant. The place had water and electricity, but the electricity had been recently shut off. Cisco was paying the water bill, but from the sounds of it, no one in town knew he owned the property. Two large chest freezers were found there, which had three more bodies, all with heads, feet, and hands removed. The state forensic team found blood stains on the floor and in the drain. The thought was that Cisco would move a dead body from the nursing facility, take it to that garage, cut off the appendages, and stuff the body into the freezer. He would later come back and remove the body to bury it.

Investigations continue, and there is some thought that the staff may have been taking money to keep quiet. Residents would know there was a death, and Cisco would remove the body himself and push it out on a wheeled gurney to a white van. He was the only one seen with the van; that was the only time staff reported it on the property. The van was found parked in the garage. Cisco only did this at night, stating it was bad for businesses to do it during the day. It is unclear why the staff did not ask why there were formal death announcements, like an obituary or a family member calling about the death.

He ensured the residents had what they needed or requested. He recently upgraded their televisions and offered them free HBO. He also added a shuffleboard table after they asked for one. There were 14 rooms, and only eight were occupied at the time of the shooting. Records showed that 18 residents were currently living there. Cisco would claim double occupancy in the larger rooms (all rooms had the exact dimensions).

Syd asked if we needed a refill, and Paul politely asked if we had a beer.

I smiled, "Paul, it isn't even noon."

Paul looked at both of us, "Emily, when I got the news of the shooting, I broke down and cried. Marcy just held me in her arms. All I could think about was making that call to Syd and trying to explain that the woman she loves was hurt or killed during a routine visit to a damn nursing home. Then, call Jay's parents and explain why the events turned so quickly and why he was placed in harm's way. Jay wants to propose to Andrea after being together since high school. He hadn't told anyone yet but planned to get down on one knee during Christmas to surprise her."

Syd blurted out, "Paul, this is no fault to you or M or Jay."

"I was the one who placed Jay in that predicament. It was my fault," was all I could get out after choking up.

Paul looked at us, "It was great police work, and trying to belittle that as dumb luck won't fly with the Governor." Paul wiped his eyes and said, "The Governor will submit your name for the highest award a law enforcement officer can earn. The ceremony will be next spring. Jay will be honored as well."

"I don't want that; you know I do not welcome any awards because what comes with them is scrutiny. Jay can be honored. I will not take that from him."

Syd looked at Paul, "We still have to be careful with our relationship."

Paul said he understood, but the Governor will not take no for an answer.

We said our goodbyes. Paul patted our girls on the heads and headed out the door. We walked with him when he turned to us and said, "Oh, please don't tell Jay about our conversation. I know he is driving up tomorrow to visit and will meet me after that. Also, the engagement is a big secret."

We both nodded, and Syd kissed Paul on his cheek.

Jay visited the following day, driving up from Wilmington with his girlfriend. She was tired of hearing my name numerous times in the past year and did not have a face to put a name to it. It was a great visit, and Andrea was perfect for him. I thought how easy it must be for a straight couple to let everyone know their feelings for each other.

After all visits were done, Syd walked around the house, night and day, with her laptop. She took this family tree journey very seriously, and I knew she was all in when starting a new project. She was off for a few weeks with me, calling old friends and drawing up a process map of where my mother had originally been born. Our formal dining room was now a war room. She did not have many facts because the paperwork was a closed adoption, and it was sixty years ago. She would start with my grandparents and the adoption and work backward to answer all the riddles she had laid out. Syd also had some political pull since she worked on campaigns, and the following year was an election year for our House Representative, whom she knew very well.

My confidence was growing, and I was getting a little excited to have information about my family that always went unanswered by my mother. I would look at all the papers Syd had posted around the dining room, and I was pretty sure all questions would be answered. I saw Syd had put the word Columbus on one of the posters with a big question mark. We didn't even know if Lynn was born there or adopted and then taken there. Lynn couldn't even recall if they moved around when she was a little girl or what city she lived in. We would not ask or think of telling her what we were up to. I didn't know if it was an act or if she didn't want to find out about her birth parents. I hypothesized that she always thought the worst, that her parents were terrible people and sold her for money, or they left her on a church doorstep. My mom watched too many movies and never used common sense why a woman would give her child up for a better life for that child, one the mother couldn't offer.

Syd talked me into a short trip to the mountains in the western part of the state. One of her political connections had a cabin, and after he heard about the shooting, he offered it to us.

He told us to bring the dogs since there were many hiking trails. There was a small rowboat and a couple of bikes, but we needed to take groceries because the closest store was over ten miles away. Thursday morning, we loaded the dogs in our SUV, a couple of coolers of food, our favorite snuggle blankets, stopped at our local coffee shop, and started our three-hour drive. Within thirty minutes, Syd pulled out her laptop and powered it up. She told me she wanted to read a few news articles and wanted my thoughts. I asked if this was part of her PhD project, and she said no, it was part of her Lynn project.

Article one was from The Plain Dealer out of Cleveland, Ohio, which read the following;

January 5, 1958

Yesterday afternoon, Mr. and Mrs. Bill and Bonnie Holland were killed when their vehicle crossed the center line on Route 82 and hit an Ohio State (ODOT) snowplow. Bill Holland (67) was driving the car while his wife, Bonnie (62), was in the passenger seat. Authorities believe there was a thin layer of ice, and Holland lost control of his car after it started fishtailing. The snowplow operator tried to stop the snowplow, but Holland's vehicle picked up speed and hit the plow head-on. Fire Department personnel arrived at the scene and had to use the "Jaws of Life" to rescue the couple. The couple was pronounced dead at the scene. Further investigation will continue.

Article two from The Columbus Dispatch out of Columbus, Ohio, and read:

January 7, 1958

Last Saturday, the 4th, Bill and Bonnie Holland were pronounced dead at the scene after a two-vehicle accident. The Hollands were traveling too fast for the conditions, crossing the center line on Route 82. The weather was reported to be foggy and ice on the road. The State Police is investigating the snowplow driver operating the state-owned truck. There is no evidence that the driver of the plow was at fault. The driver of the car was not speeding but was traveling at a higher speed than warranted. We will continue to follow this story.

Syd closed the laptop and said, "That is all I got right now on the adoptive parents, but it is a start. I have the date and location of the accident and your grandparents' full names. I know Lynn never shared that detail with you."

I didn't know what to think or how to feel. I never felt a connection with those people, and to be truthful, I had no connection with my mother. I had always hoped that I was the one adopted, but I never shared that with anyone, including Syd.

"That is very interesting. I had no idea the fire department had to cut my grandparents out of the car, meaning it was a pretty bad accident."

"I searched on Jaws of Life because I had no idea what that was and was too embarrassed to ask you."

I had to laugh because I couldn't believe I knew something Syd didn't.

"What are you laughing about?"

"Oh, thinking what a computer nerd you are, and will research if you want to learn something new. While I hate the research part."

"That is why we are a great team; I will tell you where your great-grandparents came from and when your family arrived in New York."

"I am fascinated that you really think you can find all this information by hitting keys on the keyboard."

Syd busted out laughing. "Honey, I have been working the phones, and it ain't just about hitting the keys on this here little, old laptop."

"Are you cashing in on some old favors?"

"You better believe it, and how about for the next few days, we stop talking about the past and start talking about the future? We should get serious about what we want from life and how to get there."

I raised her hand, which was clasped to mine, and kissed it.

"Let's make the best of this time, and those two sleeping in the back better get their rest."

Syd looked over at me, and I could see a tear in the corner of her eye. I know what she was thinking: if I would have died in that decayed parking lot, she had no right to anything of mine. It was a constant battle in her head that she was in fear Lynn would do whatever she could to create havoc if I died. And she would, but I did not want to admit that to her. Hopefully, marriage laws will be changing in the future.

Our vacation ended quickly, and we had a blast. We were out for morning hikes; the weather was excellent, and we sat on the deck looking out at the beautiful mountains in our hoodies. I brought books, Syd had her PhD work, we had logs burning in the fireplace, and we found old movies on AMC to pass our nights. The four of us would try to find space on the couch, and the dogs seemed always to win. We would stretch out in the master bedroom, put the same old show on, and fall asleep, never finishing the movie. I had no dreams or woke up in the middle of the night. It was the first time I felt content with my life and career. I had some clarity but did not know why. I chalked it up to fresh air, quietness, and having my three favorite things next to me without interruptions. Going home would change all of that.

Syd's war room was becoming remarkable. She had data, graphs, Venn diagrams, and newspaper clippings. She was the data person everybody wanted to work with. She was so good at stats that at 42 years of age, she got an invitation every year to play fantasy football by one of the local fraternities. She won the league two years in a row. The reason for the invite was that she was a student teacher trying to explain statistics to a class that was predominately boys, frat boys, to be exact. They claimed beer and football were their two most essential things. Plus, it was fantasy football draft time.

Syd used her magic to explain the capacity of a keg and the size of the plastic cups they were handing out for $5 apiece. She wanted to know how they decided on the price of the cup, and of course, they laughed and said, because it is $5 every year. She then showed them how to make sure the cup cost was paying for the price of the keg and tap. They built a model on how much alcohol should be in the keg and how many cups should be sold. Syd was their new star, received lifetime draft invitations, and the cups were sold at $7, with an increase each year based on the cost of the keg. They laminated their framed statistical chart and hung it in their activity room.

Looking at our dining room walls, I sat down and tried to understand her work. Syd came in and looked at me, looked around the room, and looked at me again.

"Are you okay?"

"Yeah, I am trying to understand how you collected all this information."

"I want to collect as much as possible first, then start building the story from there. It will not make much sense to you because beauty is in the eye of the beholder."

"Maybe there is something you could do for me?"

"Sure, baby, you name it," she winked at me.

"Could you give me one small section in the office and set it up as a war room, like you have done with the Lynn project, so I can put this Anna Boyd case to rest?"

"Oh babe, are the dreams still there?"

"Sometimes, but I need another run at all the evidence on the wall like I did after the case went cold."

"Sure, and if you remember, I took pictures of the display just in case we would ever need to set it back up."

"You are amazing."

"Naw, I just love my girlfriend."

Within 24 hours, Anna Boyd was back on the office wall. Syd included her school picture, a family picture, and school pictures of JR, Marigold, and Daisy. She had a map with miles from the bottling plant, grade school, bus route, and more. She also posted pictures of the house and the outside property. I pulled a chair up, looked at every picture again, and focused on the maps. Syd put all the times when the different family members arrived home and the paths they traveled. I noticed a picture of the horses Anna loved and wondered which one was Rocket. I never realized that picture was there. I was also aware that I may have the only pictures taken of the old home, on the back of the property, or the "shabby" they called it. I hated that name just as much as I hated this case.

I looked for the colored markers Syd laid out for me. Syd was big on what colors must be used if I needed to write any notes on the posters. Syd had a legend, and pink was the color that outlined tasks to do. I picked up the pink marker and wrote, "Call the photographer. Are there any pictures from the inside the Boyd's main residence?" I had pictures that I had taken, but all of them were from outside the home. I looked at the photos of the yard, the front ditch, and the white rock that made up the driveway. Many cars and traffic were parked everywhere, and I am positive no evidence was collected, or if so, it came from the cops, not the suspect. I wrote in pink, check evidence locker. Then I remembered I needed a weather report for that week. Syd came in to see me and made that sound of gratification, one I knew well.

"I see you have some work to do. The pink is a nice addition."

Syd looked over my comments, took the pink marker from my hand, and added a check mark by the weather report.

"I will get your weather report and will look for January of that year, up to the day Anna went missing and for a few months after. I know you too well, and if I only give you a month, you will ask for more." She added dates to her checkmark and put today's date down, meaning she would get that information for me as soon as our conversation ended.

"Yes, I need a short visit to West Virginia. The family still lives on the property. I checked a few weeks ago. I want to retrace my steps, but I know I will not be welcomed. Paul will have to get me a warrant if I want to do some snooping."

"Will you be doing an exhausting search on the silver Ford? Or looking at pedophiles while you are there, or just focusing on the property?" she said with a snicker.

"I will visit their headquarters, pull the evidence, maybe run a new search on silver mid-size Fords. I want to talk to the bus driver again. He is not a suspect, but I want to contact him with some details and his memory. And get a better timeline for when each family member came home. Thank you for putting the times up with the mileage, but it bothers me, and I don't know why. Witnesses backed up every reported story."

"Well, if the times were off by five or ten minutes, would that make a big change to the timeline?"

"Probably not, and sometimes I wonder if I have spoken to the killer. I think it is a family member, but the evidence does not point that way."

"Will you be taking anyone with you or going alone?"

"Alone, but I will pick up a resource when I get there because I doubt if Paul will give me an officer for a cold case not in our state."

"Ask; it never hurts, plus he loves you."

I laughed and said, "You think everyone does."

"Not really. I question your mother's motives."

It had been 30 days since the shooting, and I was bored. I took a few more trips to the shooting range and spent three days in a seminar, driving back each night to be with Syd. I was working on some old cases and monitored the phones one day for a donation event at the college. Syd was working on her thesis, and her fall semester started strong. She had been spending a lot of time in her war room and covering her work on the wall with a clean sheet of paper. I know she did not want me to see her work, so she must be working hard and did not want to spoil any surprises. I continued to work on the Boyd case, rereading all documented reports more than once. I was getting antsy and wanted a call to get out in the field soon. Syd asked me to have dinner with her because she wanted to talk to me about something serious. Of course, I said yes and thought it was strange. It could be anything, and since we had a trusting relationship, we only held serious conversations for later when it usually involved work.

That night at dinner, Syd told me she had been thinking a lot about the shooting, our future, and her job. She wanted my thoughts on her going from a full-time job to a part-time job with the consulting group. They would allow her to do so, and she would be home 100%. Syd gave out a big breath and told me she wanted to go all in with her political work and wanted to lead our Senator's electronic marketing site for the 2000 campaign, which would end in November of that year. Her salary would increase with the move. She would not travel, and they promised that if the Senator were re-elected, they would give her a 20% bonus.

The one hiccup is that Syd would have to go on my insurance as a reported partner relationship. We did not see that as a problem, but she felt the paperwork would be filed in a state agency and would always be there if someone wanted to hold it against me for future promotions. I was happy for Syd and agreed 100%. The insurance was null, and who cares at this point? We are no longer young women. Syd's dream is politics, and this move would help her launch her political career. Plus, I liked our Senator and thought it was exciting that he reached out to her personally. She wanted to call her parents this weekend and give them the news, and she wanted me to be on the call. Syd lights up when she is happy, with almost a glow and a twinkle in her eye.

I waited until she was done and said, "How is the research going with the Lynn project? I noticed you have started covering some things up."

"I don't want to get your hopes up, so I need to address some things before I show my hand. Also, I do need a trip to Illinois soon."

"Please tell me you are not looking to squeeze that Chicago trip in without me."

"Not really, but would stay with Alice, but then travel from there. Nothing weird, just some paperwork."

"Would you like me to stay out of it?"

"Well, right now, I may be on a long goose chase, but Alice knows the area I need to snoop around, and she has volunteered to travel with me. Another set of eyes and hands would be fantastic for my research."

"Interesting; please don't tell me if I am related to John Dillinger."

Syd did not laugh and went silent, which made me wonder, but the phone rang, and I forgot my thoughts. I hoped it was the good news I had been waiting weeks for.

"Agent Wolfe, this is Agent Slater."

"Oh, please tell me this is not a setback."

"Agent Wolfe, your search warrants have been issued for the Boyd case."

Syd watched me, and I put my fist in the air and whispered to her, "Yes!"

Paul informed me that I have the approval to visit the Boyd's, search their property, and question anyone related to the case.

"Also, a West Virginia trooper named Gray has requested to work the case with you. He was there the night Anna was reported missing, and he feels strongly that the local police were investigating the wrong person. He is waiting for your call, and you leave next week. Take two weeks, then let me know if you need more. I will ask if you need more than three weeks. Both governors have the same strong friendship they had three years ago. And you know, our Governor will support you if I ask for more time."

"Thank you, and I am feeling good about this. Syd set up a war room for the Boyd case, and I have found a few new things to review once I get there. Having the trooper will be of great help. I cannot thank you enough for believing in me."

"Just so you know, the family will make it difficult on you, so find a hook. Also, half the town will support you, and the other half will detest you. I am sure they kept your picture when it was in The Daily Star. The day you left empty-handed."

"You don't have to remind me; it was three years ago, but it feels like three days."

"Travel safe. Tell Syd I said hi. Senator Battle called me today and asked how you were doing. He told me a new ad that Syd did and how excited he is."

"I will let her know, and again, thank you."

I looked at Syd, "Let's move this party to the hot tub. We need to celebrate."

Syd yelled, which caused the girls to bark, and we had to laugh. Tension from last month was wearing off, and both of us could enjoy some good news.

I took all my documents from my war wall the following week and headed to West Virginia. Trooper Gray had set aside time to be with me 24/7. Once I arrived, he would have a conference room at the state police district headquarters held for us to compare notes. He would collect all evidence from the case, including the casework from the local and county police, and have it for me. I planned to arrive late Monday night and meet him the following day. Gray invited me to have dinner with him and his wife at their home as soon as I arrived. He also wanted to have a private conversation concerning the case.

I checked in at the Holiday Inn and headed to Gray's home. His wife, Sharon, was so happy to meet me. She said her husband spoke highly of me and was confident we would find Anna. Sharon immediately apologized, and I told her it was okay. I also put much hope in us, and we can still close the case.

Jerry Gray was an outstanding officer with very high morals. This I knew because I got the low down on him before traveling to West Virginia. I was informed that he would not let the investigation go, and he was told to stop asking. The local police would work on the cold case. If they needed help, the state would get involved, but the locals already agreed to refrain from asking for that help. I asked him why our paths hadn't met three years ago when his wife shot me a look.

"Wait, are you the trooper relieved from the case in the first few days?"

"Guilty. Guilty due to asking too many questions, I was upstaged by the locals, telling me the Boyd home should not be treated like a crime scene."

"So, you think the family may be guilty."

"I don't know, but I think someone is hiding something. The locals did not start their search the night Anna went missing, and the next day, the father went to work, and the kids went to school."

It was nice that he called her Anna, which told me he cared about her. I also wondered if he was having nightmares.

Jerry unloaded his thoughts about the case and how suspects were questioned. He disagreed with the local police because he felt their police force could not find Anna. They wanted to treat it as a strange person swooped in, grabbed her, and then took off. They did not press anyone other than the bus driver and another man who was a reported pedophile. Jerry thought both were just noise with the story, and the local police needed to expand their search in the community. He said they had tunnel vision and could not leave it alone. They could not grasp the thought that someone in the family knew more than they were reporting. He felt the bus driver, Springer, was targeted for being black and reported the times wrong when he dropped Anna off due to nervousness. The three sexual assailants all had iron-clad alibis, no matter how the cops tried to prove them wrong.

I told him about my experience when I first arrived at the scene, and I felt that the local police were skirting away from the problem, and that problem was Jim Boyd. I did not think he hurt Anna, but something was off with the family. Not having official statements from them was asinine, which hindered us from the start.

I went back to the hotel, called Syd, and told her about dinner and how nice the Grays were. I explained that they were dog owners, so it was easy to understand that they were great people. I gained confidence because I found someone who thinks like I do about Anna. And I hope the confidence continues into the next few weeks of being there. Syd told me she handed in her part-time paperwork and called the Senator. She planned to go to Chicago the week after I returned for a few days and would fly out and stay with Alice. I explained that she did not have to get deeper into my family tree if it took too much of her time. After I said that, I laughed because everyone knew Syd had a very high IQ and could finish her thesis in her sleep. She was just that good.

I was unaware that Syd had been talking to retired police officers, librarians, political leaders, and officials at different county facilities. She was building a story, and I had a feeling it was taking her in a direction where she could not turn around. I also felt she had invited her family in on the saga because I have been noticing more calls from them and usually short conversations, giving Syd information that she writes down and sticks in her bright yellow binder. I made sure I did not ask any questions, and many times when she was on the calls, I would excuse myself to take the girls out to play ball.

1995 – Anna Is Missing

Emery was running the investigation and assumed the little Boyd girl was most likely hiding from her parents. He had been to the home a few times after marks were reported on one of the kids, but he could not remember which kid. Also, the school principal commented that Daisy had covered up a black eye on more than one occasion. He knew Jim had a drinking problem, especially on weekends, only drinking at home to hide this fact from the community members.

Trooper Gray, on the other hand, had no experience with the family but would later comment that he thought something terrible had happened to the little girl. He had mixed feelings about the father. Gray was not pleased with how Emery was handling the case.

Emery did not treat the Boyd's home as a crime scene. He lacked experience with crimes of this magnitude (if this was one of those) but had found kids running away from home more than once with his 10 years of police experience. Daisy reported the entire story from start to finish as they sat at the dining room table while she drank her coffee and borrowed her husband's cigarettes. She cried as she told the officers how each family member made it home that day and the time they did so. Jim would tell her to stop crying and question her when she reported that Anna rode the bus home that day, and JR went with another family to the Piggly Wiggly. Jim became irate and would yell at her. Who allows a little girl to ride a bus alone and come home to an empty house? What kind of mother does that? Trooper Gray would glance at Emery like he was in favor of cuffing him and getting him out of the house. He just needed that nod from Emery, which he never got.

After an hour of collecting all the information, Emery made a grave mistake by telling the family it was too late to start a search party and that he would come back in the morning with volunteers. They would begin that search by combing through their acreage. Jim told them there was no reason to search the property. He had already done that after dinner. They needed to do their jobs and find Anna. Emery told the Boyd's that they should get some sleep because tomorrow would come early. Gray asked if he could talk to the children, and Jim said no. Gray asked why, and Jim just looked at him with no answer. Jim then asked both of them to leave because they were not helping, and he was getting angry with their questions. He was not a criminal, and they made him feel like one.

Emery had work to do and wanted to question the bus driver as soon as possible. He still thought the little girl ran away from home and took advantage of getting home from school when no one was there to stop her. He fears that she did not pack warm clothes, which may be why she will return tonight.

Gray was the opposite. He wanted to take all of them in for questioning and separating them before they could make up a story. Emery told him he had watched too many crime movies. Gray called dispatch and started collecting information on sexual offenders in a 50-mile radius. He did not believe someone would have had the advantage of grabbing Anna when she didn't ride the bus home on a regular schedule. They would have been there for Henry but grabbed a little girl instead. That made no sense. Pedophiles have certain desires, and rarely change their motives. They had no history of missing children in this county or surrounding counties. Gray decided not to wait and started his investigation immediately. He was beginning his search for Anna tonight. Gray told Emery that he would meet him back at the house at 0700 hours in the morning. If anything changes before that, he will call him and expect Emery to do the same for him.

Emery told him that he would call the school principal and get the bus driver's home phone number. If he learned anything, he would call Gray on the WVSPERN radio, a shared channel all the local police can transmit over. Gray turned his cruiser's takedown lights on and engaged his spotlight on the driver-side door. He started driving the ditches, up one side and down the other, directing his lights into the fields and pastures. He stopped at Henry's house to solidify the times Daisy gave him. He believed Daisy, but he needed to understand if the little boy's parents could give him information concerning the Boyd's.

Gray drove up their winding driveway and kept his lights on the house. He was looking for movement and possibly a little girl. Families have been known to rescue or save a child when they felt the family environment was unsafe.

Gray heard his radio crackle.

"Officer Emery to Trooper Gray, go to channel 3."

"Trooper Gray here, go Emery."

"I spoke to the bus driver, Allen Springer, a black male, 44 years of age, employed for eight years, but first school year on route three, which is the bus route Anna took. Anna was the last one to get off the bus; she was alone, and he claimed it was around 4:15 p.m. when she left the bus. He remembers no vehicles in the area and did not pass any vehicles when traveling back down Pembroke. I also called his supervisor, who told me the school district did not employ the bus drivers. They are employed by Boucher Bus Service, which operates out of Pennsylvania. They have had that contract for over ten years but lost it in year two due to contract talks stalling. Parents had to find a way to get their kids to school, so carpooling became popular. They do not conduct background checks on their employees but have had no complaints about Springer for the eight years he has been employed. He did say Springer did not like the new bus route and made that known, but he never said why. Management assumed it was due to something he was not used to. I did get Springer's address and want to speak to him in person tomorrow."

"Great information. I just pulled up to the little boy's house and will speak to his parents. I would like to know if they saw anything, even if he was not on the bus. Maybe he remembers a car from a previous day, just a hunch."

"Okay, I will see you at 0700 at the Boyd home; if anything changes tonight with your search and interviews, please contact me by radio."

"Will do, Gray out."

"Emery out."

After informing dispatch, Gray exited his squad car and left the takedown lights shining on the house. He was aware of residents having guns and did not want to get shot. He started to knock, but the Sullivan's already knew his presence was at their home. Kirk Sullivan answered the door and allowed Grey into their home. By looking at their home, they lived modestly. Kirk was a civil lawyer while his wife, Juanita, sold Avon. They had one son, Henry, who knew Anna well even though he was not in her class.

Gray announced why he was there and understood Henry was most likely in bed due to the late hour. Kirk and Juanita both agreed and hoped they could answer any questions. Gray read from his notes verbatim what Daisy Boyd reported, and he understood Henry was not on the bus today. Juanita agreed and explained that he had an optometrist appointment for new glasses. Kirk asked what they could do to help find Anna, or did the Boyd's think she was missing? When asked to elaborate, Kirk looked at Juanita, and she gave a slight nod of her head. Kirk claimed that, as a civil lawyer, he spent much time at the justice hall, where the district attorney and other lawyers had offices. He said he hears things. When Gray asked to clarify, Juanita just stated that they knew the Boyd household could be difficult for all of them to get along.

Gray then asked if the Sullivans would harbor Anna if she asked for help.

Kirk said, "If we thought Anna was in harm's way, we would take her in, call the police, and notify her parents that she was safe."

Gray replied with an affirmative nod.

Gray did have a question concerning their son and his habit of riding the bus.

"How many days a week has Henry ridden the bus since the start of the school year?"

Juanita replied, "He rides the bus home almost every day. Today was the only day he did not, this semester."

"Do you meet him at the bus stop, or does he walk home?"

"Sometimes I walk down; other times I may drive."

"Do you ever see Anna get off the bus by herself?"

"Anna usually rides home with her mother since she works at the school. Or, all three kids will get off the bus together. I don't think I have ever seen Anna alone, but I may not have been at the bus stop daily to see her."

"Would it be possible to stop by tomorrow after school and speak to your son? I want to see if he remembers seeing the same car or truck waiting around the bus stop or following the bus."

"Sure, we need to be here when you ask him those questions. Do you think someone picked Anna up off our road?"

"We just want to look at all angles and leave no stone unturned. We hope that she will be found safe and is not far away. One more thing: When Henry rides the bus home, do you know the times, when he gets off the bus or when he gets home?"

Juanita said, "Oh, that's easy. The bus drops off at 3:40 p.m., like clockwork. I could set my watch by it. And then maybe 10 minutes to walk home. Henry likes to start his homework before 4 p.m. to be ready for dinner at 5. We like to eat early since Kirk sets his own hours."

Kirk chimed in, "That's true. I want to be home to watch the local news at 5:30."

Gray said his goodbye's and continued to drive around the area, still looking for Anna.

At 7:00 a.m., six officers were at the Boyd's to start the search. Daisy was home, getting the other two kids ready for school. Emery asked if the kids could stay home to assist them with some questions. Daisy told him that Jim Sr. had already been picked up for his job at the bottling company and would not be there. He gave strict instructions that the police could not speak with the kids.

Trooper Gray stated, "Mrs. Boyd, it is unusual for the family to leave when we really need to speak to everyone and help find Anna."

Emery shot Gray a look that told him to stop talking.

Gray and Emery stayed outside while JR and Marigold started down the driveway to walk to the bus stop. Gray told Emery they had a trooper stationed at the bus stop but would not interact with the bus driver or the children.

Daisy took Emery and Gray to Anna's room, which she shared with Marigold. They had Daisy go through all of Anna's clothes, shoes, coats, hats, gloves, etc., and wanted her to report if any clothes were missing. They also asked her to go through the other kids' clothes and do the same. Other officers were canvassing door to door and questioning neighbors. Another trooper was questioning sex offenders in the area, and there were three white men between the ages of 22 and 55 who made that list. Two state detectives were called to the county to assist with interviews. Three other troopers were walking the family fence lines, bringing one canine officer with them.

Daisy was crying while taking clothing inventory but swore the only clothes missing were the ones Anna had on in school yesterday. Gray asked if there was anything she had forgotten to report from last night after they had communicated the missing child bulletin throughout the state. Daisy said no and kept to the list she gave them the night before: black gym shoes, dark socks, black pants, a black warrior school sweatshirt, a dark blue windbreaker, and she had a bright purple hair ribbon in the back of her ponytail.

One of the state troopers came to the bedroom doorway, looked at Gray, nodded his head, then left. Both Emery and Daisy did not see the trooper.

Gray excused himself and said he needed to check on his troopers.

The trooper led Gray to the garage. The garage was small, with one stall for a car, and there was a washer and dryer in the rear left corner. A rope was stretched across the garage, most likely used to hang wet clothes. He walked to the washing machine and saw wet clothes in the drum. The trooper wore gloves and took each piece of clothing out while another took pictures. The clothes were sitting in water, almost as if someone had opened the lid of the washer before the spin cycle could finish. The water appeared to be very dirty and muddy. The water had no smell, so they knew the clothes were recently placed there. There was a pair of black Converse high tops, kids' jeans, and a white kids' sweatshirt. At first look, Gray guessed the clothes belonged to the son of the Boyd's. After documenting and taking pictures of all the items, they placed them back in the washer and shut the lid but did not finish the wash cycle.

Another trooper entered the garage and said, "Investigator Thomas is trying to reach you."

The state police sent Thomas to question a local man who may be of interest. Mark Collins, a 35-year-old, had a history with young girls but not as young as Anna. One of those girls was 14, and Collins was arrested for sexual assault. Those charges did not hold up in court because the girl told Collins she was 16. Thomas got the make and model of his car, a silver Ford Taurus, and his employment status. Gray noted that he wanted to speak to the Sullivans and Springer again concerning the silver Ford.

After 72 hours, Anna was still missing. Focus was being spent on the bus driver, Springer, who reported different times when he dropped Anna off on that fateful day. Gray thought it was a simple mistake due to the train holding the bus up, which had not happened before. It was a new route, and he probably forgot to mention it. Someone had leaked it to the local paper, where it was picked up by the AP[6] and sent across the state and beyond.

Community members would stand out in front of his house. Some would have signs that labeled him as a child killer. The bus company put him on paid leave. He could not afford an attorney to avoid the chaos, and the cops were fanning the flames. Gray was sure the local cops were the ones who made that call to the local news. Gray was not happy with Officer Emery, who wanted to point the finger at Collins, one of the pedophiles, because he drove a silver car. Two kids on the bus stated they remembered seeing a silver car following the bus that day. And claimed they had seen it before. Within days, that was the hot topic in school, and twelve more kids came forward about the silver car.

Along with the students came their parents, who demanded justice for Anna. None of them could describe the driver, and suddenly, the story grew. The car had tinted windows, a loud muffler, and a West Virginia Mustangs football logo on the front plate.

Gray did an exhaustive search for the car, where tinted windows were against state law, there was no Mustang football team, including college and high school within West Virginia, and the vehicle was never located. He believed someone saw a silver car, heard about Collins, and wanted to think he picked up Anna, even though that was not his modus operandi. He had an alibi, but it was kept quiet. Collins drove a garbage truck with another employee. He was on his route that day until 3:30 p.m. He arrived at the garage, and the employer had showers

---

[6] Associated Press

in the locker room. Collins was reported always to shower for 15 minutes after clocking his timecard out. The videotape shows him leaving the premises at 4 p.m. If he had picked up Anna, he would have arrived at 4:30 p.m., missing her entirely departing the school bus. Collins met his 18-year-old girlfriend, Rhonda Masters, at a local eatery. He paid for drinks and an appetizer with his charge card.

On day four, the West Virginian Governor reached out to the North Carolina Governor due to their past relationship and asked if they could spare an agent who could look at the evidence and give them a different point of view. He asked for a female agent since all the officers working were male. I got the call and spoke with Emery, who gave me all the case's particulars. I headed over the following day and checked into the Holiday Inn. It was day six since Anna went missing.

The following morning, I went to the local police headquarters and met with Emery. He laid out the evidence and told me they were concentrating on a bus driver and a local sexual pervert (his words) who liked kids. They interviewed both of them and have video of those interviews, but they had no plans to interview them again due to possibly scaring them off. I disagreed with this tactic, but I knew better than turning my nose up at their completed work. Emery put me in a room with the VHS tapes of the interviews and asked me to review them. When I asked about the families' interviews, he told me they did not complete official interviews but documented their statements, which were in evidence. I asked to see those as well.

FAMILY DIRT

Hours later, I finished the videotapes and learned nothing I could use. I also read the families' statements from the night Anna went missing, and that added little value, but I asked for copies of my own. I felt the police emphasized the two possible suspects and those two were more scared of getting charged for a crime they most likely did not commit. Both men were threatened with arrest. The interviews were poorly done. Detective Wallace completed the interviews but is now off the case due to illness. Rumor had it that he knew he had cancer before he was assigned the case but didn't share that with the police force. He was currently receiving weekly chemo treatments for twelve weeks, followed by radiation for another eight weeks. I then asked for his phone number and was told they could not give it to me. I could see I was working uphill and felt Anna was in terrible hands with this group.

I requested to go to the Boyd's, meet the parents, and walk their property. I was told they would have to ask Jim Sr., and it would be later that week. I was starting to feel unwelcome. Emery told me he would call me later that day and find time to connect with the Boyd's. He told me I could leave for the day or watch the videos again.

I left and drove right to the Boyd's. I parked off the road leading to the back of their property. I changed into my work boots, put on a baseball hat, and placed my shield around my neck. I threw on a hoodie with the word POLICE printed on the back, just in case I needed someone to see that. I started looking at my map with the measurements plotted out. I had a small flashlight because it would get dark in a few hours. I started my grid search from East to West, taking small steps. I expected to find nothing besides the sanity I was trying to keep. I carried Anna's school picture in my hoodie pocket.

After around 30 minutes, I saw a dilapidated house in the back of the Boyd's land. There were no pictures or notes about the property, which surprised me. If I were a child, this would be where I would spend my adventures. When I entered the opened door, well, the doorway, where there was no door, I could hear the glass breaking under my feet. All the glass windows had fallen out or broken out some time ago. There were five small rooms; the roof caved in on two of them, and there was a powerful, musty smell. I could make out striped wallpaper or water stains from traveling down the walls after it rained. I continued to move slowly and concentrated on the floor. There was wood from the ceiling and branches lying on the ground. It looked like a tree was sprouting from the living room.

I found the kitchen cabinets, where the doors had fallen off or ripped away. I always carried a small 35 mm Canon camera and started taking pictures. I could see where the dust and dirt were lacking in one of the cabinets, and it appeared something may have been stored there. I started looking for shoe prints because I knew someone had been there not long ago. Could it be Anna hiding? After gently moving from room to room, I called her name, taking pictures of everything. I had just put my camera in my hoodie pocket and heard a noise that startled me. I jumped.

I turned around, and a man was staring at me. Jim Sr. should be working, but that was the man I was looking at. He had bloodshot eyes and had grown a very untidy beard from the picture I had of him.

"Who are you?" he demanded.

"I am Agent Wolfe, and I was sent here to investigate Anna's disappearance."

"No one told me."

"I'm sorry, maybe someone forgot. I was not going to talk to you and your family until tomorrow. I am just getting an early start on the lay of the land."

"Well, I don't want you back here. You can get hurt and then sue me for everything I have."

I wanted to tell him he didn't have anything that fit my taste but thought better.

"I am really sorry, and I apologize for my actions." I knew his type and how to play him.

"You have any kids?"

"No sir, I was not that lucky. God has other plans for me, apparently." I knew that he took his kids to church every Sunday, and I also knew he beat his wife.

"Are you going to find my little girl?"

"Sir, I am going to do everything in my power to do so, and I pray every night that I do." If Syd had heard my comments, she would have laughed at how this conversation was going.

"Since you are here, do you have any questions about my property? Anna isn't here; she has never come back here. She was a scared little girl and only loved horses and purple dinosaurs. You can see neither of those are here."

I wanted to tread lightly, and I knew the local police were not pressing the family or had any valuable information. "Sir, I read that your son, Jim Jr., loved to use the rope swing, or I think that is what it may be called."

"You don't know what a rope swing is?"

I bit my tongue and felt blood. "Well, sir, there was one in my neighborhood, but girls were not allowed, and if I would try, my daddy would beat my ass."

He laughed, and I could see happiness in his eyes.

"The rope swing has been here for years and is over by the gulley about one hundred and fifty yards from here. It was there when I was a boy. It is on an old hickory, and one of these days, that tree will fall. The kids are not allowed on it. You are standing on my grandparents' property; this was their land, followed by my parents, and now it is mine. The government can't have it."

I knew this was a lie, and Jim Jr. used it the day Anna went missing. I also question why the government would want this land. Note to myself: check if taxes are owed on the Boyd's property.

"Okay, sir, I am going to walk out the way I came in, and maybe I will see you tomorrow."

"We have nothing to talk about. You find my Anna. My wife may make time for you, but you better tread lightly."

"Sir?"

"She is a mess and had to start taking some head pills from the doctor. And I don't want anyone to know that. Do you understand me?"

"Yes, sir. I won't say a word." Because you are embarrassed about your wife's mental health, I would love for this man to take a swing at me, so I could cuff him and put his ass on the ground.

I checked to make sure my camera was still in my pocket before heading out, wondering if he saw me taking pictures. If so, he would have demanded that camera, and I did not have a search warrant for his property. I excused myself slowly and headed for my car. He just stood there staring at a hole in my backside. I started to wonder if he would pull out a handgun and shoot me, even though he knew who I was. He owned two long guns, a 12- and a 20-gauge shotgun. He also had a .357 revolver. I tried to find out if Jim Jr. had a gun and was told no. But, the search was for legal firearms, and most guns were purchased from local gun shows, where no paperwork was recorded. West Virginia had no state law concerning at what age a person could purchase a gun. If a six-year-old had cash in hand, they could buy a firearm. But deep down, I knew he did not hurt Anna. His words were too affirmative, and I could tell by his face that he wanted her back home. Or, I was wrong, and he is a psychopath. I was wrong once before and was shot, so I will tread lightly concerning Mr. Boyd.

The next morning, I got a call at 6 a.m., and I could have predicted the conversation. Emery was on the other end of my cell phone, informing me that Jim Boyd was angry. He called the chief to complain that I was on his property last night.

"Is that true? You went to the Boyd house without me?"

"You know it's true, and you should know I do not want to waste time looking for a little girl after eight days. If you do not want to get down to business, I will."

I could hear him stuttering and unable to put his words into coherence, trying to string a sentence together.

"Agent Wolfe, I do apologize, and I am sure you work much faster in North Carolina than we do in West Virginia, but I swear we want to bring Anna home."

"Great, we both agree. Can we meet with the mother today and maybe the other children?"

"Daisy Boyd will meet with you today, but Jim Sr. said you cannot talk to the children."

"Do you know why the father is protecting the children? We can have a state psychologist, medical doctor, teacher, or anyone they prefer to come and question them. The parents can be in the room during the questioning."

"We explained that many times and were told to drop it. Jim said no and stopped asking. He claims we are wasting time, and the family has no idea what happened to Anna. He wants us to arrest Springer, the bus driver."

"Why?"

"Racist mentality is all around us, and they don't want to think about a black man touching a little white girl. This is a powder keg; we do not need Jim Boyd lighting that wick."

"Okay, let's sit down with Daisy. Also, I would like you and me to walk the Boyd property, especially by the rope swing and the older home that has partially fallen down."

"We can do that. Why don't I come by and pick you up?"

I knew that would be a way to control me and how long I would stay at the Boyd residence. "Well, I have a few errands since I forgot some female items. After that, I will meet you at the Boyd's in about an hour." I knew he would not argue. Using the term female things always gets men.

"Will do. But please stay in your car if you arrive before me."

"Sure will." I am always glad people cannot see my face when I think less of them.

I interviewed Daisy, and she solidified the information she had given Emery. Nothing different, and she commented that she knew Anna had not come home after school. When I asked how she could be sure, she said nothing was in the house that Anna had that day. Her backpack and shoes have never been found. Had she come into the house, she would have sat down and turned her favorite show on, Barney. She probably wouldn't have even put her bag away, but she would have taken her shoes off because that is a rule in the house.

I asked about Jim Jr. and his whereabouts when he got home. She relayed the same information: he went outside, played, and came in before her husband got home.

"I read in the notes that Jim Jr. was playing on a rope swing."

"Yes, he was, but he knows better than being out there alone."

"Are you sure he was by himself? Could he invite a friend over without your knowledge?"

"No, Phyllis dropped him off at the end of the drive, and he was alone."

" Has Anna been on the rope swing?"

I got a look like I was crazy. "Anna? My lord, she was scared to jump off the stairs on the front porch, and that was two feet. She would not go to the woods or get on that stupid rope."

"Would you allow me or someone else to ask your children a few questions?"

Daisy started rubbing her hands, and suddenly, she got nervous.

"No, Jim said, absolutely not. They have no information on Anna, and you cannot speak to them here or at the school."

"Can I look around the house and outside on your property? I did hear some horses nearby. Did Anna like horses?"

Daisy started crying, "She loved Rocket and would bring him apples. She was not supposed to go over there, but I would watch her sneak to see him."

Emery said, "We spoke to all the neighbors, searched the pastures, and walked the fields nearby."

"Officer Emery, did anyone search the area around the rope swing or the house falling apart on the back of the property?" I asked.

Emery shot me a look, and Daisy said, "The shabby? Anna would never go there."

"Is that what you call it, where the grandparents once lived? Well, why don't we rule it out anyway."

Daisy shot me a glance, wondering how did I know about the grandparents' home.

"No, I told you Anna would not go there."

I took Emery outside so Daisy would not hear my next questions. I had to ask if they confiscated the guns in the house.

"Are you crazy! Their child is missing, and you want me to act like they are under suspicion?"

"No, I just want you to do your job." Like I said, I could be a smartass if people were not accountable for their actions.

I was told I could not walk the property, but I knew I wanted to return to where I was last night. I told Emery I would be in touch, drove up the road, took a left on Apple Blossom Lane, and headed to the gully. I found the rope swing attached to a 12-foot wooden ladder leaning against an old tree. I know these swings and have been on them myself. I do not see Anna climbing the ladder, but she may grab the rope and see if she could hang on to it. I went to the gully and looked down. It was unbelievably deep, and if there was heavy rain, a person would slide down and not get back up the hill. The area looked pretty dry. I got on my cell phone and called the state barracks to see which trooper was in charge of the Boyd case. I was sent an automatic voicemail message from Trooper Lee. I left my name and number, why I was calling, and wanted to find out if the gully and the old home, the shabby, were searched.

I wanted to get all the pictures I took yesterday and develop them immediately. I tried to avoid having them done at a local place of business because I knew people would talk, and it would stir up problems for the Boyd family. I drove 50 minutes away and found a one-hour development service. I was lucky that I could wait and get them back quickly. I picked up a Sports Illustrated and got comfortable.

An hour later, I had two dozen pictures, including the shabby, rope swing and gulley. I drove back to town to lay everything out in my hotel room, and I needed to get creative. I plan to go to the state barracks tomorrow to talk to Lee, who has not called me back. I was getting the feeling I was already overstaying my welcome. The only person that wanted me here was Anna. I stopped at a local diner, the only place in town, The Chili Grill, that served homemade chili and apple pie. I listened to the people eating their dinner, and they told stories about the Boyd family and how they needed to pray for them. They would also claim that it was the bus driver and he was hiding the little girl or killed her and dumped her somewhere. They said he had left the country. I just sat by the large glass window and looked on the street. I saw raindrops starting to fall, and I wished I was home with Syd.

The following day, I met Trooper Lee at the West Virginia police headquarters. He told me he liked the bus driver for the kidnapping. When I asked why he thought it was a kidnapping, he said he felt it in his chest. That was a new one for me. I don't think I have ever felt something in my chest about a potential murderer. He told me they were sitting on Springer and watching his every move. Apparently, he acted suspiciously by staying at his home and never leaving. They took pictures of a woman delivering groceries to him, waiting an hour, then driving away. It was his sister. They later picked her up and claimed that she was driving erratically. They had to let her go after a few hours. I asked him why they didn't already know who his family was and where they lived. He gave a surprised look on his face, pulled his little notebook out of his uniform shirt, and wrote that down. He told me I had no reason to be there and was not invited to the Boyd property. The news crews had been there for a few days, and the state police gave daily announcements on Anna, trying to keep her in the forefront. I was told to return to North Carolina within three days of my arrival. And I did just that. I was not aware that I would be back in three years.

1998 – Finding Anna

Three years had passed, yet I was still eager as day one. I brought my binder, maps, and pictures. Jerry had me lay all the pictures out so we could go through them individually. I explained each picture and circled areas that caught my attention. Syd put my photos in plastic sleeves so I could write on them without ruining them. We could see dust removed in one of the cabinets, meaning an item had recently been removed, but what would it be? We guessed it was something round by the circumference. Jerry looked at my Mountain Dew can.

We both said at the same time, "A can."

I showed him the footsteps, which appeared from muddy shoes.

"I did some measurements, and it appears to be a boy-size seven child's shoe. I also have weather data for that week Anna went missing. This side of West Virginia was in a drought—no rain for over 45 days. Meaning it was dry, but these prints are muddy."

Jerry looked at me and put his head into his hands.

"I got pictures of shoes inside the garage, but they were never turned over."

FAMILY DIRT

"What do you mean you have pictures?"

"One of our troopers went into the garage and found clothes in the washer, and it looked like the washer had just stopped without spinning. It may have become unbalanced and stopped mid-way through the cycle. We carry those throw-away cameras in case we need to document something. Let me grab the pictures out of the locker."

Jerry returned with a stack of pictures they had taken outside the home and inside the garage.

The garage was one stall, and Boyd's vehicle, a Dodge minivan, was parked inside. To the left was a washer and dryer and a side-by-side refrigerator. One of the pictures had the refrigerator door open, filled with cans of Budweiser beer. It had to be Jim Sr.'s alcohol stash, and it was filled from top to bottom. I could see clothes in the muddy water in the following picture. After that, I reviewed the images of each piece of clothing lying on the garage floor. I looked at the shoes, then back at my picture, and realized the muddy prints came from those size 7 Converse.

I kept flipping through my pictures and back at Jerry's.

"One of the pictures I took in the shabby kitchen always perplexed me. I did not see it when I took the picture, but something shiny was next to the old stove, between the stove and the cabinets. The stove bottom broiler door was missing, and it might be the handle of the missing broiler door. Look at this and tell me what you think. I have never figured this one out," pointing to the area I had circled.

"Boy, I don't know what that is. It could be a handle, it is definitely metal. We got a magnifying glass. Let me go grab it."

He came back in a few minutes holding the tool, and I just stared at him

"What's wrong? Did you figure it out without me?" He let out a laugh.

I held up the picture of the washer full of clothes.

"Why were these pictures never entered into evidence?"

"Like yours, we didn't have a search warrant, so we took the clothes out, took the pictures, and put everything back like we weren't there."

"Please tell me what color you see?" I pointed to the muddy water at the top left inside the washer.

"It looks like purple, but we didn't take anything purple out of the washer."

I flipped through my notes and put them on the table, pointing to one sentence. I read it out loud, "She had a purple ribbon in her hair. She loved Barney and could not wait to watch him on television. Anna was home, and I think someone in her family hurt her."

We looked at the picture of the old stove with the magnifying glass, and we could see the silver items, which were crushed beer cans.

We had to start building a case; something purple and beer cans would not get us a search warrant. Jim Jr. was most likely stealing beer, taking it to the shabby and drinking it. The impression in the cabinet was a mark from a beer can.

Did Anna find out JR was drinking beer and threaten to tell her dad?

Would JR kill his sister for something that foolish?

Were there more secrets in the Boyd household that we didn't know?

Did JR get his clothes out of the washer?

Who finished the wash, and did they find the ribbon?

Is the purple ribbon in their house?

I was so confused that someone in that family may know JR was involved but kept it a secret for three years. It didn't make sense.

Jerry and I looked at each other and said, "Search Warrant."

We would have to see a judge and get a warrant, but we needed a solid strategy if we were looking for Anna, buried or her body hiding on Boyd's property. The search warrant I was given were not for the shabby, and we wanted to make sure a local warrant would stand up in court.

Jerry called his Lieutenant and asked to meet with him to discuss the case. We needed direction, not politics. Jerry and I were pushed off the case three years ago, and we did not want that to happen again. I knew my leadership was in my corner if push came to shove.

The following day, we had a search warrant for the Boyd property. It was limited to the shabby, but we already secured warrants for the residence so we were happy. I had suspicions about that place on day one and thought of it often.

Jim Sr. was livid when we announced ourselves. Daisy and the kids were gone at the school carnival and would not be home until later that afternoon. We asked Jim if he wanted to come with us, and he said no, we were wasting his time again. Truth be told, we didn't want him to be with us, and we documented that we asked.

We brought a cadaver dog and started our walk to the shabby. I still hated that name and was telling myself, please don't let that little girl be buried there. I was getting a sick feeling and started to get nauseous, which was a first. The dog, Louie, was a beagle with an excellent nose. He had won major awards and was quite good for only two years old. He started outside the perimeter and was taken around the shelter on more than one trip. I was getting nervous. We may be way off on this one. I didn't know how to be happy or sad. I wanted her found but found alive. Louie's handler started room by room as we waited outside. Within 8 minutes, we heard a howl. Then another howl, and then a bark. The handler came out with Louie and said, "We got something." My heart skipped a beat.

Anna was found almost three years from the date she went missing. We took tremendous care in excavating her body. We called for state experts and followed evidence-collection protocol throughout the entire process. We would not allow to lose this in court for shoddy police work. Jim Sr. was taken to the police department and held for questioning. State troopers went to the school and told Daisy to get the kids; they needed to go to police headquarters because Jim Sr. had gotten into trouble and needed her to come and bail him out. That was a lie, but they did not want to cause a scene. Once they reached headquarters, they were all separated and sat alone in interrogation rooms. Police officers stayed with JR and

Marigold but refused to question them. Only asking them if they were comfortable and needed a drink.

Anna was buried under the floor in a bedroom of the shabby. Pieces of wood from the ceiling and branches covered her burial site. She was at least four feet underground. She was found at the bottom of the hole, where a natural spring was located. The state coroner was taking pictures and documenting every move she made. Megan Chandler was one of the best; I knew she could build a story on what happened to Anna. Megs was known throughout the East Coast as the most brilliant forensic expert. I had all the confidence in the world that she would make the case against the suspect with no questions unanswered.

She told us she wanted to get the body back to the "garage," as she called it, and it appears Anna was shot in the chest by a shotgun. She was buried with one spent slug and one shell never fired, along with her book bag and a beer can. Megan put the items in evidence bags, put dirt in a container, and we lifted Anna very slowly and placed her in a small, black body bag. I wanted to cry, but all feelings left my body, and I had no tears. Megs zippered the bag up very slowly, with tears in her eyes. She asked Jerry and me to carry Anna to the van parked at the back of the property. The paparazzi started to arrive, where we had closed the road. I could hear their excitement blocks away.

Megan ordered officers to bring in lights and set up for a long night. She would start evidence collection with the body but wanted to return to the shabby when she was done. Megs asked for a full excavation of the shabby and told us that after that was completed, we would take the shelter down. She wanted to ensure no other bodies were underneath it, and I had never allowed that thought to cross my mind.

Later, I stepped aside and called Syd to tell her Anna was found. After hearing the story, she started crying.

"The pain Anna felt and to be buried in a backyard, laying in the dirt, while her family went on with their lives. I hope you hang every damn one of them."

I explained that we did not know who the killer was. Time would tell, and they were possibly being interviewed as we spoke. I told her I loved her and asked her to please kiss the girls for me, and I would call her in the morning because I had no idea how long we would be on the site.

We had the complete story within 4 hours of the events of that faithful day.

Anna arrived home, dropped her bag at the door, ran to the television, and turned it on because Barney had already started. JR came home next and wanted to know why she was there. Anna was not aware, but she was ruining her brother's day. JR changed his clothes and started out the door with his dad's 12-gauge shotgun. Anna knew the house rules: guns cannot be touched, ever.

"You better put that back; Dad is going to be mad!"

"I can have it. Dad lets me, and he just doesn't tell you."

"I am going to tell Mom when she gets home."

"If you tell Mom, I will tell her you left your shoes on in the house."

She screams, "You better not, she will tell Dad, and I will get a whooping."

"When are you going to grow up? You can't be a cheerleader if you are still a baby."

"I am not a baby!"

"Who is watching a show for babies? Barney is for babies!"

"I am not a baby; stop saying that."

"Come with me, and you can watch grown-up stuff."

"You won't make me swing on that swing, will ya?"

"No, just come with me, and we will be quick. Then we will walk over and give an apple to Rocket."

"Goody, let's go!"

JR shut the television off and told Anna to grab her bag. That way, Mom wouldn't know she didn't follow house rules. All backpacks had to stay in the bedrooms.

The two headed out the door and towards the garage. JR needed to get something, so he told her to wait. He went to the refrigerator in the garage and took a beer and grabbed a box of shotgun shells off the cabinet.

He walked out carrying both.

"You're going to get into trouble," Anna said with the voice of a five-year-old.

"Only if you don't keep your mouth shut! If Mom and Dad find out, you may never see Rocket again. I would hate to miss my target and shoot him."

Anna started to whine, "Don't hurt Rocket. He is my best friend."

"I am joking, but keep this a secret, and I mean it. Or you won't have a best friend."

They walked back to the shabby, and JR opened his beer. He took a couple of swigs and placed the can in the cabinet.

"I'm scared. I don't like this place, and it is haunted."

He laughed, "Haunted? Only babies believe in ghosts."

JR and Anna left the shabby with the gun and gunshot shells stuffed in JR's jeans pockets. He gave one to Anna so she could look at it.

He made her stand behind him, loaded four shells at the bottom of the 12 gauge, and then asked her what he should shoot at because he had no targets left on the property. All the empty beer cans were hidden in the shabby, and he was too lazy to get them.

Anna pointed, "That tree."

"That's boring, but okay, put your hands over your ears. This will be really loud. And don't scream. If you scream, you can't be a cheerleader."

Anna did what she was told.

JR squeezed off one round in the old hickory about forty yards before him.

With the loud bang, they saw a squirrel jump from the tree to another tree.

JR aimed at the squirrel and squeezed off another shot. Birds flew off, chirping and scaring Anna.

"What did you do? Don't hurt the squirrel," as she took off running to the dead squirrel lying on the ground.

JR started shouting, "What a shot! I can't believe it!"

Anna turned around and looked at JR and then back at the dead squirrel, which was missing its head. Anna was startled, but she turned back to JR, "You killed it, and I am telling Dad. You are going to get the belt tonight."

JR pointed the gun at Anna, "If you say anything, I will shoot you and that damn horse."

Anna said, "You're the baby, and you'll cry." Anna started walking towards the house. JR was unaware, but their mom would be home ten minutes later.

JR yelled at her, "Anna, look!"

Anna turned around and was shot in the chest by her big brother.

JR dragged Anna into the shabby, where a huge hole was under the scrap wood. JR knew that because he had dug it last year to get to a spring below the hole. He wanted a place to hide beer cans and gun shells while he used it as an underground fort. He filled it with dirt, but it would still be loose since he put some boards down before filling the hole.

He dumped everything in the hole, including her book bag. He needed to get home, change his clothes, and get the gun back under his parents' bed. When he got to the house, he could see the minivan in the garage. He dumped the gun in the back of the van and planned to sneak out later to get it and put it back before his father would know it was gone. He heard his mom come out of the house, and she saw him and made him change his clothes. He stripped down to his gym shorts and dumped everything in the washer. JR was unaware that Anna's hair ribbon had come off when he tossed her body in the hole. It was caught up in his back pocket. He was in such a hurry that he had no idea it was there.

Had the cops searched that night, they would have found a recently fired shotgun and the purple ribbon in JR's jeans. JR was getting nervous when he heard the cops with his parents. He had to wait for them to leave and sneak out to the garage. His mom did not go to bed that night, so he could not go out and get the gun. He soon fell asleep, and the gun stayed in the van. The following day, the cops were at the house. He did not know what to do except go to school and act like nothing happened.

The night after Anna went missing, Daisy entered the garage because she had left her purse in the van. She was exhausted from talking with the police all day and needed a cigarette. When she walked by the washer, she noticed the muddy mess. She grabbed a shop towel and wiped the washer clean. She then remembered seeing JR and how muddy he was. She opened the top washer and saw the mess. She was sure he did not put detergent in with his clothes. She turned the dial to spin, draining the muddy water. She pulled up a chair and got a cigarette out of her purse. She was worried about Anna, but she knew that her son had done something terrible to her. JR was a troubled child and had a history of hurting small animals. When she would tell Jim, he ignored her.

"Boys will be boys; leave him be. He ain't growing up as a fairy. No boy of mine is going to be a girl."

JR hated his sisters and continuously teased Anna when his father was absent.

Daisy was in turmoil because she did not want to tell the police that JR might be possible for Anna's disappearance; it made no sense, and she was embarrassed for even thinking of it.

The spin cycle ended. She opened the washer door. A purple ribbon lay on top of one of the Converse shoes.

Daisy sat down and cried. She couldn't believe it.

What could Anna have done to her brother that he needed to hurt her?

Where is she?

She started to look around the garage and found a flashlight. She was prepared to search the property and did not care what time it was. She went to the van, sat in the driver's seat, and cried. She didn't know what to do. Should she drive around town and look for Anna? Should she call the police or wake up Jim?

Should she wake up JR and ask him where Anna was?

She finished her cigarette, flipping her ashes into a cup in the middle of the front seats. She snubbed the butt out and decided to wake up JR. She looked in the rear-view mirror, and something caught her eye. She got out of the van and walked around to the back. She saw a small muddy hand print on the back glass of the van door.

She opened the door slowly, and she saw the gun. At that point, she knew Anna was dead.

Daisy admitted to hiding the gun after Jim went to work, and the cops left later that day. She cleaned off the mud and put the gun back under their bed in its case. Daisy had to decide whether to lose one child or two. She decided she could do nothing for Anna and saved JR.

JR was arrested and taken to a juvenile detention center. Charges were pending for Daisy, but the charges would never hold up in court. Jim wanted nothing to do with her. The community could not grasp what happened, but the talk in town, they wanted JR never to see the light of day. Four days later, I was driving back to North Carolina and promised never to return to West Virginia. That was a lie, and I had a funeral to attend once Anna's body was released from evidence.

1998 – Branches Emerge

After the Boyd case was closed and I returned home, Syd left for her trip to Illinois. We had planned that after she returned, I would head to Ohio to spend time with my mother.

She was flying into O'Hare, picking up a rental car, and meeting Alice and her family for their favorite pizza. I was unaware, that Alice was helping much more than Syd let on with my family tree. Both have collected quite a story, but much more work had to be done. She never offered any information to me, and I noticed she took everything off the wall in her war room. Syd told me she had to make a few side trips south of Chicago. She was excited because she was sure she found where my mother had been born. Syd needed to visit a few county courthouses and state agencies. She promised to check in a couple times a day during her travels.

Paul had me working from home for the next 2-3 weeks. He wanted me to rest and take some time to breathe. I returned to my cold cases and followed up on the Cisco and Boyd indictments. I spoke to state attorneys and police agencies many times each day. I would have loved to be with Syd, but I knew I wasn't welcome. Since coming home from finding Anna, I felt Syd acted like she had a lot on her mind. Her thesis was likely making her indifferent, but I was afraid it might be me. Syd was always happy and showed a lot of emotion, and when we spoke, she always paid attention. I called it listening with her eyes. That had stopped this past week.

Syd called me after dinner and was excited that she had chosen to stay with Alice, her husband, and their two boys. They ate pizza and talked about their hockey team and, of course, the Blackhawks. They wanted her to attend their next hockey game in a few days. Syd made her airline ticket one way because she did not know how much time she would need. She planned to be away for three days, and she was trying her best to stick to it.

Syd was heading out early in the morning after connecting with a county clerk who was able to send her a few documents with the names and dates of possible grandparents of my mom. I asked her how she could confirm that the information was correct. Syd said she had her ways because everything had to fit the script. I did not know what that meant, but Syd was great with math and statistics. She would not crank the lever if the dates and names didn't add up.

When Syd hung up the phone, she picked up the two documents emailed to her. She hated lying to me, and it was something she was not proud of. She feared I would make her stop if I knew the story before it was finished. People don't want to learn bad things about their family. She did not need me to lose confidence in myself and have it affect my career. I had made comments that Lynn's parents may have had to give her up due to an unexpected pregnancy. The family could have been poor and could not afford a child. Syd did not want to be the one to prove that wrong, and she had mixed feelings about how to propose the story to me. The story was still in progress, but she was finding that she wanted better results. Syd had been speaking with Nancy and keeping her involved with each step. She also used her as a sounding board when she needed clarification on family generational timelines.

Syd had a grandmother on her dad's side, who was 89. She called Helen with a few questions, making it a habit for historical clarification. Syd had difficulty believing life could be harmful for people born in the 1920s. Helen reminded her that many people are still treated unfairly and women rights have slightly increased since that decade. Syd started questioning humanity and how women have been mistreated throughout history.

The next day, Alice and Syd headed off to a few towns southeast of Chicago. They were able to collect much more information than they first thought. Alice had done much of the work because she had an old college friend, Tad, who was a genius at mapping out family trees. He was working with a startup company, Tree Roots, that specialized in tracing generations and the history that went with it. Their goal was to offer a product where users could tap their databases and build their own family tree. Collecting the information was the start phase, which took an extensive amount of time. He gave Alice an abundant amount of information and was excited to do so free of charge.

"So, you and this guy ever hooked up?"

"Who, Tad? Syd, please, are you crazy!"

There was a reason Syd liked Alice so much; she was very animated, and Syd would find ways to excite her.

"Tad seemed very interested, almost too interested. And believe it or not, a real nerd, not a nerd like us, but like a nerd on steroids."

"You didn't find that attractive?"

"Well, one night, we were working late in the computer lab, and he flat-out asked me if I would date him." I looked at him and said, "Tad, two nerds should never be in a relationship. Could you imagine what our kids would look like?"

"Alice!" Syd blurted out.

Tad looked at me and said, "I wasn't talking about kids. I just wanted to get a hamburger with you."

"When Tad found out he was helping Emily after that little Boyd girl was found, we can ask him for anything. He is your ace in the hole."

They spent their time zipping in and out of county courthouses, a lawyer's office, three libraries, and a driver's license facility and ended up eating their way through town. They learned more at every stop but were more perplexed than when they started. They rolled through microfiche and dusted off old newspaper clippings in large dusty scrapbooks. They knew they might have to travel farther downstate, so they came prepared and made hotel reservations. The next day, the visits were the same, and they added some pictures to their stack of treasures. A librarian at the local library was very engrossed in the story and was able to have state records faxed up from Springfield, the state house in Illinois. She sent Syd and Alice to the local newspaper, which had existed for over 75 years. They kept their own library, and she knew the person in charge.

They headed a few miles away to the newspaper facility, which had a history of Emily's family. They spent a few hours there and packed up, realizing they had worked eight hours straight and missed their lunch. Due to Alice's boys' hockey game, they needed to return to Chicago. They left their names and phone numbers with everyone they met and was told, if any other stories were found, they would notify Syd.

Once Alice and Syd got in the car, they stared at each other, holding folders crammed with documents. Syd started crying. Alice soon followed. The story they found was not joyous, and eventually, Syd knew she was walking barefoot on glass. She needed to think if the journey should be stopped. Alice and Syd had a quiet ride back to Chicago. They stopped at a drive-thru for a cold hamburger and fries and eventually started talking about their day. Alice offered to investigate a few areas Syd needed closure and felt Tad could pull that together for them. Alice asked Syd what she was thinking and if she was still flying out tomorrow. Syd said she was, but she was heading to her parents. She wanted to speak to her mom and grandmother in person.

"If I come back in a few months before the weather starts turning colder, I would like to go to the cemetery, even though it is supposed to be difficult to find. I need to visit the grave site. I need closure before I wrap this in a present with a bow to Emily. I love her way too much for her to find out."

"Syd, count me in. I would be honored too, and I cannot imagine finding that place, let alone the grave."

Syd called her mom, explained that she needed to see her, and gave her a synopsis of my family tree. Nancy was happy to see Syd and told her everything would be okay. Syd called Helen and asked if she could visit when she came to town tomorrow. She needed help with a few details of her project.

Helen could hear Syd's voice crack, and Helen said, "Families are not kind to each other. One should never be embarrassed because they are related to someone that is a jackass."

Syd had to laugh and told her it was the first time today that she could crack a smile.

Syd called me and explained that she needed to fly out the next day and head to her parents. She lied again and said her grandmother was ill and felt it would be a good time to fly down and spend a day or two with her. Again, Syd had to feel uncomfortable offering up false information, which was happening more and more. I asked if she needed me to fly down, and Syd started to cry. She said she missed me and everything was fine. She and Alice had a great time, and they found some interesting things, but she did not know if the items collected added value to the project. Syd winced because she felt she was lying more this past week to me than in the 18 years we were together. Syd had to go due to the hockey game but promised she would call tomorrow morning after she got to the airport. She had a 9:10 a.m. flight to Birmingham and would have to fight the traffic to O'Hare. I knew something was up, but I wanted to give Syd space. I had no clue my family secrets were driving her to her limits.

Syd was picked up at the airport by Nancy and Mack.

"What a surprise, I feel honored."

"Oh, honey, we both want to welcome you home." Said Mack.

Nancy shook her head in agreement. "Let's go get some breakfast at your favorite diner."

Syd explained to her parents some of the stories she found concerning my family. She did not want to explain every detail but gave a CliffsNotes version. She told them about Tad and how he was helping her build out the family tree. Mack asked if she needed any funds, and he would give her whatever she needed.

"Thank you, Dad, but I am okay. Tad is with a startup company that is using new tools to see how it will function. Alice has been a lifesaver. Also, I met some great historians and librarians in Illinois, and if they find anything, they will call me. I have been blessed that this is happening right now when I need it the most."

"How is Emily? I called after Anna was found but have not spoken to her for a few days."

"She is doing very well, much better than expected. She didn't get much time to rest after the shooting, and then the Boyd case swooped her up. That has been a good thing."

Mack looked at her. "We need to plan a vacation with the whole family. I want you to think about where you want to go. We can have everyone come to Alabama, go to California, Colorado, or North Carolina, or we will pay for everyone to go anywhere you want."

"Dad, that would be fantastic. After I put this to bed and my thesis in a good place, I can give it some thought."

"You do that and think about the weather. If you want cold or hot, we can even do lukewarm," he let out one of his big belly laughs.

Syd and Nancy went to visit Helen later that day. Syd had Helen explain how she grew up and what expectations were put on women. Syd had asked if she could use her tape recorder to interview her, which Helen found comical. Syd asked about women's rights and health, transportation costs, living wages, and parent's expectations after childbirth. Syd really wanted to pay attention to what her grandmother told her. Helen grew up very poor, and she told her that was why Mack was so good with money. They didn't need much, so they were able to save money and help him and Nancy start a good life.

When Syd and Nancy returned to the car, Syd felt happy.

"Emily's grandparents and great-grandparents lived much like gramps. It was tough, but they just went in a different direction due to one man. Oddly, you can be a good person, but one person can change your trajectory in life — for good or bad. I really want to finish this for Emily. She deserves to find out who her family is. She lived with a mother who did not show compassion, a father who was an alcoholic, and no grandparents. Her coworkers treated her disrespectfully when she was first hired as the only female cop. Then she got shot due to them leading her into a deadly situation. I am so disgusted with society right now. I need to get this right."

"Are you feeling better about the story you are working on and can spin it in a good light for Emily?"

FAMILY DIRT

"When we get home, I will sit with you and Dad. I have yet to tell you the entire story. Mom, I won't lie; it is sad, horrendously sad."

Syd could relax and feel more open with me in her phone calls the next day. She caught up with old friends, went shopping with her mom, and even stopped by one more time to visit Helen. Syd was happy; she understood that my family had no reflection on who I was. In a way, they do, but not in a bad way. She looked forward to flying home, and I would pick her up with the girls. I told Syd they missed her, and I planned to cook her a nice dinner when she returned. Syd was starting to feel everything was right in the world. They could put Anna Boyd to rest. I was cleared from the shooting, and things were starting to get back to normal.

Her phone rang with an area code 206. It was from the Seattle area. It was Tad.

"Hi Tad, how are you today?"

"Hi Syd, I have something that I need to send you. Can you get by a computer? I am going to attach an article to an email."

"Sure, I am working on my thesis now, so send it over."

Tad heard the familiar ding, meaning Syd received his email.

"Are you sitting? Things are about to get really crazy."

Syd read the title of the article from The Tennessean, "Local Man Missing, Foul Play Expected."

Syd looked at the date, August 7, 1973.

Syd said, "Oh, no."

We were so happy to see Syd when we picked her up at the airport. The dogs greeted her with some howls and barks. Even though I was leaving the next day for my family visit, we would make the best of our short time together.

After dinner, I was packing to leave in the morning for Pickerington, a small community outside of Columbus. My mom was currently living there, and it was where I grew up. I had put off the trip as long as possible but knew I had to see her and discuss future plans.

Syd could see my hesitation as I was tossing clothes in my bag.

"You know, you could just fly and get it over with."

"The drive is short, and I will leave early in the morning and be there in seven hours. You know I love to drive and hate for airlines to control my time."

Syd laughed because she knew I wanted control of everything except her.

"When will you head back."

"I called Paul and told him I may be heading back on Monday, so Friday night to Monday morning should be enough time for Lynn and I to hate each other more than usual. If I stay longer, we may kill each other," I grinned.

"How about you take Ruth with you? She can keep you company, and your mom will be excited to see her. Taking both may be too much, but Ruthie would love it."

"That is a great idea. Ruth can pack her food and snacks, and I will show her what a quick trip to Ohio feels like."

"Great, I will pack her favorite ball and stuffy, and she will be excited to go with you."

We both looked at her as she lay on our bed, staring at the suitcase. She knew I was leaving. Keaton, on the other hand, was running through the house with her favorite stuffy toy in her mouth, squeezing it as loudly as possible. We always remind Alex that she is an enemy of ours since sending the girls new toys for no reason. Alex knew they had loud squeakers, which was why she chose them.

"I am going to the supermarket and pick up a few things to put in my cooler."

"Can I give you a list? I want you to pick up a few snacks for Ruth at the pet store. Is that okay, or will it slow your packing time?"

I said, "Please, I can pack in less than five minutes for a week-long trip."

"Oh, I know. I have two bags always to your one small bag. You should be working for Conde Nast Traveler."

"Okay, smart ass, get your list ready, so I can be back before the game night starts. And I would like to know how your Clue skills have been so good."

"Just following in the footsteps of my future wife."

Later, I was picking up a few things from the supermarket, and I grabbed some mustard for Syd. I then realized why she was so good at Clue. Her research skills have been on steroids.

Syd picked up the phone and dialed a phone number.

"Kris, it's Syd."

"So, when is she leaving?"

"She leaves in the morning, back on Monday evening, is her plan."

"How do you want to do this?"

"I told you I would pay. You just need to let me know."

"Okay, I will be fair. I don't live that far from there. I will keep to the plan. I will head there in the morning. How deep do you want me to dig?"

"I just want you to collect as much information as you can without pissing anyone off."

"I can do that. You can trust me."

"I trusted you once, and you screwed around on me, remember."

"C'mon Syd, you are being unfair. We were never a thing, and besides, that was high school," she said, laughing and sounding like she was choking on her drink. "Does Emily know about me?"

"Of course not. I have no reason to tell her about old flames, especially straight girls. Plus, it was awkward in the '70s and seems like an eternity ago."

"It was an eternity, but I still think of you, maybe a little."

"Well, I can safely tell you, I am glad it didn't work out because there is no way I would live in that conservative state that bans books."

"C'mon, it was one book, and we are doing our best to get people to be more accepting of others."

"Orwell, should never be banned."

"I agree, but now I read him, so it didn't work."

"You keep trying, and tell Smith I said hi."

"Oh, don't worry, he is helping me with this rendezvous."

"Nice, and Kris, thank you for doing this."

"You are always welcome, and I would love you two to visit one day."

"Let's see how this ends, and we can talk."

Syd had to stop and think about whether this was a good move and if she would be sorry for getting Kris involved. She felt as though she was drowning and just needed reassurance that what she was doing was going to work. Syd trusted Kris, and she could go a year without talking to her, and nothing changed in their relationship. She did not have the time to travel to Tennessee, but she would if she had to. It was a hunch, not a story she felt needed much attention.

She looked down at Keaton, who had a ball in her mouth.

"You and me, kid, for a few days. That means a lot of walks, and you watching me work."

Keaton just looked at her and continued to slobber on her ball.

The following day, Syd helped me load Ruth in the SUV. I always leave a map with the route I am traveling and would check in every few hours. Ruth would need a couple of stretch breaks. The weather would be good with no rain so it would be a nice drive there and back. I asked Syd if she had anything she wanted me to share with Lynn about her family heritage. I just got that look from Syd, who told me not to add drama to my visit. Ruth was more than happy to go with me. Keaton whined, but I suspected she was about to walk to the coffee shop and get a pup cup, and she was a dog highly motivated by food. Syd told me to wait a minute, "I think you forgot something." She ran into the house and came back with a plastic bag. Syd updated my favorite hoodie with a new one.

"I thought that old UNC hoodie had seen enough slobber. Let's keep it, but not out in public," she said with a huge smile.

I immediately removed the old one I was wearing, passed it through the car window, and put on the new Carolina blue.

"Thank you, fits perfectly!"

"Oh, baby, if I don't know your size by now, I never will."

Ruth and I went down the drive, honking as we pulled away.

As Syd watched the SUV leave her view, she looked at Keaton and loaded her in the Lexus. She had a package waiting for her at the Federal Express store. If she was lucky, the missing piece may have been found. They drove the few miles to the campus store, and Keaton sat in the backseat watching her favorite person enter the store. Syd collected a box that was heavier than she expected. They made her sign for it, which surprised her, but that was good mojo. She jumped in the driver's seat and pulled out a knife that she kept in the console. She cut through the sealed box, reached in, and took out many documents and pictures.

There was a note attached from Tad.

Syd read it out loud,

Syd, I got as much as I could, and I was shocked by the material that was not secured, so I grabbed everything. I will tell you again that this is a vulnerable story, and you will see in the pictures and the records what happened in that god-forsaken place. Please read slowly; don't give up! You can burn or shred these when you are done. I have all the copies and can email you anything you need. I know you do not want Emily to see these, and I understand why.

Godspeed, Tad.

Syd leafed through the documents, stopping at medical records and some black-and-white pictures. She pulled out a piece of paper with the numbers and names corresponding to that number. More than once, more than one name matched to one number, which Syd imagined was a mistake. Tad circled the name she was looking for. Syd caught her breath. The sheet of paper had a paper clip on the side of it. She turned it over. There was a picture attached, facing backward. She pulled the picture off and turned it over. It was a small grave marker with the number 817. A coldness came over her. She looked at Keaton in the back seat, who was letting out small growls. Syd looked around, but no one was around the car. She looked back at Keaton, still growling and staring at the picture Syd held in her hand. Syd put everything back in the box. She was well aware; she opened the bottle, and the genie was not going back in.

She immediately went home, kicked off her shoes, and went to her war room. Keaton grabbed her ball and laid it down by Syd's feet. Syd emptied the box of documents and started putting them in different piles. The papers went back three generations: Lynn, her parents, and her grandparents. It included many different locations, including Illinois, Indiana, and Tennessee, just to name a few. Other documents were a hodgepodge with no direction on what pile they should be placed in. Syd started the story on one side of the wall and taped the necessary documents to her giant timeline. She soon found out her future wife was of Italian/Scottish heritage. Appeared some German and French as well. Even though she had hoped for Australia, Italy would be a nice vacation place.

1912 – Meet The Martin Family

William and Ethel Martin were living the American dream. William was a patrolman in Peoria, IL., and earning a decent salary. He was 28 years old and had been married to Ethel Johnson for one year. She was 23. Ethel was lucky enough to be hired as a police matron at the local jail when she turned 21. She had an uncle who was a police captain who helped her immensely secure that position. Women were rarely arrested, but Ethel would be called upon to assist when they were. If no women were being housed in the jail cells, she would do secretary duties, making coffee and filing paperwork. The police officers loved Ethel and treated her well. They feared that her uncle would fire them if he heard of any nonsense. Luckily for them, he would be retiring in the next few years.

William was considered a handsome, polite young man striving to be a police sergeant. Ethel's uncle thought highly of him, and William courted Ethel for over a year. Of the nineteen police officers on the force, William was by far the best. He was of Catholic faith, as was Ethel, and they made a perfect pair. Between their two salaries, they felt they could afford a lovely home with a white picket fence and welcome children into their family.

One year after William got down on one knee, the two were married at St. Joseph's. It was the event of the year, bringing all the Catholics in the city, which included most of the police department. William and Ethel were deeply in love and had big hearts for their community. William wanted Ethel to quit her job and do something she enjoyed. He felt they had enough money hidden in their floor safe and could not imagine doing something so foolish as to lose those funds. They both wanted to start planning a family and looking forward to being parents.

During the first year of marriage, Ethel didn't get pregnant, even though the couple had tried. The doctor told her not to worry, to spend as much time outside getting fresh air, and, more importantly, to pray. Ethel and William agreed and put in a garden to keep Ethel occupied. She soon discovered she had more food than they needed, so she learned how to canned food and use their old cellar to its fullest advantage. She felt it was essential to do so, to show God that she cared about her husband.

William and Ethel agreed that they should donate to the local soup kitchen if there were more food than they needed. Olivia Underwood was an advocate for the poor, and she would set up on Main and Second Street twice a week, offering soup and bread to anyone in need. She hooked up her horses to an open wagon and would lead it to the corner without missing a day, even in the rain or snow. Olivia invited the police officers to spend time with the less fortunate community members. Once Ethel learned about Olivia, she asked her husband if she could volunteer. She felt that this offering to God may help her get pregnant.

The second year, Ethel continued with volunteering at the soup kitchen, which had now moved into the basement of St. Josephs. Ethel was thrilled to spend more time with the homeless and poor. She would then go upstairs and assist with making sure all the bibles and hymn books were clean and placed in the pews. She prayed to God and asked for a child before she left. She wanted a boy, of course, for William and hoped one day he would follow in his father's footsteps as a man of the badge. She saw how people in the community looked at her husband with respect. She wanted that same look to be cast on their firstborn son.

In 1915, Ethel and William had their prayers answered, and Ethel was pregnant. They were elated! All their dreams had come true. They had an elegant home and a plentiful garden, and they purchased their first car, a used Ford. This was a big purchase for them, but William wanted the best for his family.

The following year, Melvin was born. Doc Jones was brought to the Martin home and delivered a healthy 6 lb. 2 oz boy. William had chosen Melvin because it was the name of his great-grandfather, who was reportedly a very fair man. Ethel wanted a Catholic name for her firstborn and believed the church expected that. She knew her husband was brilliant and agreed that a family name was much more important than a saint's.

Ethel was happy to be at home and answer to every whim Melvin yearned. At first, William was pleased with the mother-son relationship, but he would explain to his wife that she shouldn't pick him up every time he cried. He even brought Doc Jones home to explain that Melvin needed to develop strong lungs. He told her Melvin would not learn by picking him up every time he cried. This could keep the boy from attending school or hold him back due to his underdeveloped brain. Ethel was angry and did not want men to tell her how to be a mother. She would have been happy if Melvin stayed home and never attended school. That scared William, and he asked Doc what he should do. Doc told him to have as many babies as possible. That way, Ethel would want the boy to attend school so he would not take up her time with new babies. And pray for a girl.

William listened to the Doc, and within the next three years, Ethel gave birth to two more children, Florence and Elizabeth. Melvin was now five and difficult to contain. He was jealous of his sisters and would do cruel things to them, including pinching, pulling their hair, or telling them they were ugly. That continued as the girls started to get older, but they could eventually tell their parents what he was doing to them. Ethel would send Melvin to school, giving her and the girls time together. Melvin would come home from school and find out they went to the local candy store or ice cream parlor without him. He would throw things at Ethel, yelling that he hated her. William had Doc pay house visits to watch Melvin's mentality, and they were worried something was wrong with him. They knew he had a severe disease because there was no other reason for the angry outbursts. Doc told them the boy was not sick; he was spoiled and needed to understand he couldn't treat girls like that. William asked what should he do, and Doc asked if he owned a belt.

Melvin was a bright child. He learned how to use people to get his way. He adapted to school and was always polite to the teachers. Behind their backs, he was the opposite. He would bully kids and find ways to try and look up girls' dresses. He carried this same mannerisms when he was home with his sisters. They would tell on him, and he would swear they were lying, knowing they would get soap in their mouths. He was sent to St. Joseph's every other day to pray. Ethel told William she could not take it anymore. Melvin was not proper with the girls, and she was afraid he would hurt them one day.

William was tired of coming home from work every day to chaos. He was doing his best as a sergeant and caring for his patrol officers. Prohibition had started, causing crime to skyrocket in the city. Chicago mafia members were being seen and rumored to be running liquor stills right under the noses of the city officials. William was hard-pressed to admit that the city officials were taking money and allowing it to happen. This scared Ethel since they lived downtown and could see the crime element increasing when the sun went down. The city got quite loud, with music and women of the night sauntering down the sidewalk. Ethel demanded they move from the area; she did not want her children to witness the crime when they stepped outside their front door.

William agreed and moved the family six blocks from the main square. It was closer to the school the children attended, and now, all three of them went simultaneously. Ethel volunteered at the school to watch the kids and report any crime she would see in the area, which was minimal. The move did the family well, and Melvin was starting to grow up and not be a pest to his sisters. He hung out with other boys, playing kickball and stickball every weekend after school. Ethel and William started to see that those activities brought him maturity, and they felt more potent as a family.

In the summer of 1926, William decided he needed to keep Melvin busy. With school ending, he feared Melvin would get into trouble, and Melvin was now allowed to earn a wage. He was ten years old, and William stressed that Melvin had to be the man of the house when he was not present. It was time for him to act like a grown-up. The family did not need money, but William understood the budget was getting tighter, with all the children growing out of their shoes and clothes much quicker. Melvin was not happy because he wanted to spend his entire summer outside, playing with his friends. There was a nearby park, and he wanted to play cowboys and Indians and build a tree fort. William did not want him in that park. He knew a crime was occurring in the woods surrounding the park, and he did not want to worry about his son getting into trouble or hurt. That accelerated Melvin's need for his son to start a job.

Within a week, William stopped by a local grain mill about half a mile from his residence, next to the Illinois River. The Aster Wheat Mill operated by having farmers bring their grain, which they would process and send up the river to Chicago. Employees unloaded the wheat, stacked it inside three grinders, and operators fed the grain into the grinders until it was pulverized into flour. Stackers had to sack the flour and stack it, which would then be taken to a barge that came from downriver. Loading was a tough job, and most of the employees who had to stack and carry the flour were the newest and youngest in the group. These boys and young men didn't last long, and after a few months, they would eventually quit. Hourly pay was poor, and the way the men treated the new workers was even worse.

William had connections with Alvin Aster, who owned the mill. William was the officer who arrived when Alvin's son got his hand stuck in one of the grinders. His son, Leroy, lost his hand, but if William had not arrived and, put a tourniquet on his wrist and rushed him to the hospital, he would have bled to death. William had left for the day and heard the call on the radio. He was only a few blocks away and sped to the scene. When Leroy passed out, he got Leroy's hand out of the grinder, breaking his wrist on purpose. He took off his belt and tied it below the broken wrist. He then took a mill bag made of heavy burlap and put it around his hand, tying it and controlling the bleeding if the tourniquet failed. They carried Leroy to William's car and sped to the hospital. Leroy learned how to run a mill with one hand and continued to work six days a week. Alvin felt he owed William his life because he wouldn't be able to live without his son.

After speaking with Alvin and him hearing that William had a ten-year-old son who could use some growing up, he immediately hired him. The mill needed a stacker, and it may be difficult for Melvin, but it was a job. He would work ten-hour shifts, starting at 6 a.m., with a fifteen-minute non-paid lunch, six days a week with Sundays off to attend church. His wages were set at 22 cents per hour. He would be paid in cash on Saturdays at the end of his shift. If he missed work or was late, no wages would be earned. If he was hurt at work, he would be fired immediately. He had to follow every rule, including no swearing or smoking. If he damaged a bag while stacking or carrying the flour, the cost would be deducted from his pay.

When Melvin was told about his new job, he cried. He claimed he would run away, and it was unfair that he had to work when he was supposed to have the summer off. None of his friends had to get a job, so why did he? William sat him down and told him it was time to grow up and that he would get to earn his own money. He would have to turn his wages over to his mother, but he could keep a small amount each week for the candy store. Melvin was still upset after dinner and went to bed early, crying himself to sleep. His sisters could hear him through the sheet that separated their beds. For the first time, they actually felt sorry for their big brother. Soon, his dad was standing over him, holding a candle. He was told to get up, and it was time to get to work; he was driving him to the mill.

That summer, Melvin learned to hate his parents. His father made him work, and his mother did not stop it. The job was difficult for a young adult, let alone a boy. Melvin would stand by one of the grinders, grab a flour bag, and put it under the chute. He would reach up and grab a lever to dump the flour. He had to be careful not to spill the flour and make sure all the flour was put into the burlap bag. Once full, the 35 lb. bag would have to be picked up and moved to the bag sealer, where another worker would seal the bag with heat. Melvin would then have to pick up the bag and carry it over his shoulder for over 50 yards. He would then lay it in a pile 12 bags high by four bags wide. He would have to count the bags as he continued throughout the day. In the last thirty minutes of the day, all workers were to clean up their areas. If they were not finished cleaning, they were not paid for any time after their shift. If they got done before their thirty minutes, they were allowed to leave but did not get paid for doing so. Melvin was always last because the men made him clean. The men said that was the rule: new hires had to be the last workers out of the mill.

The men found ways to harass Melvin and did whatever they could to make his shift miserable. They would walk behind him when he was carrying a flour bag and poke it with a knife. When Melvin went to stack his bag, he noticed a trail of flour behind him. When that happened, the partial bag of flour was then charged back to him, which was a loss of wages. Melvin would get deductions in his pay for the first few weeks until he could find a way to carry the bag in front of him. His parents started asking him why he was not bringing home the wages that he was promised. He told his dad what was happening at the mill. William wanted to avoid reporting the problem to Alvin; he tried to find another way for his son to collect the wages he was promised. William made it a habit to walk on the shop floor when he drove Melvin to work or when he went to pick him up at the end of the shift. The men soon found out Melvin's dad was a police sergeant. That made them hate Melvin more, but they knew he was off-limits.

For six straight days, Melvin would have to put up with the men harassing him relentlessly. But that made Melvin work smarter. Even though he would not be returning to school, Melvin's learning did not stop. He became smart in his own way. Working with older men, he started to learn things he was unaware of. The one day a week, Sunday, Melvin was free to do as he pleased after he attended church. He would tell his family that he would play at the school grounds, but he had found another way to make money without his parents being aware of his movements. He learned many of the men had side hustles, from picking up envelopes from nearby businesses or dropping off money envelopes to women living in an old deteriorating hotel. The men would give Melvin a small amount of money for every envelope he collected or dropped off. He was told he couldn't tell anyone, ask any questions, and needed to sneak around without having the attention being cast upon him. Melvin was good at sneaking and learned how to be a fantastic liar.

As summer turned into winter, Melvin's second job evolved into new opportunities that involved smuggling liquor from one place to another. He stole a wagon, put a wooden box around the frame, and laid blankets on top of the liquor bottles. If he was stopped, he would tell people he was collecting blankets for the poor. People knew his mother's history, so they believed Melvin was a nice young man who helped his mother with her clothing drives.

Melvin now made more money than he earned at the mill since he was moving alcohol, even though it was against the law. He would take his cash and bury it in his family's backyard when no one was watching. His sisters never paid attention to Melvin; their time was spent with their mother. William was always working, giving Melvin more freedom on his one day off. He could not tell his family he was saving money. He knew his parents would take the money from him and buy gifts for his sisters, which he felt was unfair. Besides, he had grandiose plans waiting for him.

Soon, the wagon was turned in for a sled once snow arrived, making his route a little more challenging. He had to find other creative ways to deliver the liquor. Once, he had a fifth of whiskey fall off the sled and break into two pieces. He knew he would be in trouble and needed to find a way to hide it. At the end of the day, all bottles delivered had to be full, unopened, and unbroken when the counting was completed. When the glass bottle broke, he lost much of the alcohol but could put the top of the broken piece back on the bottle. The bottle still had the cap on it, so it appeared never opened. Melvin placed the bottle square in the middle of the other bottles and made sure he had to be the person who checked it in. He would need a plan for taking the blankets off the bottles once he arrived at the warehouse.

He was already late, and Bruiser would be waiting on him. Melvin pulled the sled through the snow and slushed to the back garage door at the old warehouse. He knew the game. Smack the door twice, count to ten, and smack the door again, this time three times. When someone asked who it was, the answer had to be Preacher James. Bruiser would then take the chain on the other side of the door and start pulling on it, lifting the door to rise. Melvin was supposed to take his load to the corner and Bruiser would stack it with the rest of the deliveries.

"Boy, where you been? The truck is going to be here any minute, you fool."

Bruiser was an old man, tall as a giant, wearing bib overalls, a dirty white t-shirt, and a tan jacket. He wondered if Bruiser was living in the warehouse despite there being no electricity or water.

"I had to stop and hide, coming around the corner on Aiken, 'cause cops were there with the ladies."

"Cops shaking the girls down on a Sunday?"

Melvin lied but knew he had Bruiser, hook, line, and sinker.

"Yeah, they were standing around on the corner, acting like they were looking for someone."

"We need to be careful. Let's get to unloading so we can hide if the cops start snooping around."

"I can do it myself. Why don't you grab your newspaper and tell me something smart since I don't go to school? I need some education."

Bruiser stopped walking with Melvin and turned around to get the paper. His plan worked.

Melvin hurriedly removed the tarp from the other deliveries, then took his wooden box holding 12 bottles and placed it on top of the others. He then put another wooden box filled with bottles on top of his. Hoping that, when found, it would appear as though it had broken during shipment to the new location. Melvin understood that if it was found broken while he was there, Bruiser would beat him, and he would lose his job. His money would be stolen as well. He still had six dollars in his pocket from earlier envelope runs.

"The paper is talking about St. Joseph's and wanting people to bring clothes to the basement so they can give them to the poor people."

Melvin said, "that's where I go with my family."

"You Catholic?"

"Bruiser, you're not?"

They heard a vehicle pull up at the door. Bruiser acted scared and looked at Melvin.

They heard the familiar two bangs, then three, and the magic words. Bruiser told Melvin to hide; no kid was allowed to be there during pick-up. Melvin ran up a flight of steps to a platform that led to an office that overlooked the warehouse and laid down on his belly. Bruiser started pulling on the chain, and a light blue Ford truck pulled in. There were words on the side, but Melvin couldn't make them out because he was too far away. The man driving was short and fat, with a funny hat on. He could hear them talk but could not hear their words. Melvin watched them load all the liquor bottles in the back of the truck. The man then covered up the bottles with wood planks that were in the warehouse. Melvin heard another vehicle outside, and he got nervous. He listened to the same pattern of smacks on the door and watched Bruiser start pulling the chain. Bruiser glanced around like he was looking for Melvin because he didn't know where he was hiding or if he slipped outside through one of the broken windows. Bruiser was hoping Melvin would make it out of the building for their safety. Melvin watched as a cop came walking through the door. It was his dad's boss, Lieutenant O'Leary. Right when Melvin thought Bruiser was going to jail, the guy in the funny hat pulled out an envelope and gave it to the cop. They all laughed about something, and then Melvin watched the truck leave the warehouse carrying the liquor. He could see out the window that O'Leary got into his cop car and drove behind the truck, following, without stopping the driver, who had illegal alcohol. He watched Bruiser lower the door after the men left the warehouse. Melvin learned a valuable lesson, and he did not need Bruiser to read it to him in the newspaper. Bruiser yelled out Melvin's name, but Melvin stayed hiding on the platform. Bruiser looked around, took his newspaper, and left the warehouse, walking towards the train yard. Melvin guessed Bruiser wasn't living in the warehouse after all.

Melvin continued to turn over his wages to his parents, saving his Sunday cash for something bigger. He had heard stories about the city of Chicago. More liquor could be moved in quicker trips, making him rich. He knew his parents would never allow him to leave. He was now thirteen but far from being a man. He had learned to be street-smart and kept his nose out of any business while sticking to his routes. The one thing he did do was pay attention. He listened to the way men talked and how they used hand gestures. He wanted to be just like them and less like his father.

For three years, Melvin thought about telling his father's lieutenant that he saw him take money for illegal alcohol. Maybe he would give him money to keep his mouth shut. But he was afraid O'Leary would tell his father, and he would get the belt and would have to quit his side hustle. Melvin did not know it, but his life was about to change, and his second job would not be that damn important to him.

William decided that Melvin needed to return to school because he wanted him to have a career as a cop. William felt his family was not following the Catholic faith, and he had robbed his son of the privilege of an education. He felt guilt while watching his daughters flourish in their studies, and Melvin deserved that same respect.

William was unaware that his son was a criminal and wanted to stay a criminal. He would talk to Ethel about having Melvin return to school the following year and have his daughters help Melvin with his studies.

William was working at the jail, helping detainees since they had seen an increase in arrests during the summer months. The court was backed up, overfilling the jailhouse, with men being arrested for multiple charges, primarily related to alcohol, prostitution, or gambling. He did not like working behind a desk but understood he had no choice. William had taken an assignment at the county jail to learn the faces of the criminal element in his community. Since Prohibition, the police force had spent much of their time making surprise visits to all the speakeasies in the downtown area. William knew they were serving liquor but could never prove it. Someone on his force was a rat, tipping everyone off on their secret plans. He didn't trust the City Mayor or his top brass. He wanted to find a way to catch the rat but needed a big piece of cheese—money—that he did not have.

At the end of his shift, William was leaving the jail. He had just gotten into his car when he heard a call over the radio about a possible burglary at the waterfront area in a stockyard's warehouse. He knew the owner who ran the stockyards, and while there was cattle feed, there was nothing else worth stealing. Why would anyone want to rob that place where the owner used a drop safe, and most business was done on a handshake? William called dispatch on the radio and said he would take the call since he was on his way home. He was asked if he wanted backup, and he said no.

William parked off the side of the warehouse and decided to go on foot. He quietly shut his door and started looking through the dirty windows. He didn't see much due to the darkness outside and the bags of feed stacked inside as high as the ceiling. William went back to his car and grabbed a flashlight. He walked to the back of the warehouse, where the delivery trucks parked. He saw a van but assumed it was owned by the warehouse owner. William could hear two voices but couldn't determine what was being said. He thought one voice sounded familiar, but the other had an accent he didn't recognize. He planned to sneak in on the other side of the warehouse and return to the delivery dock. He picked up the pace and started looking for an unlocked door. When William couldn't find one, he returned to the dock, but on the other side, where the door was partly open. He was able to sneak in under it without being seen. The two voices were farther away, but he could see the light on and shadows moving about. William hid behind the tall food bags stacked over twelve feet high. He could hear clanging and smelled a familiar odor—it was an illegal still.

William realized he would have to return to his car radio to call for help, but he didn't want to move too quickly. He could hear the two voices coming toward him. Then, he realized one voice was Lieutenant O'Leary's. Maybe his boss was there to arrest the man running the still. William listened to their conversation and heard them talking about moving the liquor to Chicago later that night. That's when William realized his lieutenant was in on the crime.

William emerged from the darkness, displaying his gun and pointing it at the man with the accent. The man was tall, slim, and had bronzed skin. Lieutenant O'Leary told William to lower his firearm. William refused.

"I said, lower your firearm, Sergeant!"

"Why should I? This man is breaking the law."

"Sergeant, do you see me in uniform? Do you understand you just blew my cover?"

The bronze skinned man turned to O'Leary and said, "What?" in broken English.

William then felt embarrassed and realized he wasn't aware his lieutenant was involved in undercover obligations.

"I said, holster your firearm, now!"

William lowered his gun and started to put it back in his holster when the bronzed skinned man pulled a revolver from his jacket and shot William.

William fell to the ground and rolled backward to get behind the stacked food.

He knew he had been shot, but it was in the upper shoulder of his non-shooting hand.

The bronze skinned man started to run back to the still when William heard O'Leary scream.

"You fucking goombah! Now you screwed us!" as O'Leary ran, following the man.

That's when William realized O'Leary was in on the crime, just as he'd first thought. He got to his feet and ran to follow them. O'Leary took two shots at him while running to his new hiding spot. O'Leary ran back to the room that contained the still, and William saw O'Leary shoot the other man in the head. O'Leary destroyed the still by knocking it over and lighting a match. A fire started, and O'Leary ran to find William. William was trying to get to his car when O'Leary took one more shot and hit William in the back. O'Leary ran from the warehouse, where he had parked his car a few blocks away. He knew Sergeant Martin's body would be found, along with the other man. People would think Martin was a hero and died while finding the illegal still. He would be buried with honor.

William had been shot twice, but he was still breathing. He managed to crawl on his belly to the outside of the delivery dock. The fire had grown, and the warehouse was fully engulfed. A local newspaper delivery man saw the fire. He drove down to the warehouse, hoping to get a story, when he realized there were no cops or fire trucks in the area. When he went around the corner, he saw a cop lying on the ground. He jumped out of his truck and ran to the cop. He turned him over, grabbed his shoulders, and dragged him to his truck. He noticed the wide trail of blood as he pulled the cop across the pavement. He opened the back of his truck and threw William in. He sped up the hill toward the hospital, driving as fast as he could, not hearing a sound from the bleeding cop. He drove to the Emergency Room entrance, slammed his truck into park, and started honking the horn.

A security guard ran out to see what the commotion was when he saw the bleeding cop in the back of the truck. The men grabbed William by the shoulders and ankles and took him inside to the nearest gurney they could find.

Within minutes, police officers arrived at the hospital to check on their beloved Sergeant. One of them left to pick up Ethel so she could be with William. He was in surgery, and no one would tell the patrolmen if William was alive. Other officers were helping fight the warehouse blaze with the local fire department. Ethel arrived at the hospital and demanded to speak with the doctor. He told her he didn't know if William would make it through the night. He had not gained consciousness, so they didn't know who shot him. Ethel sat down and cried; she did not know what to do without William.

When the warehouse fire was finally extinguished, they found a body and remnants of an illegal still. They assumed William had seen the man with the still, and a shootout had ensued. William killed the man and was shot during the scuffle. William was called a hero.

That night, Ethel returned home to tell her children that their father had died. She woke all three and gave them the horrific news. She explained that no one could speak ill of their father, that he had surprised a burglar and been shot but had killed the thief. Melvin knew what this meant for him, and he was not ready to be the man of the house. He had a dream of leaving, and this would make it easier.

William's funeral was held at St. Joseph's Church, where William and Ethel had married. The place that had marked the happiest day in Ethel's life was now replaced by her saddest. People were standing out in the street because there was not enough room in the church. Everyone was talking about how William was a hero. He was one of the most outstanding officers in the entire force. His eulogy was given by Lieutenant O'Leary, the same man who had killed him. Melvin locked eyes with him when O'Leary stood at the podium to speak. O'Leary looked down to read but realized he had seen the younger Martin running money for the same gang that had the illegal still. He wondered if Martin's son knew he was involved in his father's death.

Leaving the church, the family walked behind the horse-drawn hearse to the neighborhood Catholic cemetery. Ethel and the girls were walking alongside two police officers outfitted in their formal dress, carrying the United States and Illinois State flags. Melvin walked behind them, hanging his head. O'Leary came up and put his hand on the back of Melvin's neck, giving it a squeeze. Melvin did not need to look up; he knew who it was.

O'Leary said quietly, "I know what you do."

Melvin kept looking down and replied, "I know who you are and what you did," in a loud and demanding voice so the people around them could hear the conversation.

O'Leary took his hand off the boy's neck and slowed his walk to put space between him and the family. He wondered if the kid would be in trouble and if he might have to call in a favor.

That night, Melvin waited for everyone to fall asleep. He went into the backyard and dug a hole to retrieve his money. He put on three layers of clothes, a wool hat, gloves, and work boots and walked down to the riverbank next to the mill. As the barge left to travel upstream, Melvin jumped onto the barge, heading for Joliet. He understood O'Leary had given him no choice. He could hear O'Leary's voice, that he was somehow involved in his father's murder. Melvin was positive that O'Leary had shot his father and would come for him next. O'Leary knew that the younger Martin boy would hear the comments already being made on the street. Rumors had started that a cop had set Sergeant Martin up to be murdered because he would not stop investigating illegal alcohol sales. If Melvin did not leave now, he may never get another opportunity to do so.

1922 – Meet The Conti Family

The Contis welcomed a baby girl, Lillian, their first and only child. The couple was originally from New York, where Phillip and Louise's ancestors had settled once arriving from Italy. Phillip graduated from NYU and landed a great-paying job at a financial institution. Louise had never worked, and her only goal was to be a mom and look stylish, no matter the time of day. They settled in Naperville, IL., due to Phillip's new job, and bought a nice home in an influential area. They purchased a newly constructed three-bedroom home, mortgaged through Phillip's employer. They had a spacious backyard with a large oak tree, perfect for a swing. Louise spent all her time singing, playing her violin, and dancing in front of Lillian. She read to her, took her on long walks, allowed her to fall when she tried to stand, and let her put dirt in her mouth if she wished. Louise wanted Lillian to understand that she could be as bright as any boy and did not need a boy to tell her what to do. Both parents felt that education was the best thing a parent could give a child. Girls were not given the same opportunities as boys, but Louise could see that times were changing slowly, and she wanted to make sure her daughter was given every chance to earn a college education. Her dream was for Lillian to attend Juilliard and be a violinist or ballet dancer—high hopes for an Italian immigrant.

Lillian started school when she was four years old. She could read, recognize her colors and numbers, recite the alphabet, and tie her shoes. The school advanced Lillian to the first grade within the first month of the school year. Louise volunteered at the school and ensured Lillian gained confidence while the teachers treated her as a gifted student. Lillian advanced one more grade the following year, which was considered a phenomenon. When at home, Lillian started playing the violin and started reading music. Not only was she the most brilliant child in her class, but she was also the best dressed. Louise would take her shopping since money was never an issue. Lillian learned to take care of her belongings, ensuring everything had a place and was neatly organized. She could draw and paint at a much higher level than her age. Phillip would take her artwork to his bank and show it off while bragging to anyone who would listen. He loved hearing them call his daughter a future Rembrandt. The Contìs knew that one day, Lillian would make them proud and would be the first in her class when she graduated. Lillian was very popular with her classmates, always treating them respectfully and bringing them to her home to play in the yard. She was much younger than her classmates but more mature than they were, so the age difference was not noticed. She was the perfect child; her family could not ask for anything more.

In 1930, the Contìs hit rock bottom very quickly. The Great Depression took no prisoners. Phillip lost his job, and the housing market dropped by over 75%. They couldn't sell their home or purchase another. There were no options. They would eventually go into foreclosure and lose the down payment they had placed when they bought their new home. They had to make a plan, take their cash, and leave the community they loved. They packed up and started to drive. Lillian cried because she had to leave her home and all her friends. It was traumatic for an eight-year-old, and she did not understand why they had to go. They promised her that one day they would move back; this was just a small thing, and everything would work itself out. They decided to move to a rural area because living would be cheaper. They could try to do small jobs and make money to survive. Phillip could try to assist others with their financials, like stocks and life insurance, and how to cash those in if there was an option. Louise felt that she could clean people's homes or maybe sew. They also thought it would be safer for Italians to stay away from the crime that was taking place in the larger communities. Keeping Lillian safe was their primary concern. She was already two grades ahead of her age, and they did not want her to lose any knowledge she had gained. Nor did they want her to go backward at a new school so they decided not to allow the school to find out her true age. Their dream for her was to still attend college, and that would never change, no matter how poor they became.

The Contis knew other Italians had settled in Joliet, IL., thinking that would be the best place for them. That community had grown, and more Italians were moving to the area each year. They found a trailer that was sitting on an acre of land. The owners before them had moved out and foreclosed on the property. The bank was happy to unload it to Phillip, even though he paid too much. He had cash, so the bank was glad to have it out of their possession. The Conti's were happy they had a roof over their head, which was a dirty and dingy side-by-side trailer but a home. They learned to stick to a budget, only buy the necessities, hang blankets over the windows when it got cold, and spend as much time outside when it was hot. It was a different life than they once had, but the community around them was caring and helped bring food to starving people and furnished clothes to needy children. Lillian did not like the change but liked the school she attended. She breezed through grade school, her popularity did not waver, and every child wanted to be her or her friend.

When she was 12, she would be starting high school. Her classmates assumed she was 14 or 15. And if a stranger looked at her, they would agree. Lillian understood that she would meet new students, teachers, and obstacles, and she knew the importance of never allowing anyone to keep her from what she wanted, which was happiness.

In 1934, Lillian was off to a great start at her new high school. She was considered gifted, and the school asked her parents if she could participate in two classes above her grade level, reading and math. Phillip and Louise were ecstatic. They agreed and felt Lillian needed to be challenged to keep her interested and not let her mind wander. Lillian soon learned that she was not the smartest in her class and that math could be complicated. She wanted to return to her old math class with her friends but was afraid to ask her mom. Louise had been sick for quite a while, and she did not want to bother her. She knew not to ask her dad because he wanted his daughter to work in a bank like him, so math was essential. Even though her dad was now working as a bank teller, he knew he would eventually be back in his original management career. Phillip dreamed of overseeing a bank and having his daughter work for him.

Louise got sicker, so Phillip took her to the free medical clinic. The family did not have health insurance, and he was ashamed that Louise had been sick for weeks. He thought she may have just been under the weather, but now he understood she was unwell. Louise lost weight, had a daily fever, and was too weak to eat. Phillip was apprehensive about his wife's illness but hoped it was just influenza, which many people were contracting within the community. The doctor took some blood and told Phillip he would mail the results to him, or he could come back and pick them up the following week. He didn't need to. Within that week, Louise was admitted to the hospital. Phillip had to take her to the emergency room because she was experiencing shortness of breath, and her lips were turning blue. Louise's friends demanded that Phillip take her to the hospital that day because she was critically ill.

The doctors told Phillip his wife had leukemia and would die soon. He couldn't take her home, so he brought Lillian to the hospital. They prayed as they sat at her bedside. Lillian was too young to lose her mother. There were so many things she needed to learn from her. Who would she talk to about boys? Help her with her homework? Do girl things with? Was her dad even capable of taking care of her?

Louise died two days later. They had a small service at the local Catholic church, and all the Italians attended to grieve for the family. Lillian knew she would never recover. She really only loved one parent, and now that parent was dead.

Lillian returned to school, still grieving and struggling. Her scores steadily declined. She was removed from the two acceleration classes and put back in with her original classmates. Phillip went to the school multiple times to speak to the principal. He wanted to stress the importance of helping Lillian from failing and wanted direction to keep her in school. She had difficulty getting out of bed in the mornings, and more than half the time, she refused to attend school. Phillip had advanced with his position at the bank and wanted to eventually move from Joliet and take Lillian to a new school. Lillian was spending every weekend sitting at her mother's grave and crying. Phillip thought it was unhealthy and was trying to manage his life with his daughter, knowing he was failing as a father.

Lillian was a sophomore in high school and no longer had her mother. People treated her more like her high school age than the age she actually was. Louise's friends tried to counsel Phillip and explained that the best thing for Lillian would be to take her out of school, allow her to rest, and start school the following year. They all agreed she needed time for herself. Phillip needed to guide her into a family of two, not three while grieving for Louise.

Phillip was against that and felt moving her to a new school would be the answer. Even though Lillian was dealing with depression, her father knew she was a good child. She stayed out of trouble, listened to her father, and did what she was told unless it dealt with her mother's death. Months passed, and the Contis did not celebrate the holidays. Neighbors dropped off food, wrote notes and cards on how much they missed Louise, and invited the family to Sunday mass. Phillip and Lillian stopped going to mass when Louise died. Those Sundays were now spent at the cemetery. Lillian would always brush the leaves and snow from her mother's headstone. She never wanted to leave her mom. And no one could make her.

Phillip was told a new opportunity was waiting for him. His bank was purchased by a larger financial institution, and they wanted him to join their team. The economy was growing again and had stabilized. The American Dream was once again within his grasp. The only problem was that he would have to relocate to Florida. Phillip was ecstatic. The new position would allow an increased salary so he could afford to buy a new home for Lillian. He didn't stop and think that Lillian would be heartbroken leaving her mother, her friends, and her high school. Phillip could tell her no more cold weather. She could enjoy the sun and the ocean. Phillip waited a week before he broke the news to Lillian. He accepted the job and had one month to relocate to Florida. He knew if he changed his mind, he would be fired and never get this opportunity again. He waited for the weekend before he sat Lillian down to tell her about their new adventure.

Lillian was horrified; her dad asked her to leave her mother in Illinois while they moved a thousand miles away to Florida. She didn't care about the sun or the ocean. No matter how much her dad tried to talk her into it, she wasn't going. Lillian told him she would run away if forced to move. If she was brought back, she would run away again. Phillip did not know what to do; he could not leave his daughter alone in the trailer. Phillip spoke to some of Louise's friends and wanted their help with a plan. He could only foresee options to have Lillian stay after graduating high school and then move to Florida to be with Phillip. He dreamed of her attending college in Florida and following his footsteps in the financial world. Louise wanted Lillian to attend college in New York, but Phillip could not have her living so far away from him in a big city, unattended.

Louise's best friend, Theresa Bertonelli, told Phillip that Lillian could come and live with her and her two girls. Theresa was a single parent due to her husband had died nine years into their marriage. He was in the military and fell off a platform during paratrooper training. Theresa collected a small monthly pension to support herself and her daughters, Katherine and Angela, while she worked at a nearby grocery store. Theresa had to pay a babysitter for her girls when they weren't in school. This was a significant expense. She wished she could quit her job to stay home with them. However, her job offered health insurance for both her and the girls, so she needed to remain employed. Katherine was eight years old, and Angela was six—too young to stay alone.

Theresa asked Phillip if Lillian could remain with them. Lillian could stay at the same school with her friends, and Theresa requested that Phillip send monthly funds to help her buy things Lillian might need as a young woman. In return, Lillian would watch the girls after school and during the summer months and help them with their homework. Phillip wasn't crazy about the idea but felt it was the best plan. He would leave it up to Lillian to decide what she wanted to do. Phillip saw no harm in allowing Lillian to stay in Illinois but would expect her to follow the rules while separated. It would only be for a few years, and when Lillian graduated from high school, she would be shy of her sixteenth birthday. Once she completed high school, she would move to Florida.

Phillip sat Lillian down and explained her two choices. It was up to her to choose; his feelings would not be hurt if she decided to stay. Lillian broke down crying and told her father, "Thank you," adding that she wanted to stay where her mother was buried. He told her he expected her to move to Florida once she finished school, and he needed her to promise him she would. Lillian promised but knew she might never see her father again. Once she graduated, she planned on leaving town and heading north to Chicago, where Lillian could be anything she wanted.

Within weeks, Phillip closed the trailer, took all his wife's clothes, and donated them to a local church. Lillian helped him, crying the entire time. She kept her mother's favorite dress and hoped to wear it one day, possibly on her wedding day. She also took her mom's violin, even though she had forgotten how to play. Phillip dropped Lillian off at the Bertonellis' home, hugged her, and thought it was strange that his daughter did not shed a tear when he said goodbye.

Lillian was granted her own bedroom, which made her happy. The school would end in a few months, so she felt she would have a little freedom before reporting for babysitting service. She was wrong. Theresa gave her a list of duties each day, which included preparing meals, walking a mile to the grocery store, helping with the girls' homework, and even doing the family's laundry. Lillian knew she was being taken advantage of and had to report to Theresa every step she took when she wasn't in school. At first, Lillian liked the girls but soon found out Katherine would do whatever she could to get Lillian in trouble with Theresa. Both girls had not been stellar in school before Lillian moved in, and that continued afterward, with Theresa blaming Lillian for the girls' poor performance. Theresa told the other women in their community that Lillian was becoming a bigger problem than she anticipated.

That summer, Lillian was not allowed to leave the home, and she found out that the only time she was granted permission was when Theresa would take her to Louise's gravesite and drop her off for a few hours. When Theresa picked her up, the girls had bags from area department stores filled with new clothes and shoes. Lillian wondered if her dad was paying for the latest outfits. Lillian would write her dad, but Theresa was the only one with his address. She would ask for the letter, put his address on it, stamp it, and take it to the post office. Lillian was positive that Theresa was reading the letters. She could tell by her mood swings when she said something negative or positive about the family. Lillian would never get a returned letter from her father, which she thought was strange.

Lillian had passed the eleventh grade and would be starting her final year in high school. She was not doing as well as she could, but she learned that just doing the minimal was all she needed. She started using the girls against Theresa, and Theresa felt Lillian was evil for her girls. She would hear Katherine say words like "damn" or "hell," which caused chaos in their home. The girls no longer wanted to attend church and said they didn't need to go, as they could just pray at home. Theresa was distraught with her home environment and wondered about sending Lillian to Florida to be with her dad. Since he left, the two had never arranged a visit because it was too far of a distance to drive. Theresa still didn't want to lose her babysitter for the summer and hoped this final year would go by quickly. She was saving the money Phillip was sending and had created a nice savings account for herself. She, too, was buying new clothes and shoes and wanted to start dating now that the girls were getting older.

School started, and Lillian always managed to skip class. At lunch, she would sneak off and walk into town, and no one paid much attention. Most adult women who knew her were either at home or the supermarket. As long as she stayed away from the grocery store, Theresa would never see her. She would say they let her leave at lunchtime if caught, but she had to return to class. Lillian would secretly take money out of Theresa's purse so she could go downtown to Woolworth's and sit at the soda counter. She wanted to drink her favorite malt milkshake while batting her eyes at the young man working the soda fountain. Lillian was beautiful, and over the past year, she could turn not just the heads of high school boys but also those of adult men. She was only fifteen but looked older than eighteen. She understood that she looked just like her mother: nice olive skin, dark hair, and big eyes, and had that Italian flair when she walked. Had she spoken Italian, strangers would believe she had just arrived from New York via Italy. Lillian knew she had sex appeal, and she took that in stride, hoping that one day she would meet a wealthy man and move to New York.

Willie was the young man working the soda fountain. He was of German ancestry and would speak German when Lillian came to sit at the counter. He thought this made him more attractive than he actually was, but it didn't. He was unaware that his parents had given him an American name to hide his German heritage. Willie had little going for him as a potential suitor for Lillian.

"Hallo, Miss Lillian," Willlie said with a smile.

"Hello to you, sir Willis," Lillian replied flirtatiously.

"Should I assume your usual drink?"

Lillian gave a wink of an eye and slowly reached into her purse to pull out her coin purse. "I don't know, Willie. I may not have a dime, but only a nickel. What can a poor girl do?" she said with a hint of playfulness.

Lillian knew the answer and had played this trick before. She would always manage to get out of paying for her drink, at least for a little while.

"You keep your dime, Fraulein. I will give you the drink if you can keep it a secret," Willie smiled.

"You know I am good at secrets," whispered Lillian as she grinned sheepishly.

One afternoon, Willie sneaked Lillian into the walk-in freezer and kissed her. Lillian blushed, then told him to be a man and kiss her properly. He became embarrassed, so next kiss was harder and deeper. Lillian felt a warmth come over her body, even though they were standing in below- freezing temperatures. Willie was smitten with Lillian and wondered what her parents were like. Would they favor their daughter dating and marrying a German? Lillian never spoke about her parents or where she lived. He did notice that she would turn and look when someone walked into the drugstore. He wondered if it was due to the bell above the door ringing every time it was opened. Or was she hiding from someone?

Lillian never told Willie that she was a high school student and wasn't even sixteen. She was afraid that might scare him off. She was not attracted to him, but the kiss did make her feel like she could use him to her advantage. She did not want to marry a boy who worked at a drugstore, scooping ice cream. She tried to keep the con going as long as possible because, at that time, she was not allowed to date nor could have boys over to Theresa's house. Theresa would remind Lillian that she was a Catholic girl, and her mother wanted her to marry a Catholic boy and be a virgin when she did.

Lillian kept the ruse up for weeks, showing up for a chocolate malt and a slight make-out session. Willie slowly discovered that he couldn't afford this Italian bombshell, but he didn't have the nerve to tell her. Whenever he asked Lillian to speak to her father, Lillian would make up an excuse. Willie was hoping Lillian would bring Mr. Conti to the drugstore so he could ask Lillian out on a formal date.

She acted as though her family had money, but she couldn't afford a dime soda. This gave Willie mixed messages, but he was positive there were good reasons. Lillian complained that her parents kept all the money because they needed to send it back to her grandparents in Italy. Her nonna was sick and needed some type of operation. Lillian would tell him, "Now was not the right time to ask." Willie continued inviting Lillian to the freezer to steal a kiss. If Lillian was being truthful, she was just there to watch the effect she had on Willie after getting that kiss.

Winter was just getting over, and Lillian had not been spending time at the soda counter due to the bitter cold. It was now March, so she decided to skip class and visit her "soda boy," as she called him. She walked into Woolworth's, sat at the soda counter, and found no one behind the counter. She waited for Willie, but he did not show. After a few minutes, a short man with glasses appeared and asked her what she needed.

"Where is Willie? He usually makes my malt for me," she asked.

The man, with a name tag that read *Robert,* looked at her and smiled. "Willie doesn't work here anymore."

"Where did he go?"

Robert took a breath, looked Lillian in the eye, and said, "Willie was caught not being honest and taking things he shouldn't have."

Lillian let out a gasp. "He would never do that."

"Well, he did. Do you want something or not?"

1937 – One Woman's Mistake

A man appeared from the freezer area. He had dark hair and beautiful brown eyes and wore black boots, blue pants, and a striped white and blue button-down shirt with his name embroidered over the left chest: Mel. Lillian noticed he had cigarettes in his shirt pocket. She also saw a tattoo on his right forearm, but she could not determine what it said.

He looked right at Lillian. "Afternoon, miss," as he tipped his head to her.

"Robert, I have your milk and ice cream; I'm going to need you to come and count so you can sign your name to the order."

"Go back and get to unloading; I'll be back there in a second after I'm done waiting on one of my customers."

"Excuse me, ma'am, I didn't know."

"That's quite all right, sir; I thought a chocolate malt sounded good."

"You know, that does sound good. Robert, make that two." He pulled out a money clip, and Lillian saw the massive wad of dollars.

"Sir, that is awfully nice of you, but I can't have you do that."

"Tell you what, once Robert here gets them made, why don't you bring mine to the back where my truck is parked, and we can share our lunchtime together?"

Robert rolled his eyes.

"Sir, that sounds very nice. Thank you."

"The name's Mel," he said, pointing to his name on his uniform, "and I'm glad to meet you."

"Hi, Mel, my name is Lillian."

Mel made a fake bow, turned around, and went to unload the truck.

Robert started making the two malts.

Lillian watched Robert, but all she could think about was Mel and how lucky she was that Willie wasn't honest with his employer.

Mel was still unloading his truck from the back alley when Lillian arrived with his malt. He told her to get comfortable in the cab; it had a bench seat. When Mel was done, he slammed the door to the back of the truck and locked it. He came around to the driver's side door and jumped in. Lillian had already started using a spoon to eat her malt, while Mel decided to use his straw.

They didn't speak for the first five minutes; they just looked at each other.

"You Italian?" Mel asked.

"Yes, is that going to be a problem?"

Mel just watched her and nodded his head, indicating no. He had a feeling this girl was going to be trouble for him.

"How long have you been driving this truck?" Lillian asked.

Mel didn't want to tell her that he had just started. He was trying to collect a bet the driver owed, and he took off running when he saw Mel. Mel caught him and beat the crap out of him. He emptied the man's pockets and took whatever he had. The guy then ran off and left the truck. Mel didn't want to leave the truck, nor did he want to steal it, since it had the word Swanson in large blue letters, which was the name of the creamery that owned it. Mel took it to the owner and told him he found it in a back alley. When he did, the owner asked him if he wanted a job. Mel said, sure, and the rest is history. That was three weeks ago.

The story he told Lillian was quite the opposite of the actual events. He explained to her that his family owned the creamery, and his last name was Swanson. He was learning the ropes to understand the routes before the business was his. He claimed he had two sisters, but they could not own the creamery because of some legal issues. Mel was 22 years old but told Lillian he was 26. When he asked about Lillian's age, she lied and said she was 19, even though she was not quite 16. Lillian told Mel she was between jobs and hoped to be a nurse. Lillian thought that would give her some credibility with a man who would one day own a creamery. This would be the dream she wanted – a man who made enough money, and she would never have to work. Mel did not look like the kind of man who needed children. This could work for her.

Once they finished their malts, Mel asked if he could see Lillian again. He had a car and could pick her up if she told him where she lived. Lillian explained that her parents would never allow her to date a man his age. He wanted to know how they could make it work so he could spend more time with her. She told him she could meet him when he delivered at Woolworth's, and then they could plan how to see each other in secrecy.

Twice a week, Lillian would sneak into Mel's truck when she saw it in the back alley of Woolworth's. She would lie down on the seat to surprise Mel when he jumped in from the driver's side. He would take her with him to finish his route more than once, and they would drive to the park. Mel discovered that Lillian was unlike the other girls he had made out with. She would tell him what he could do and what he couldn't. Lillian loved to sit on his lap and kiss him, putting her hands in his thick hair. This continued for weeks, and Mel asked Lillian if she would come home with him. He knew she would say no, and he didn't want to take her to the boarding house where he shared a room with another man. Lillian was expecting a quaint home from the son of a creamery owner, not a dirty, one-night motel.

Mel was starting to get impatient with Lillian. She was the prettiest girlfriend he had ever had, but she was still a kid. He imagined she would eventually stop coming around, and he could quit this job. He was still collecting wages from men who wouldn't pay when they lost their bets. He also protected the prostitutes if their pimps requested him to do so. He could no longer run liquor because it had become legal years ago. He did not want a job like everyone else. It was easier to lie and make money.

Lillian was preparing to graduate high school in June, and Theresa told her she would be moving to Florida. Lillian did not want to go. Phillip had gotten remarried the year before and did not tell Lillian until after the wedding. Lillian was heartbroken. Phillip and his new wife, Mary, had plans for Lillian to move in with them and attend college close to their home. Lillian did not want four more years of school. Her plans were not to work or go to school. And now, she had met the love of her life, Mel, whose family owned a creamery. Lillian wanted to tell Theresa she was not moving to Florida and leaving her mother in Illinois. She would move in with Mel when he eventually proposed to her. She didn't want to tell anyone about Mel yet because she was afraid they would not allow her to see a man who was so much older than her and possibly not Catholic.

Mel explained to Lillian that he was tired of sneaking around and making out in a truck. Lillian did not have an answer but did not want him to stop seeing her. Lillian started crying because she was afraid Mel would move on to another girl, which was what he wanted, but he didn't tell her. Mel only dated girls for one thing—sex. He didn't want to pay a prostitute, which he had done more than once. He would also use his power against the prostitutes when making collections, giving them more time to pay if they performed sexual acts on him.

He felt that if Lillian wasn't prepared for sex, he would move on to someone who would. He also understood that one day, Lillian would figure out that he was not the son of the creamery owner and most likely would break up with him anyway.

Mel decided to tell Lillian it was over. As usual, she was waiting for him in his delivery truck. He took her right to the park, not finishing his deliveries. Lillian wanted to know why he wasn't finishing his route, and he told her he had something more important to do. Lillian had to contain her excitement, knowing he would ask for her hand in marriage. He parked the truck under their favorite tree in the back of the park. They needed as much seclusion as possible.

Lillian jumped into Mel's lap and planted a big kiss on his lips. "So, what's so important? Do you want to ask me a question?" Mel let out a sigh. "I told you I was tired of sneaking around. I'm a grown man. I need to be with someone who wants to be with me."

"What do you mean? Of course, I want to be with you."

"If you want to be with me and one day be my wife, I need you to act like it."

"I don't know what you mean. I would love to be your wife, but how do I act like that? Is it because you haven't met my parents?"

"I don't have to meet your parents, but I need you to prove that you love me and only me."

Lillian looked at him, and a tear came from her right eye. "I wanted to be a virgin on our wedding night. I want you to respect me."

"As long as you're a virgin now, it doesn't matter if you are on our wedding night."

"Are you sure that you would still want to marry me once we have sex?"

"Of course, baby, I will take care of you. If that makes you happy, I will let you stir the ice cream before we pack it. And all the malts you want."

That day, Mel and Lillian had sex in the front seat of the delivery truck. Lillian cried but knew she had no choice if she wanted Mel to marry her. She knew nothing about sex nor what to do, so she just lay on the dirty bench seat and allowed Mel to do what he wanted. It was nothing like she had imagined, and it was over in minutes.

Afterward, Mel lit a cigarette and asked if she wanted him to drop her off back at the drugstore or if she wanted to walk home. Lillian thought that was odd because he always took her back to town. She told him that she needed to go back towards downtown so she could walk home. Mel took her back to town, kissed her forehead, and said he would see her next week.

Lillian got out of the truck and knew something was wrong. She watched Mel drive away. He didn't honk like he usually did. Lillian would never see Mel again because another man took over his delivery route. She would ask the man about Mel, but he would say he was new and did not know anyone by that name. Lillian tried to explain that he was the owners son, but the new driver would just shrug his shoulders and say he didn't know him or where he went.

Ten weeks later, Emily was graduating from high school. Phillip and Mary were driving up from Florida to see her graduate. They were staying at a local hotel and arriving the day before. Theresa was glad to see Lillian move away and have her home as it was before she arrived. Theresa bought a special dress for Lillian to wear to her graduation. Lillian did not want to wear the dress because she had saved her mother's favorite dress, and that was what she wanted to wear. Theresa told her to put the dress on and model for her. If she needed seamstress work, Theresa was highly skilled and could make the dress fit perfectly.

Lillian put the dress on and noticed it was tight in her belly. Theresa looked at her and said, "Lillian, are you pregnant?" Lillian burst down crying. Theresa demanded to know who the boy was that she had sex with.

The next day, Phillip and Mary arrived in Joliet. A message was waiting for them at the hotel. Phillip had Mary settle in while he drove to Theresa's. When Phillip saw Lillian, he was furious at Theresa and his daughter. He wanted to know how this could happen. His daughter was not even sixteen yet! Theresa looked puzzled. "What do you mean, she is not sixteen?" Phillip looked at his daughter. "Who is this boy? Tell me right now!"

Lillian told them about Mel and that his parents owned a creamery. They met one day when he was delivering ice cream to Woolworths, and he bought her a malt. They started talking and spending time together after her school day ended and he finished his deliveries. Phillip told her to get in the car, and they were going to the creamery. Lillian needed to find out where it was, but Phillip did not need directions. He was going straight to the police department.

Phillip made her sit in the car while he went inside. Lillian thought he was getting directions, but he wasn't. Her dad came out, got in the car, and she saw a police officer get in a cruiser. The cop pulled out, and Phillip started following him. Lillian thought it was strange that a police officer wouldn't just give her father directions. Within a few miles, they were pulling into the Swanson Creamery. Phillip told his daughter to stay in the car. Lillian started to cry because she did not want Mel to get into trouble with his father. Phillip and the police officer went to the front door, and the police officer took his baton and knocked on the door. Lillian saw a man come to the door but could not hear the conversation. She rolled down her car window and strained to hear.

The cop made the man come outside. Lillian was in horror. If that man was going to be her future father-in-law, and this is how her father treated him the first time they met, it was unacceptable. Her father looked very angry and his face was bright red. She prayed that Mel would not be home to see this behavior from her father.

"Are you Mr. Swanson, and is this your place of business?" the police officer asked.

"Yes, it is, and why are you here?" Mr. Swanson replied.

"I am Phillip Conti, and that is my daughter," Phillip said, pointing to the car. "I demand to speak with your son."

"Why do you want to speak to my son? He's twelve; what could he have done?" Mr. Swanson asked.

"Twelve? Don't you have a 26-year-old son named Mel?" Phillip asked.

"That bum! I assure you, sir, he is not my son. I am not old enough to have a son that age, let alone a criminal like him," Mr. Swanson said.

"That's the kid I hired months ago, and he left my truck on a county road weeks ago. I reported the truck stolen, and one of your officers found it and returned it. The truck was wrecked, and all the inventory was spoiled. If he is found, I want him arrested."

Phillip's face turned pure white, and he felt dizzy. He broke down and started crying.

Lillian watched her father cry, and she started crying too.

Mr. Swanson wanted Mel arrested for stolen property and theft of money he took.

Phillip wanted Mel arrested for making his 15-year-old daughter pregnant.

Phillip only had a few days in Illinois, and he wanted Mel found before he had to decide what to do with his daughter. His prayers were answered, and the cops caught up with Mel as he was trying to flee to Chicago. The cops knew he would want to make collections with the city prostitution ring, and they knew Mel due to being arrested for minor crimes. Phillip was brought to the jail so he could speak to Mel. Phillip wanted to press charges but realized his grandchild's father would be in jail due to him. Mel reported to the police that Lillian told him she was nineteen years old, not fifteen. The police told Phillip they could not arrest him if that were true. Phillip was so mad that his face turned a bright red. He told Mel he had to marry his daughter and be a father to their child. Mel told him he couldn't care for Lillian, let alone a child. Phillip told him he had no choice.

They would get married the next day, and Phillip would give them his trailer that he never sold. It needed work, but Mel would have to get a job and use that money to repair the trailer. Phillip wanted to know how much money Mel had because he was told Mel was collecting illegal bets and prostitution wages. Mel claimed he did not have any money. However, the police reported that Mel had a suitcase full of clothes when he was arrested, and they confiscated a large sum of money. Phillip asked for $50 from the funds they confiscated. He told the Sergeant to keep the money, and if he made a visit to his daughter's trailer and saw his grandchild in squalor, make arrangements to take the baby somewhere. Phillip would leave his address where he could be reached.

Phillip went to Theresa's house to deliver the plan. Lillian would marry Melvin Martin, have his child, and live in their old trailer. Melvin was required to get a job, make repairs to the trailer, and agree to regular visits from the police to ensure he was taking care of Lillian. One of the officers had lined up a construction job for Melvin, and if he didn't accept it, he would go to jail. That was part of the agreement. Melvin also had to pay for the damage to the Swanson delivery truck, with monthly payments to avoid being detained and sent back to jail.

Lillian was crying uncontrollably. She didn't want to marry a bum. Mel had lied to her, which wasn't how life was supposed to be. Phillip told her there was no way she was moving to Florida and making him and his new wife take care of her and a child. Melvin was the father, and he was responsible for doing his part.

Furious at Lillian's poor judgment, Theresa also felt sadness for her. Phillip, however, showed no sympathy. He told Lillian he would pick her up at nine o'clock the following day to take her to the courthouse. After the wedding, he would hand her the keys to the trailer, and they would be on their own. He added that Melvin was lucky—because he wanted to kill him with his bare hands.

Turning his anger on Lillian, Phillip said she should be ashamed of herself and demanded, "What would your mother think of you being a whore?"

Theresa was outraged and told Phillip to leave her house, insisting he had no right to talk to a child that way.

Phillip, his voice dripping with disdain, fired back, "She's no longer a child but a whore who spread her legs for the first boy that came along." Then he stormed out, leaving the room in silence, with Lillian sobbing and Theresa shaking her head in frustration.

The following day, Phillip pulled up at Theresa's house. Theresa came out and told him she was taking Lillian to the courthouse. Theresa had stayed up all night fixing the dress that Lillian wanted to wear. She would not allow Phillip to ruin the wedding even though he was angry. Phillip slammed his car in reverse, spinning rocks, and turned the car towards downtown. Theresa went in, gathered Lillian, and told her everything would be ok. Theresa called the electric company to make sure the trailer had heat. She also called the water company so the couple would have a working toilet. Theresa had a group of Italian women from the neighborhood go to the trailer during the wedding and scour the place like new.

When Lillian arrived at the courthouse, she noticed her father did not bring his new wife, meaning he was embarrassed by his daughter. Melvin came, and he had scrubbed up well. Theresa could see why Lillian thought she was in love with this man. He wore a button-down white shirt, blue jeans, and work boots. The police officer who went with them to the creamery also showed up. Lillian thought that was nice of him. She was not aware that if Melvin did not go through with the vows, he was there to arrest him. Right at nine-thirty, they were ushered in to see the judge. He had them repeat after him, and they signed their wedding license within minutes. Theresa was the maid of honor, and Phillip refused to sign as the best man, so the police officer printed his name. Phillip walked over to Lillian and handed her the keys to the trailer. He said very low, "How dare you wear your mother's favorite dress. She was a pure woman, you are not." With that, Phillip turned around and walked out of the courthouse. He picked up Mary at the hotel, and they started their drive to Florida. Phillip would never see or talk to his daughter again.

Melvin was working as a roofer, which allowed him to be off in the winter, starting in November. He spent his first winter drinking at the nearest tavern. Lillian had her first child in January, and Melvin was not at the hospital with her. Theresa took her to the hospital when her labor started. Theresa tried to find Melvin but she could not. Lillian told Theresa that she wanted her child adopted and asked Theresa to please call the state officials so they would come and pick up the child after birth. Lillian did not want to know the sex of the baby or see the baby. She was careless and did not want her child to be raised in the same environment she was living in. Theresa told Lillian she was doing the right thing and that the baby would go to a couple that wanted a child. Lillian was in labor for over twenty hours, and when they prepared for her to give birth, the doctors told her that the baby was breech and that they would have to prepare her for a cesarean section. Lillian was scared and started crying. Theresa held her hand and cursed Phillip and Melvin for being the men they were. Leaving a sixteen-year-old girl to give birth alone.

Theresa expressed to the nurses that they should make a call to social services and inform them that the baby would be put up for adoption. Lillian did not want to see the child or know the sex of the baby. Please leave a note for all nurses not to bring the baby to Lillian, even if she requests it. The father of the child was drunk and abusive, and he should not see the child as well. Theresa wanted the baby moved as soon as possible out of the hospital so Lillian would not change her mind.

The nurses listened well, and when Lillian was discharged three days later, she left without her child. Lillian had given birth to a little girl, severely underweight due to her mother's poor health and her father's abuse. The baby was still admitted to the hospital, and would remain there for over two weeks, and eventually adopted to a loving family. Melvin never visited Lillian in the hospital, commenting that he hated hospitals. When he was told their baby was given up for adoption, he was elated. When the timing was right, he was planning to walk out on Lillian.

Lillian's plan was for the child to grow up in a safe home without violence. She then decided to leave Melvin as soon as she could; she would try to hide money to gain her freedom. She was too young to be a wife or a mother. Lillian did not understand that freedom was not hers to choose. Women did not have the luxury of earning a living wage and making decisions that affected their lives. Lillian's life did not get better. Melvin was still working as a roofer, which meant he only worked half a year; the other half, he drank. When he was intoxicated, he would assault Lillian, both physically and sexually. Lillian would soon have two more children, a boy she named Daniel and a girl named Sally. She knew she could not give up on them as she did her first child. Lillian was barely scraping by but doing everything she could for her two children. She worked with other Italian mothers to trade kids' clothes so children would have winter coats and boots. She also learned to do things that most women did not have those skills, like putting in a vegetable garden or how to turn a wrench to fix a leaky faucet. She understood Melvin was no help and wished he would not come home from his job. She would be ashamed of herself for praying he would walk off the side of the roof and die. Lillian knew that was not Christian of her, but she didn't care. Spring was arriving, which meant he had to return to work, and she looked forward to spending that time with her children.

She knew her husband was sleeping with other women. She could smell it on him. She refused to have sex with him for fear of getting pregnant or acquiring a sexually transmitted disease. That caused fights on many occasions. When he came home drunk, he would pass out, and she actually looked forward to those nights because she didn't have to speak to him. Melvin was usually angry, and he would hit Lillian. He made sure he never left a mark where people could see. If that happened, Lillian would wear heavy makeup. The women in the neighborhood knew that Melvin was beating Lillian. They would visit with her and explain that she did not have choices. He was the father of her children. He did no harm to the children, who were now three and one. If he harmed them, they told her to take them and leave at once.

Lillian dreamed of packing them up and leaving but had nowhere to go. She had the trailer and wondered if she could sell it, take the money, and run away with her children. Lillian talked to Theresa about how she would be able to do it. Theresa had to explain to Lillian that the trailer was hers, but her father did not sign the property title because she was a woman. He refused to sign it to Melvin, so the title remained in her father's name. Lillian started crying, something she was getting very good at. Theresa told her the only choice in her life was to take care of the children, and when they got older, maybe she could find a job and leave Melvin. Lillian told her that she could not take the abuse anymore. She was tired. She was 22 years old and had never experienced life. She made one mistake, and why should she have to pay for that every day of her life? While Melvin is working half a year, drinking and sleeping with other women, she is cooking his dinner and washing his clothes. Theresa said Lillian's life was unfair and that all women were trying to survive. Lillian was not happy with that way of life. She was embarrassed to take her children to the grocery store and pay with brightly colored fake dollars given to her by the federal government. That told everyone she was poor and on welfare, and she could see how the women behind the counter would sneer at her when counting out the paper. Melvin refused to pick up work in the winter months, or allow her to try and find a job.

That summer, Melvin worked six days a week, ten hours a day. On the sixth night, he would stay out all night, come home in the early morning hours, smelling of women and liquor, and beat Lillian if she protested. Lillian had heard rumors that her husband was spending his time and money on one of the local prostitutes, Brenda Brown. Lillian was tired of her husband not being a husband or a father and decided to visit Miss Brown.

Brenda was not surprised to see Lillian. She knew Melvin was married with children, but she didn't care. She didn't want a husband; she just wanted a man to care for her, and Melvin was doing that. Lillian politely asks her to stop seeing him and send him home to be with his family. Brenda said no, it was not her fault that Lillian could not keep her man happy. Lillian wanted to punch Brenda but was aware that she could be arrested and put in jail. Lillian thought of a better way to stop the affair. Lillian told Brenda that she would go home, load up his children and clothes, and return them to her. She could be their new mother. With that, she turned around and walked to her car. Lillian would never give her children to this woman, but she thought that scaring her to be a mother might get her to stop seeing Melvin. Lillian started crying as she started walking to her car. Her two babies were napping in the back seat, and she realized how sad of a life they had.

The next night, Lillian stopped by Theresa's and asked if her kids could stay the night; she had something important to do. Theresa told her not to do something foolish. Lillian went home and waited for her husband. Melvin showed up at four o'clock in the morning. Drunk and screaming at Lillian. He started pushing her and slapping her in the face. Brenda told him Lillian had come to the motel and threatened her to stop seeing Melvin. He was screaming so loud she knew the neighbors could hear the fight. Lillian was screaming back as he was trying to punch her and grab her by the hair. He was so drunk that he had a difficult time keeping his balance. He would throw a punch, hitting nothing, then falling over. He knocked Lillian down and tried to kick her. He missed once and kicked the bedpost with his stocking feet. He screamed in pain and called Lillian a bitch, and he was going to kill her. The next swing landed on the side of Lillian's face, knocking her over between the bed and the wall. She lost consciousness. Melvin was hoping he killed her. He plopped in bed and fell asleep.

An hour later, Lillian woke up. She could hear Melvin snoring in bed. She crawled out of the bedroom on her hands and knees trying not to wake him. Her face and head hurt so much. She reached the bathroom, grabbed the sink, and got to her feet. She grabbed the cord to the light and pulled it. She looked in the mirror and realized why she couldn't see; one of her eyes was swollen shut. Her nose looked broken, and she had dried blood in both nostrils and on the front of her shirt. She put her hand on her head and felt a huge lump. When she removed her hand, clumps of hair fell from it. Lillian looked down in the sink and was shocked that much hair had been pulled from her head. She made a decision that would change the path of her life and others.

Lillian went to the kitchen and grabbed a cast iron skillet. She then went out to Melvin's truck and found some rope. She walked slowly back to the bedroom, where Melvin was passed out and still snoring. He reeked of alcohol. Lillian took the rope and tied his hands to the bedposts. She took the skillet and hit Melvin five times as hard as she could in his head and chest. He stopped snoring, and Lillian could not hear him breathing. She turned the light on next to the bed and saw blood on the sheets and walls. Lillian had killed him.

She froze and needed to think about what she would do next. She dropped the skillet, pulled her clothes out of her dresser drawers, and put them in a plastic bag. She grabbed some shoes and a coat. She took out Melvin's billfold and took all the cash he had. She went out to his truck and found some dollar bills. She threw everything into her car and started driving. She didn't know where she was going and knew she would be arrested if she were found. It would be foolish to get her children and put them in an unsafe environment. She did not know where to go, and for a brief second, she thought she should drive towards Florida. She wanted to turn herself into the police because she knew this plan would fail, much like she had done her entire life. She continued to drive and never looked back. She had a tank full of gas, and did not know how to read a map, or understand the highway system. She needed to go as far as she could. Eventually, she would see a sign that said Welcome to Indiana, but that would be hours away.

The following day, Theresa brought Lillian's two children back to their home. She did not see any vehicles at the trailer. She became nervous because it was not like Lillian to be gone this early on a Sunday morning. She left the kids in the car's back seat and went to the door. She noticed blood on the door, not a lot, but it worried her. She turned the doorknob, and the door opened. Theresa called Lillian's name but got no response. She went room to room, ending in Lillian and Melvin's bedroom. She caught her breath and looked at the mess. There were dresser drawers pulled out, clothes tossed about, a mirror broken, blood on the walls, and a cast iron skillet with blood lying on the floor. It finally happened: Melvin killed Lillian.

Theresa ran out and got in her car. She went right to the police department to report a murder.

Theresa pulled into the parking lot and saw a familiar truck, Melvin's. He must have turned himself in. She decided to take the children back home and wait for the police to call her.

Melvin was at the police department to report that Lillian tried to kill him. He explained that she tied him up and beat him with a baseball bat. Melvin didn't want anyone to know that a woman got the best of him, so he had to lie. A frying pan would not make a good story, but a bat would. Melvin was beaten pretty badly, and he was told after giving his statement that he needed to go to the hospital. Melvin said no, but the police told him the charges against Lillian would be more believable if he went to the emergency room and sought medical treatment. That would send a message to a jury that his injuries were severe. Melvin demanded that the police get a warrant and arrest her for trying to kill him. The police agreed to do that and wanted to know where Lillian would go. Melvin was positive she was heading to Florida to take the kids to her father's house. That day, Melvin was treated for a broken orbital bone, fractured nose, thirteen stitches above the eyebrow, three teeth were missing, and both eyes were nearly swollen shut. The police officers laughed at him while watching him from behind the two-way glass. How does a man allow a woman to beat his ass? They were calling him a pussy and making cat sounds. Melvin, of course, could not hear their words.

Theresa never got that call, and she would get no answer when she called Lillian's home. She did not have a phone number for Phillip or a current address to tell him his daughter was dead. After four hours, Theresa returned to the police department. Melvin's truck was gone, which baffled her. Did they move it to an impound yard? Did they let him go? Theresa went in and spoke with Officer Wegman, where she told him everything that happened that morning and what she saw at the trailer. Wegman told her they already knew what happened, and Melvin reported it. They informed her that Lillian had beaten Melvin and fled the area. Theresa faked a frown. But then, she realized Lillian would never leave her children. She knew Melvin had done something to her. The police told Theresa a warrant had been issued, and they would start looking for Lillian. Theresa told them she had Lillian's children and she didn't know what to do with them. Wegman told her she had to return the children to Melvin at once. Theresa explained she could not do that. Melvin may hurt the children. Wegman told her to get the children and that he would meet her at Melvin's home. Theresa got in her car and cried.

Theresa pulled up to Melvin and Lillian's home, and the police cruiser was parked next to Melvin's truck. There was still no sign of Lillian. She took the two babies out of her car and walked slowly to the front door. Once inside, she gasped when she saw Melvin. He looked like a man who was beaten by a gang that used brass knuckles and baseball bats. She immediately knew why the cast iron frying pan was lying on the floor. Melvin started yelling at Theresa and wanted to know what she was doing with his kids. Theresa explained that Lillian had dropped the kids off the night before at her home, and she had been told that Lillian needed some time to herself. Melvin let out a laugh.

"Oh, she needed time to herself, all right. There is no way I am taking care of these kids!"

Wegman said he needed to make arrangements because the state officials were not taking them. They had a father, and he needed to start acting like one.

"Look at me; I won't be able to work for a week with this face!"

Theresa said, "Well, I guess you won't need a babysitter then."

"You bitch, I know you talked her into this."

"I didn't; I wish I would have, much sooner than today."

Wegman put his hands up and told them to stop.

Theresa put the kids' bags down and looked at them sitting on the couch, scared.

"I am so sorry, babies. I love you." She turned around and walked out.

Wegman turned to the door and started to walk away. He turned back to Melvin.

"You are a sad excuse for a husband and father. You never deserved Lillian. I watched her grow up and saw her in pain when her mother died. You got her pregnant, and that is the reason you are here. You are a leech."

Melvin just stared at him, watching his back when he walked out the door.

Melvin had no idea how to care for his children. He never changed diapers, bathed, fed them, or was an actual father. He tossed the children in the truck and headed for Brenda's motel room. He was expecting her to be a mother to his children. She owed him. When he showed up, he left the kids in the truck. He banged on the door to room 222. Brenda answered it, leaving the security chain on the door. She peeked out and saw Melvin's face.

"Open up."

"Damn, boy, what happened to your face?"

"Don't worry about it, I said open up."

" I can't; I am working right now."

"On a Sunday?"

"You know Sunday means nothing to me, sugar."

Melvin kicked the door in, breaking the chain. He saw an overweight, sixty-year-old man sitting on the bed in his underwear, T-shirt, and socks.

"Get the fuck out, now!" yelled Melvin as he grabbed the man's clothes and threw them out in the hall.

The man did what he was told and never looked back. He started running to the stairs to get out of the motel as quickly as possible.

"Grab some clothes. You are coming with me."

"Maybe I don't want to come with you."

Melvin forcibly grabbed her by the arm and told her that her face was going to look like his if she didn't get her ass moving.

Brenda reached for a bag and threw some clothes in it, and they headed for the door.

When they got to the truck, Brenda wanted to know why there were kids and who they belonged to.

Brenda stayed with Melvin's kids while he went to work. He made her cook, clean the trailer, and, most importantly, care for the children. He did not want the state to make a surprise visit and place him in jail for child neglect. Melvin was aware Wegman would make that phone call. Brenda told him this was not the proper life for the kids and that he needed to put them in an orphanage so they could be adopted.

Melvin was now fighting with two women about his children. Theresa had repeatedly stopped by and asked if she could take the kids, but Melvin refused. He knew she would find a way to give the kids over to Lillian, and he wanted to ensure she never saw them again. Brenda told Melvin she was not a mother and needed to get back to work — just let the damn woman have them. Melvin told her she wasn't returning to work and that he would eventually marry and take care of her. Brenda laughed, saying she would never marry him. Enraged, Melvin backhanded her across the face, leaving her with a nosebleed.

Melvin came home from work the following day, and Brenda was gone. She had left his two kids sitting in a playpen with dirty diapers. He knew he could not care for the children without a woman in the house. Gathering all the kids' clothes and toys, he stuffed them into plastic bags, loaded everything into his truck with the children, and headed for St. Augustine's Orphanage — the only orphanage he knew of.

He dropped them off at the orphanage, signed some paperwork, and walked away, never to see his children again. They had his last name, but that was all they would ever have from him. Melvin told the nuns that their mother had an arrest warrant for attempted murder, and the children could not be released to her. He instructed them to call the police immediately if Lillian Martin showed up.

Without looking back at his two children — too small to even understand their predicament or what was in store for them — Melvin walked out of their lives forever.

1945 – Justice Is Not Fair

Lillian never felt safe after settling into her new apartment. She managed to get a job cleaning at a nearby hotel. Since she had no work history, she did what many others did in the 1940s—she lied. Thankfully, she had experience being tidy and highly organized, skills she owed to her mother. Despite her efforts to build a new life, she longed to go back home and visit her mother's gravesite, but she knew it wasn't possible. Jail awaited her if she returned.

Who wipes the leaves and snow off her headstone?

Who brings her flowers on Mother's Day and her birthday?

Who sits for hours and talks to her?

She hadn't meant to kill Melvin, but that wouldn't matter to the police. Women had no rights, even if they were getting the shit kicked out of them. She missed her kids dearly and cried herself to sleep every night. She had hope that one day she would see them again. She was certain Theresa was raising them—or perhaps she had taken them to her father in Florida.

One day, her children would be older, and she had to find a way to bring them to Indiana. The trip would be close if they were still in Illinois. But if they were in Florida, she feared she would never have the money to travel there, and if she did, her father would have brainwashed them. Chances were, they would only come to see her once they were adults.

Lillian went to work each day, kept her head down, and cleaned until the skin wore off her hands. The management at The Slumber Inn was pleased with her work. She wasn't making minimum wage but had to accept the 35 cents an hour. She repeatedly asked for more hours, and management granted her requests, but they didn't pay her extra for those times.

She saved every penny she earned to move as far from Illinois as possible. Indiana is not far enough. Fear consumed her—one day, the police might show up at her door to arrest her.

She had plenty of men try to take advantage of her while she worked at the hotel. She did her best to avoid making eye contact and, more than once, pretended she didn't speak English. Sometimes, men would leave her a tip—maybe just a quarter or fifty cent piece—but that made her happy. She still had Melvin's car, and she hid it in the back of the hotel. She would walk to work, even in bad weather. The staff thought it was strange but assumed it was due to repossession or jealous boyfriend.

She aimed to pack her car, leave Indiana, and head south. She wondered what Kentucky was like and if it would be cheaper to find a home there. She now had work experience and hoped that would open doors to better opportunities and higher wages. Lillian also hoped she could sell her car after moving and live on a bus route so that transportation wouldn't be an issue. This would give her a great start in her new life.

Melvin was still pursuing Lillian. He sold the trailer and land after forging Phillips' signature. Feeling rich, he quit his job, loaded his truck, and headed to Tennessee. He had spent money on a private investigator to find Lillian but always came up empty. He didn't care about his kids and thought they were better off without him. Florida had been a bust, and Lillian's father no longer lived in that state. The investigator told him he would keep trying, hoping Lillian might have contacted the orphanage. Melvin didn't know if she was that foolish, but it was worth a try. He told the investigator he was tired of giving him money for results that led nowhere. Melvin said one more month, he would cut him off after that—no more money. The investigator responded that he had a lead from the IRS and hoped to find out if Lillian was working and paying taxes, which would give him her location. Lillian had most likely changed her name, but he hoped this would point him in the right direction.

Melvin was now working construction and operating heavy machinery, which paid handsomely. However, he rarely saw the money because Patricia, his new wife demanded his check every Friday. Melvin was still legally married to Lillian, but he kept that a secret. They lived in a trailer outside Nashville, in Clarksville. He had moved there within thirty days after being attacked by Lillian. One of the guys on his last roofing job told him about the construction contractor and how they hired any man who wanted to work. He got in his truck and drove straight to Clarksville without thinking of his past life in Illinois.

He met Patricia a month later at a local bar; she was the bartender. He still had the broken bone over his eye, missing teeth, and a nasty scar next to his eyebrow. After work, he would drag himself into Shooters Bar, where Patricia would watch him flash money when he ordered his draft beer. She knew he worked outside because of the sunburn and assumed he made good money driving machines around because he liked to brag about it. Patricia thought he might be an easy catch. When asked about the scar on his face, he told her he got hurt on a construction job—something about another operator swinging an excavator bucket around and him walking right into it. Melvin never told her he was married and had two children, actually three if he was counting correctly. Patricia made it difficult to hide money, another reason to stop paying the private investigator.

Lillian was unaware that a private investigator was hot on her trail. As long as she stayed far from Illinois, she felt she had great odds, to remain free.

One afternoon, Lillian met a stranger while vacuuming the hallway on the third floor. She excused herself as he walked by, not making eye contact with the man. The vacuum stopped working, and she felt a tug on the electrical cord. She was startled and turned around to see the stranger dressed in a suit, wearing a bowler hat, with the other end of the cord in his hand.

"Excuse me, ma'am. I was just trying to get your attention, but I'm sure you didn't hear me."

"No, sir, I'm sorry, I didn't."

"I just wanted to tell you you're doing a fantastic job."

"Thank you, sir, you are too kind."

"Would you know where I could go for a nice piece of apple cobbler?"

"There's a diner at the end of the next block called Maggie's. The best dessert you'll find in this city."

"Thank you, kind lady. Could I ask what your name is?"

Lillian froze.

"Oh, I am so sorry, that's none of my business. Please excuse me."

"Sir, that's okay. My name is on my nametag."

The man looked at her shirt and said, "Thank you, Claire. My name is Charlie."

Charlie reached down and plugged the vacuum cord into the electrical receptacle. The vacuum started humming, and Lillian went back to work.

Charlie left and walked to the payphone on the corner. He made two calls — one to the Joliet police and the other to Melvin Martin.

He then walked a block and sat by the window at Maggie's diner, hoping they had cobbler on the menu.

Five days later, police officers from Joliet were sitting in an unmarked police car, watching the front door of The Slumber Inn. They needed a day to follow Lillian to make sure it was her and to get an address of where she was staying. They also wanted to understand if she was in a current relationship. They would be issuing both an arrest and search warrant. The Illinois district judge finally signed the warrants, which added a few days to their trip. The arrest warrant was not as difficult to attain as the search warrant. The judge needed extra clarification as to why the officers needed to get inside her apartment. The officers believed they could collect paperwork showing Lillian's escape path or letters informing someone about the crime she committed. They needed to take her car and return it to Melvin since his name was on the title. Melvin also requested Lillian's wedding ring because he wanted to pawn it.

Lillian finished her shift and walked home. She stopped at the diner and picked up a piece of cherry pie. It was payday, and she felt she had earned it. She never splurged on herself, always saving every cent she earned. Today, something felt different, but she didn't know what it was. She had hoped Charlie would leave her a tip when he checks out tomorrow morning. He appeared like a man of substance and it may be a nice amount. Lillian was too busy daydreaming to realize a man was following her on foot and another man in a car. She finally made it home, climbed the three flights of stairs, and put her master key in the door. She had just opened the door when she heard a man's voice behind her.

"Lillian Martin."

Lillian turned around to see who was talking to her. It was a police officer.

Lillian fainted and fell to the ground before the police officer could catch her — or the piece of cherry pie.

Melvin was ecstatic when Charlie called him after Lillian was arrested. He wanted to see Lillian behind bars. He was shocked that she had yet to travel very far and had only been living a state away. Charlie said she was cleaning hotel rooms and living in a dingy studio apartment. She had no friends, spent all her time at work, and went home, where she stayed the entire night. She walked everywhere, and he found her car parked, never moved, in a back parking lot. Lillian looked different from her picture. There was some resemblance—the eyes, the freckles—and she seemed somewhat Italian. He said she had cut her hair and lost weight. She was never a heavy woman, but now she was fragile, with her hair worn above her shoulders. It looked like Lillian tried to dye it, making it much lighter than her original color. Melvin could not wait to see her when he faced her in court.

Lillian had been sitting in a cell at the county jail for three weeks. She was told she was arrested for attempted murder. She was confused because she didn't know Melvin was alive. She found out that she had hurt him, and he had to go to the hospital for the injuries he sustained. She was also told her children were in an orphanage. She cried every night while in her jail cell. Three other women were bunked with her, and they would threaten to hurt her if she didn't shut up. They finally moved her to the infirmary so she could be watched by a nurse. The superintendent of the jail claimed Lillian was suffering from delusion and depression.

Lillian would scream that she wanted to see her children and that they needed to bring them to visit their mother. A jail matron told her that no one knew where her children had been taken after she abandoned them. Once children are placed in an orphanage, parents can't know where they are, so they don't try to come and get them. She told Lillian that her children must have been taken because she was a worthless mother.

Lillian grabbed a drinking glass next to her bed, broke it on the bed frame, and held the jagged glass to her wrist. She said she would cut herself if she didn't get to see her children. The matron told her to cut her wrist so she wouldn't have to worry about her children. Lillian dropped the glass, sat on the bed, and cried.

She then found herself restrained to the bed frame. A doctor came to see her and told her that she was schizophrenic and delusional. She would be held in the infirmary until her court proceedings were completed. Lillian just wanted to see her two children and asked every day, more than once per day, to have them brought to her. Lillian was not allowed any visitors, but only one person would try. Theresa would come to the jail on Sundays and ask to see her. The matrons would tell her that Lillian was highly medicated because she had tried to kill one of them. Theresa told them that Lillian would never do something like that. They claimed she was very hostile and had attempted to kill a man and now tried to kill one of them—she was crazy. Theresa asked them if they had met Melvin, they would understand why she took a frying pan to his head. He was the one who put her kids in an orphanage, even though Theresa would have taken them. Melvin knew Theresa would have given those babies a better life than in a dirty orphanage. When Theresa would be turned away, she would go to the local Catholic church and pray that Lillian would be safe and one day be released.

Two weeks after the glass incident, Lillian sat in court with a public defender. There was no jury, as it was a bench trial.

Her fate would be determined by one man, the judge. Lillian knew she would be found guilty because her attorney told her the injuries Melvin sustained were life-threatening. He added, "Women don't act that way; something must be wrong in your head." He also said she had left her children and didn't try to contact them. "The judge won't take too kindly to your actions."

Melvin was the only witness called for the prosecution. Lillian watched as Melvin entered the courtroom and walked to the stand. She quickly looked down and didn't want to make eye contact with him. He was dressed like a slob, and she was embarrassed that he would show up wearing rags like that in front of a judge. She needed help understanding the questions Melvin was being asked. She felt confused, and her head felt heavy. The doctor had given her a shot in the arm before she went to court, which made her feel very tired. He told her she was too anxious to speak in court, and the shot would help her. Lillian did not feel anxious; she only wanted to see her children.

Melvin told the story of how Lillian attacked him while he was sleeping. He had worked all day, came home, and went straight to bed. He woke up covered in blood, with his head bleeding. He must have been knocked unconscious with the first blow. Melvin claimed he had never hurt Lillian and had no idea why she tried to kill him. He also said he was an outstanding father to his two children and an excellent husband. Lillian did not make a sound as she sat with her head down. Melvin would later tell a newspaper reporter, "My wife was unrecognizable and ugly. When she was married to me, she was a beautiful woman."

The defense called one witness—Theresa. Lillian watched Theresa walk to the stand. Theresa sat down, staring at Lillian with a sad look. Lillian looked back down at the floor. Theresa explained to the judge how Lillian had been an excellent young woman when she first met her. She described how Lillian's life changed after her mother died. Lillian was intelligent, advanced two grades, and graduated high school at a young age.

Theresa recounted how Lillian cared for her two children while living in her home for a year. Lillian was not a violent person, and Theresa trusted her. She explained that Lillian had never been allowed to grow up because Melvin came into her life and deceived her.

Lillian was a victim. Melvin took advantage of her when she was only fifteen. Over time, Melvin turned into a drunk, a womanizer, and beat Lillian whenever he chose to.

The prosecutor asked, "If those facts are true, why didn't Lillian protect her children and report the abuse to the police?" Theresa explained that women are not listened to, and she planned to stay with Melvin until the kids were grown. Then, she would leave Melvin after asking for a divorce. The prosecutor asked, "If you knew this information, why didn't you report it to the police?" Theresa didn't know what to say. The prosecutor then claimed Theresa was making up stories and should have stepped in to help the children. He added that maybe they should find something to charge her with because she was a liar.

Lillian's head snapped up. "STOP, STOP, STOP!" she screamed. The prosecutor turned and stared at Lillian. The judge took his gavel and wrapped it five times.

"Enough! Bailiff McKenna, take Mrs. Martin back to the infirmary, now!"

The defense attorney stood and said, "Judge, I have the right to reexamine the witness."

"Court is over today, and there will be no more questions."

Bailiff McKenna took Lillian back to the infirmary, where she showed no emotion. He restrained her back to the bedframe and whispered that he was sorry.

Lillian lay there and stared at the ceiling. She knew she was going to prison for the rest of her life.

The next day, the judge called Lillian's attorney and the prosecutor to his chambers. He had decided what Lillian's punishment would be. He didn't want to send her to prison because he knew she was "sick in the head" — meaning her brain did not work like others. Lillian may have been brilliant as a young girl, but her brain had not grown as fast as her body. Melvin should have known that when she put their first child up for adoption. The judge added that she was not ready to be a parent or a wife.

The judge ordered that she be taken to the State Mental Hospital. She would leave the next day, and once admitted to the hospital, she would never be allowed to be released. It was a life sentence. The judge told Lillian's attorney to speak with her and tell her he was doing her a favor. His reasoning was that Lillian would be able to be with other women like her and receive medication, which would help her sickness. The judge said she would never be cured, but she needed help to keep her from being hostile and dangerous to others, including herself.

Lillian was 23 years old, and she would spend the rest of her life in an insane asylum that was three hours south of where she grew up.

Lillian arrived at a massive stone building on a cold, rainy day. She was taken by a police wagon and wore a cloth dress with no shoes. She had a skimpy jacket that did not keep her warm. The back of the wagon had no heat, even though the two officers bringing her were properly dressed and had heat in the front cab. Lillian could hear them laughing the entire trip.

They finally drove up to a locked gate when Lillian heard a male voice ask them to state their business. The officer replied, "What do you think? We have a crazy lady for you." Lillian heard a buzz, and the wagon proceeded into the complex. They parked the wagon, and she heard the officers leave the cab. There was a small window in each back door, and she could see both officers running in the rain to an overhang. She watched as one of them picked up the phone.

In a few minutes, a large man wearing all white came out of the door. An older man in a white jacket followed him. They stopped and spoke with the officers, and she could hear that one officer was mad and yelling while he pointed at the wagon.

The man in the white coat pointed as well. The officers came running in the rain and got into the wagon. Lillian could hear them complaining but could not make out the words. They started the wagon, and it jerked backward as it was put into gear. The driver slammed on the brakes, throwing Lillian off the seat. She hit her face on the back of the wagon, letting out a scream. The officers got out and were yelled at by the man in the white jacket. Suddenly, the doors were open, and the four men stared at Lillian, who was lying in her own blood on the floor of the wagon.

The large man dressed in all white scooped up Lillian and carried her to the door. She heard the other man yelling at the police officers. He told them he would call their boss and that they were not allowed to disrespect his patients. Lillian realized the man in the white coat was a doctor. The large man carried her through the door and down a flight of stairs to the infirmary. Lillian was laid on a bed and immediately tied to the four bedposts. The doctor leaned over Lillian's face, shining a bright light in her eyes.

"Orderly, get me some gauze and water. I need to see if Mrs. Martin needs stitches."

Lillian's face hurt, and she was in pain, but she didn't want to say anything. She was smart enough to understand that it made it worse every time she questioned something.

The doctor placed some gauze on the side of her head and put pressure on it. He poured water over the cut and applied more gauze. He told the orderly to get the nurse. When the nurse came in, she was instructed to sit next to Lillian and hold the dressing over the cut. The doctor returned with some instruments and told Lillian she was going to get stitches on the side of her head. He would have to cut some hair on that side, and she might look unpresentable outside the hospital, but she wouldn't have to worry about that inside. The doctor gave her seven stitches, washed her face, and told the nurse to take the patient to the women's ward, building C, and put her in a quiet area. The patient was schizophrenic and severely depressed. She had a history of violence, so the nurse was told to inform all staff.

In the first week, Lillian began to understand what type of women were housed with her. There were murderers, alcoholics, highly depressed women, and a large number of women who had nothing mentally wrong with them. Each group tended to stay in like-minded clusters. Lillian didn't fit into these groups, so she tried her best to get along with everyone and avoid talking too much. She met a woman named Barb, who was dropped off at the hospital by her husband. Barb claimed her husband wanted a new wife, so he got rid of her. When Lillian asked how that worked, Barb explained that by state law, it only took two signatures to have a person committed to the hospital. Many men would bring their friend or brother with them, and both sign a document stating that the woman was crazy, and the hospital would take custody of the woman. The patient would never be allowed to be discharged or have visitors unless the person who signed that paperwork wanted the patient discharged. The women were there for a life sentence and were only allowed to leave when they died. Then, their bodies were buried in a field in back of the hospital.

Lillian found this highly unbelievable. How could a husband do this and get a new wife whenever he wanted? However, she didn't question Barb because she seemed pretty strong, and it would be wise to stay on her good side.

Lillian continued to make friends and tried to help the other women. She was not violent and found ways to de-escalate arguments between the women. Patients were never allowed to go outside and stayed in one large building that housed 60 patients. Lillian found out there were other buildings — one that housed more dangerous women and four others that housed men. If any patients found a way to break out of their building, a loud alarm would sound, prompting people living close to the hospital to lock their doors. Lillian could swear she heard that alarm every other week.

Barb told her some men were there instead of prison, and they tried to climb the fence to escape. The women weren't as hostile, but once in a while, they would hear of a troublemaker who wanted to go over the fence. Barb claimed all the orderlies were men, and Lillian needed to be careful. They were known to hurt the patients for no reason, so she was told not to give them a reason, or they would take advantage of it. The patients who tried to escape always ended up in the infirmary.

Lillian explained that she had no reason to escape. She had no home, didn't know where her children were, her mother was dead, and her father had disowned her. When asked about her husband, Lillian would tell people it was his fault she was in the mental institution — he put her there.

Lillian was a stellar patient and a model for others. Doctors continued to give her daily medications, but Barb showed Lillian how to cheek them. That way, when the nurses looked in her mouth, it would appear she had swallowed the pills. Lillian had no idea what pills they were giving her because they would not tell her, even though she asked. She had told the doctor that she felt she did not need medication, and he told her she had no choice. She had a history of violence, and if the pills stopped working, they would have to use electric shock on her. Lillian had no idea what that meant, but it sounded terrible. She continued to cheek the pills and spit them out in the toilet.

Lillian would be friendly with the orderlies but not with the nurses. The orderlies were all men of different sizes and ages. They always looked good in their white uniforms and white shoes. Lillian loved all white and felt it had a nice, clean, crisp feeling. She did ask them if she could get a book or listen to music, but she was always told no. She could sit in the recreation room, where tables were set up. Barb found a way to get playing cards, and some women would come and play. Lillian would ask every day if this was how their lives would end. She was too young to live this way and needed to be outside. They only could leave their unit if they had to go to the infirmary or see the doctor. Lillian wanted to be treated like a human being, not like a crazy person, because she was not crazy. She was actually smart and afraid she was not smart anymore. She felt her mind was rotting every day.

Many days, Lillian would just sit in a chair and stare outside. She would listen to the orderlies and hear about their activities when not at work. She missed her kids and her mother. She had no one in her life. Lillian became very depressed and would spend hours crying quietly. She wanted to die because this was no life for a young woman. She would watch patients scream, throw themselves on the ground, slap the nurses, or fight the orderlies. There was constant chaos. Violent patients were not supposed to be mixed in Building C, but they had too many patients and not enough beds in the other units. Lillian was getting scared for her safety, and Barb became her protector.

At the next meeting with the doctor, Lillian explained that she could not stay there any longer. She needed to get outside and feel the sun, eat edible food, and find her children. When the doctor asked her what she would do if she could not leave, Lillian made a mistake by saying she would want to die. When asked to explain, she promptly said her life was not worth living if it was living this way. The doctor made notes and excused Lillian back to Building C.

When Lillian was escorted back, she went to her favorite chair next to the large window that looked out to the woods. Barb was playing cards with three other women and noticed Lillian crying. Barb excused herself from the card game and sat down next to Lillian. Barb looked around to ensure no one was watching, then held Lillian's hand tightly.

"What did the doctor say?"

Lillian looked at Barb, then back out the window.

"He didn't say anything. He just wrote in his notebook."

"Did you ask about your children?"

Lillian started crying but made sure she was not heard by the staff.

"I told the doctor I didn't care if I was dead."

Barb was shocked. "Lillian, don't talk like that!"

Barb saw the nurse look her way; she immediately dropped Lillian's hand.

"I told you what happens to patients when they admit they want to kill themselves."

"I didn't say I wanted to kill myself," Lillian whispered to Barb.

Barb told her to look at her. "What do you think not wanting to live means?"

Lillian looked away and continued to stare out the window.

Barb stood up and said, "Sometimes, I want to give up on you. You are too smart to be this dumb." She walked away, leaving Lillian alone.

Three weeks later, an orderly who Lillian did not recognize was standing next to the nurse during her morning medication schedule. When Lillian's name was called, she approached the nurse and waited to be handed her pills. The nurse informed Lillian that she was to go with the orderly. He would take her to see the doctor. When Lillian asked why, she was told it was none of her business and to go quietly with him.

Lillian walked out of the restricted area and was taken outside toward the stone building where the doctor's office was. Once inside, the orderly took her through a different door into a stairwell. He directed her to walk up a flight of stairs as he followed. At the top of the landing, he used his key to open a door.

Lillian saw a well-lit large corridor that smelled like it had been recently cleaned. Her doctor's office was not on this floor, which confused her. A nurse joined the orderly, and they directed her to walk down the hallway while they followed. They had Lillian stop about halfway, where a chair was placed outside a closed door. She was told to sit down. The orderly stood beside her while the nurse entered the room, closing the door behind her.

Within a few minutes, the nurse told Lillian to stand up and follow her. Lillian was still confused, and no one explained what was happening. She followed the nurse while the orderly followed behind her. A doctor was standing next to the bed, and she could see a machine beside him near the head of the bed.

"Good morning, Lillian. I am so happy to see you."

"Why am I here? What did I do? Who are you?"

"Mrs. Martin, you did nothing wrong," claimed the nurse.

The doctor took Lillian's hand, squeezed it, and led her to the bed.

"We want to help you so you are not depressed."

"I am not depressed. I just don't want to be here!"

The orderly placed his hands on Lillian's shoulders and pressed hard. He started walking her to the bed as the doctor held her hand.

Lillian started screaming for help.

The orderly grabbed Lillian around the waist and slammed her onto the bed. The doctor grabbed one wrist, and the nurse grabbed the other. There were leather belts on the side of the bed, and they tightened them so she couldn't move her arms. The orderly grabbed one ankle, tightened it with another belt, and then grabbed Lillian's other leg. She was trying to kick him in the head. He managed to grab her leg and tighten the belt down.

The nurse grabbed something and placed it in Lillian's mouth so she couldn't scream. The doctor wiped something cold on both sides of her head as the nurse held her head down. She heard a machine make a buzzing sound, and it was getting louder. The doctor told her to relax; it would be over quickly. He placed electrodes on both sides of her head, and Lillian felt all her muscles tighten. She passed out.

Lillian was administered her first dose of unmodified electroconvulsive therapy (ECT). The doctors would guess what dosage a patient should be administered. Their scientific method included past information about other patient's weights and what they were diagnosed with. One problem with this method was that the first expert guessed the dosage and time to administer the procedure to the patient. Doctors then performed the electric shock for that dosage and time. If patients were given too much of an electrical shock, they could eventually die.

The machine was shut off, the pads were taken off Lillian's head, and the leather belts were removed. The orderly carried

Lillian's body to a gurney, which was placed in the hallway. The orderly and nurse escorted Lillian back to her bed. Lillian would lay in her bed for over 48 hours, unable to walk or eat. Barb would tell others that she thought Lillian was dead, but she knew better because her eyes remained wide open.

The electroconvulsive therapy would continue for Lillian due to her depression and the fear that she would hurt herself, according to the doctor. Barb was upset that the doctor was using this therapy on Lillian and on others. Barb would see many women come back to their beds the same way she saw Lillian on that first day of treatment. Barb could not be boisterous or angry because she knew she could also become like Lillian. She felt her friend was gone — a waste of a young woman's life who could no longer have a voice to defend herself.

Lillian became less responsive to Barb. She had a difficult time playing cards or telling stories about her past. She would have very keen memories of the violence in her marriage, a memory she wished she could not recall. She remembered her mother and would sing songs they had sung together. She would ask to draw and color and smiled as though she had no worries. Lillian looked forty years old, though she was not even twenty-five.

Barb understood what was happening: the doctors were silently killing the patients. She knew they had to have vacant beds to make room for more patients. She listened to the nurses talking secretly at the nursing station. Many rumors circulated that patients going for electroconvulsive therapy were sometimes given too much, and they would die. The doctors used the patients as guinea pigs, trying to correct the dosage. Barb overheard them say that the doctor who found the medical cure would be famous, and they wanted the State Hospital to be the facility where the answer was found. The state would reward handsomely if the doctors showed results.

The hospital had its own cemetery, where patients were buried. Each headstone had a number—no names—and plots could have more than one patient. Barb was horrified that the hospital was not an actual hospital. There were no patients being cured. It was a prison where the prisoners would soon die at the direction of the doctors.

1952 – Martin Children

Daniel was now eleven, and Sally was nine. Both had to move to a new facility, St. Cecilia's, for orphans over ten years of age. Sally was turning ten that year, so she was allowed to be with her brother, as they were moved together as one family unit, which did not make much sense to Daniel since boys could not mix with girls. He only got the chance to talk to Sally on a few occasions. If Sally needed to get information to Daniel, or vice versa, they had to depend on leaving cryptic messages somewhere around the school grounds.

Life at St. Augustine's had been bad, and both children didn't think it would improve when they moved to this new home.

St. Cecilia's was an ancient building built in the late 1800s. It was always cold, even in the summer, which was nice. Daniel understood that he would be released if he was adopted or when he reached thirteen years of age. Sally would have to wait longer; if not adopted, she would be released at fifteen. There were different state rules for boys and girls. Daniel didn't know if Sally could survive without him. He had taken care of her the best way he knew how.

Daniel remembered very few memories of his parents; Sally had no idea what a parent was. Daniel remembered his mother because she would sing to him. He doesn't remember her voice anymore, which makes him sad. He doesn't know what happened to his mother, and he had hoped that one day he would find out. He would take every opportunity to see her again.

However, his father had always yelled at him, and he had no desire to see him again. He was scared of him.

The years at the Augie – that is what the kids called it – were very difficult. There were too many kids and insufficient beds, clothes, or food. Local churches would try to have collection drives, but the community always fell short. It was the same at Cecilia's but worse since the orphans were all older. The community did not like having the noise of Cecilia's or getting woken up in the middle of the night when the alarms were blaring at the highest volume possible. The alarm usually meant a child had climbed over the six-foot fence and tried to escape. They would find kids trying to break into homes to steal food. Sally was never one of those kids, yet the nuns were brutal to Sally. She was a typical girl but had a mouth on her, that led her into trouble continuously. Sally liked to use swear words and fight with the other girls. She thought that was funny; the nuns did not.

Daniel did what he was told and was a stellar child at Augie's. The nuns treated him well, to the point where he did not want to move to Cecilia's. There would be a mixture of older boys and girls, and he had difficulty climbing to the top of the heap at Augie's. It took a lot of work to become popular. He knew that if he did, the other kids would take care of his sister. And now, that security blanket was gone. He would have to learn how to deal with the new kids and find ways to lure them into his web. Daniel thought it was exhausting, but he continued to work as hard as he could so that Sally would be in a good spot when he had to leave her.

The first month, Cecilia's was difficult to master. The boys and girls were bigger and stronger than at the Augie. A rumor got started that their mother was a killer, that she had killed their father. The other kids despised Daniel and Sally, giving them nicknames like "Mama's Little Killers" or "Twins of Dracula." The names were stupid, and Daniel would tell Sally to ignore them. He was never told their mom had killed their dad. And he doubted his mother would have sucked his dad's blood out of his neck if she had killed him. His mom was too nice to do such a thing.

The boys were not as vindictive as the girls. Daniel made friends quickly because he was good at kickball. They could overlook his mother being a murderer as long as he kept kicking the ball as far as he could.

Sally, on the other hand, would get into trouble every day. Many girls would be leaving the following year since they were fifteen. Six of them had started a club, calling themselves the "Gang of Six." The gang would wreak havoc on the other girls when the nuns were not paying attention. Cecilia did not have enough nuns, and it was easy to thrive as a bully. The boys and girls were separated on the playground, and Daniel could still see his sister and how she was getting bullied daily.

Sally was not smart enough to play the game, go along with the gang, and try not to be overbearing. She made up for what she lacked in that department with her studies. Sally was one of the most intelligent girls at the orphanage. She was just the opposite of Daniel, who was not a good student but had common sense that would allow him to live on the street once he was released.

Both Daniel and Sally were curious about their parents. Orphans were not allowed to ask or talk about their families. The nuns kept them busy, so their free time had to be spent studying, cleaning, or doing yard work. Sally hated doing anything unless it involved reading or writing. The other girls would dump water on her head or throw dirt when pulling weeds. The gang would team up on Sally and pull her hair, pull her skirt down, or spit on her. This would often turn into a fight, with Sally getting the worst of it. She would land a few blows, pull out lumps of hair, and even bite a few of the gang members. Once, she even left bite marks and drew blood. The name "Dracula" became popular after that incident.

Daniel was the type of kid who would be quiet to listen to what other kids were talking about. One day, while waiting in line, he heard two boys talking - the two who were always up to no good. Billy and Carl were very well-known in the neighborhood because one or the other would sneak over the fence about eighty percent of the time. They were both popular with the other boys, as they made them laugh and could be dared to do just about anything asked of them. The two were twelve and would be released in the next few months. As luck would have it, their birthdays were two weeks apart. They had already decided how to make money once released - theft was their choice, and stealing food and money without getting caught would be the start. Their dream was to rob a bank. Daniel thought they were too stupid to pull that plan off.

They whispered that they had found the office containing the orphans' personal files. They wanted to find their parents, so they planned to sneak out late one night and break into the office. This made Daniel pay attention. He wanted to find his mom, even if she was in prison. He thought it was important for Sally to meet their mother. Daniel could have cared less about his father, and he was still optimistic that their mom did not kill their father. Carl said they wanted to break in that weekend, which was only a few days away. They needed a plan. There was only one security guard on duty on the weekends, and the boys knew he slept in a chair, waking up every two hours to walk around the grounds. They just needed to make sure he had just returned from his rounds and returned back to sleep. Billy thought they might have to get his keys without him noticing if they could not pick the lock. They decided they should find another boy to be the lookout. Daniel found his way in.

Daniel approached Billy and Carl the next day on the playground.

"I was wondering if you guys need some help."

Billy put his hands on his hips. "What help? We never asked for any help."

"I heard you say something about needing a lookout."

Carl laughed. "Why do we need a lookout?"

Daniel looked down at the ground. "Look, I need to know where my mother is. I just want to know if she's dead or alive. I need to find out before I get out of here. I don't have a home and need to go somewhere."

Carl and Billy looked at each other.

"If we tell you our plan, and you tell the nuns, you'll be the one dead," Billy said with a sneer.

"I won't tell a soul; I just need to find out where she is—that's it."

Carl explained the plan to Daniel, including what part of the plan Daniel had to accomplish. They were planning the escapade for Saturday night. Daniel had to report to the basement at two in the morning, and he couldn't be seen. Once there, he would be their lookout.

"What do you want us to find out? Where is your mom?"

"Yeah, if you can tell me anything about her or where she lived, that would be a start. And if you don't find anything, it may be in my sister's folder."

"We ain't looking for your sister. It's your folder or nothing."

"Okay, but make sure you guys don't make a mess because the nuns can send you to jail."

"No, they can't. They have to let us out on our birthday. Don't be a smart ass."

Daniel knew better but decided to drop it. He didn't want to scare them off.

"Okay, I'll be in the basement Saturday night. I'll make sure no one sees me."

"You better be careful because if we get caught, we'll tell the nuns this was your plan, and you threatened us to help."

Daniel stared at both of them. "Don't get caught."

When Saturday night arrived, Daniel was getting scared. He couldn't back down now; he was stuck. He lay on his cot, staring at the ceiling, even though it was pitch black. There was only one clock on the wall, and he couldn't see it. He was hoping to hear Billy or Carl sneak away.

Daniel went to the bathroom so he could pass by the clock. He barely made out that it was ten minutes before two. He decided to forget using the toilet and started his journey. He moved slowly down the corridor and crept down the flights of stairs until he reached the basement. He didn't realize how dark it was with no lights on. He touched the wall and tried to feel his way to the door. He slowly opened it and slid inside. He waited by the wall, too scared to move.

A few minutes later, he heard the door jerk open, and a loud squeak echoed in the stairwell. It was Billy and Carl.

"Damn, can you two be quiet?" Daniel whispered.

"Shut up, don't be telling us what to do. You're not the boss," Carl bellowed.

At that moment, Daniel realized how stupid these two were and how they would be caught in minutes.

"You stand by this door, and if you see old man Malone, the security guard, you whistle loud."

"You'll hear the door squeak, so whistling would be stupid."

Billy whispered, "Why don't we just kick your ass now and call it a night?"

Daniel said he was sorry and that he was just scared.

Carl laughed. "Don't pee your pants, little boy. Do what you're told."

Daniel stood in the back corner and watched the two boys walk down the corridor. He lost sight of them after a few seconds. Malone should have completed his rounds and be sleeping in his chair on the other side of the building. Billy and Carl made it to the office they were looking for. It was a wooden door with a glass panel at the top. Billy had stolen a bobby pin from one of the girls, and the plan was to use that to open the door. Billy was quite skilled with opening locked doors. He had been sent to the orphanage due to bad behavior. His parents had placed him at the orphanage to keep him out of juvenile detention. Billy liked to break into his neighbors' homes and take things his family could afford. It was a game to him but an embarrassment to his parents. They told the neighbors that Billy had gone to California to live with his uncle.

Billy put the bobby pin in the lock and started to turn it slowly in different directions. Carl was listening for a whistle. Within minutes, Billy heard the lock pop and turned the doorknob. They were in. They found their way to a desk and turned on a light. They knew it was highly dangerous, but they couldn't steal a flashlight from old man Malone.

They went to the file cabinets and looked for the letters R and K in the boys' section, corresponding to their last names. They pulled out their personal folders and put them on the desk. Billy realized he didn't know Daniel's last name. Carl decided to open all the drawers for both the boys and girls and find one name that appeared in both cabinets. Daniel and Sally were the only brothers and sisters at Cecilia's. Billy started calling out the boys' last names, and Carl did the same for the girls. They stopped on "Martin," and both grabbed the folders and put them on the desk. They shut all the drawers when they heard keys rattling. Billy turned off the desk light and picked up the folders. He gave two to Carl, and they stuffed them down the front of their jeans. They didn't hear a whistle from Danny, so they were confused.

Billy and Carl got under the desk and waited for Malone to open the door. When it opened, they heard someone whispering their names. It was Daniel.

"What are you doing? You're the lookout!" Billy whispered loudly.

"I have the keys. Malone was asleep and forgot them by the bathroom. I heard him walking in the stairwell, so I followed him."

Billy turned the desk light back on.

"Here, Merry Christmas, we grabbed your sister's, too."

Billy reached into his pants and pulled out two folders, and so did Carl.

They started reviewing the paperwork, knowing they couldn't take anything outside the room.

Daniel sat down and started shaking his head.

"What's wrong?"

"My mom didn't kill anyone, and she's not in jail. I know where she's at."

Carl chimed in, "Well, you better hope she's still there when you get out of this hell hole."

"Oh, she ain't going nowhere. I found her. And in two years, I'll see her."

The boys carefully put their folders back and made sure nothing looked out of place. They shut the door, locking it. Billy had the bobby pin in his pocket. The only thing they had left to do was get the keys back to the bathroom and sneak back to their cots.

The boys were unaware that old man Malone was searching for his keys. He needed his keys due to having a unique key that fits into a timing system when he made his rounds. In areas around the complex, there were red boxes on the wall, and he used the key to put it in those locks. It would record that he was in that area when he was supposed to be. Malone needed his job and had been working there for over ten years. He knew the nuns would find any reason to fire an old black man. He retraced his steps and remembered using the bathroom. He went around the corner and ran into the three boys.

"Whatcha young'uns doing out here and not in bed?"

Daniel spoke up. "We were looking for you because we found these keys in the bathroom."

"What? All three of you boys were using the bathroom together?"

Daniel continued, "No, I got scared that something might have happened to you, so I got the older boys to help me look for you."

Malone didn't know what to say. He didn't believe it, but Daniel was a good kid; the other two were trouble.

"Give me those keys, and y'all better be quiet getting back in bed. The sisters hear ya, and we'll all be in trouble. Can I count on all y'all to do that?"

Daniel said, "Yes, sir, we will."

Both Carl and Billy shook their heads. They all made it back to their cots. Billy knew he had underestimated Daniel. Carl thought Daniel was pretty damn brilliant to get them out of trouble.

Daniel laid on his cot and cried but made sure no one could hear him.

1954 – A Sons Mission

Daniel turned thirteen and was leaving Cecilia's the following day. The nuns told him he had ten minutes with Sally before being escorted off the property. The next day, Daniel and Sally sat in the same office where they had been two years earlier, on the first day they arrived. Sally was crying because she knew she had to stay until she was fifteen. She had two more years at Cecilia's before she was allowed to leave. The nun told Sally to stop crying and tell Daniel goodbye.

"Sis, it will be okay. I will come back for you."

"What happens if you don't?"

"I promise I will."

Daniel then grabbed Sally and hugged her while whispering something in her ear. He made sure he didn't use the ear that the nun could see.

"Stop it! You are not allowed to touch. Daniel, leave this room at once!"

Daniel picked up his plastic bag, which contained two sets of clothes and one pair of shoes, and walked out. The nun slammed the door. Sally had stopped crying, but the nun didn't notice.

Two weeks later, Daniel was standing outside the State Mental Hospital. He pushed the intercom button.

Daniel heard a man's voice come from the box.

"We do not take visitors."

"I am not a visitor; I was told you are hiring."

Daniel heard a buzz, and then the gate started to open. He walked through toward the pedestrian door. A big man, all dressed in white, came out the door.

"Boy, follow me, and do not talk."

The man took Daniel down a large corridor and told him to stand against the wall. He knocked on a door, which an older woman opened. She came out into the hall and looked at Daniel.

"How old are you? You're not very big."

"I am 14, going to be 15, real soon," Daniel lied.

"Let's go talk."

The woman welcomed Daniel into an office and had him stand in front of her desk while she sat behind it.

"What is your name?"

Daniel already knew he could not give his real name, or they might figure out his mom was a patient.

"My name is Billy."

"Billy, what is your last name?"

"Daniels." He blurted out, without thinking.

The woman let out a snort. "Where do you live?"

"I live down the street in an apartment with my grandmother."

"So, you're telling me you live close and could be at work at the proper time?"

"Yes, ma'am, and I will do any type of work and work any hours you give me."

Daniel did not have a home; therefore, he was homeless. He hitched rides and found soup kitchens and extra clothes from the church. He also slept many nights inside the church—any church he could find. There was a preacher's wife who took him in for a few days and allowed him to take a shower. He cleaned the church to say thank you and helped with any other chores she had for him.

The woman looked at Daniel and stared.

"Orderly, get in here."

The big man in white was waiting in the hallway, and he entered the office.

"Take Mr. Billy down to the basement, give him his uniform. Try to find something that will work for him. If it needs altering, it will be sent to Mrs. Weinberger, and she will assist. I want him to have socks and shoes."

The orderly nodded his head.

"Billy, you get your uniform on; our orderly (pointing at the big man in white) will then take you to the supply room, where we keep our mops and buckets. You are not allowed to speak to anyone and at no time come into contact with our patients. We are not allowed to use your name, so if you hear 'orderly,' you must pay attention. You will be paid on Fridays fifty five cents an hour in cash, and you can advance to a better-paying job. You will work every six days, with Tuesdays off. If you want to work on Tuesdays, and we need you, you come and speak to me personally. Do you understand what I just said?"

Daniel nodded.

"Sir, do not nod. Speak."

"Yes, ma'am."

"On your way, and you, orderly, take care of this young man, train him, show him the ropes. If I find out you are not doing your job, you will be outside that fence line."

The orderly stood at attention. "Ma'am, you can count on me. I have never let you down."

"No, sir, you have not, and that is why you have the current job you have. Let's try to keep it."

Daniel walked out and could have jumped for joy. He just needed to find a way to locate his mother.

Daniel got outfitted in a new uniform. It was loose, but the orderly said they would take care of that later. He received a brand-new pair of white sneakers. He couldn't remember ever getting a new pair of shoes before. He got three new white, heavily starched T-shirts and three pairs of white socks. They found him a white jacket if he was sent outside to work. They gave him a woman's size, but he was told not to worry — no one would know the difference. The seamstress would use a black marker to write his name on the inside of his clothes. But Daniel was responsible for washing and ironing them.

Daniel had yet to learn how to keep his uniform clean or how he would iron it. He didn't even have a bed to sleep in. The orderly must have noticed Daniel's face drop.

"Billy, listen to me. You seem like a good kid. We have lockers downstairs, and I'm taking you there next. I'll give you a locker, but you must buy your own lock. None of us do, but that's up to you."

"Thank you, sir."

"There is a wash basin and an iron. You can wash your uniforms and hang them in your locker to dry. Then, iron them when they dry. If you don't know how to iron, one of the other guys will teach you."

"Thank you because I have never held an iron before."

"That's fine; you'll get along with all the men. You won't be with patients until you prove you can be trusted. We'll start with the women first since they're the least violent."

"Violent?"

"Billy, we do things here that you can never repeat. Do you understand that?"

"Yes, sir."

"Keep your head down, do your work, and it will be okay. Do you have a place to stay?"

Daniel just stared at him, feeling like he would start crying. But he didn't. He shook his head no and immediately dropped his eyes to his new shoes.

"Listen, we'll borrow a cot and put it in the coal room next to the locker room. It will stay nice and toasty. I'll get you a blanket. When you get paid, I will give you the name of the man who runs the flop house down on Adams St., about a mile down the hill. He'll give you a room for a quarter a night, but you may have to share it with another boy. If you pay more, you can have your own room."

Daniel didn't know what to say.

"Billy, if you embarrass me, if you don't show up to work, or if you talk to anyone, I will get back at you, one way or another. Is that clear?"

"Sir, I thank you, and I will not disappoint you."

"I believe you. Let's head down to the basement and get you that locker so you can put your belongings in one."

Daniel was doing well with his job. He never missed a day and took every extra shift offered to him. He always arrived early, even though he walked a mile to work. There was a bus service, but he would only spend the dime on a one-way trip if it were raining. He was growing tall, so he started needing different uniform sizes. Some of them were pre-worn, but he didn't care. The shoes, however, were always new. No employee returned their shoes when they left the hospital, and the new shoes made Daniel happy.

He continued to scrub and wax floors in the office areas. He dusted, changed light bulbs, and was taught how to repair and paint the walls. Daniel was happy and had to remind himself that his name was Billy. He didn't always answer to Billy, and the guys would tease him. He knew which office held the patient files, but that was where the doctors were. Their file cabinets were always locked, and they carried the key in their pocket. It would be difficult to get his mother's folder. He hoped to find her through a process of elimination, but many new patients arrived daily. This made it difficult to remember who was who. He would only see them has they were getting off the bus or being taken to one of the offices. Daniel thought it was odd that he never saw patients leaving, only arriving. He was told that due to the patients being unstable and violent, there was no place to discharge them. One of the older orderlies told him that all the patients were crazy and that they could just kill all of them, and society would be better off. Daniel became furious but held his anger.

One day, Daniel was finishing waxing the floor and locking the equipment in the supply room when a man wearing a white coat stopped to talk to him.

"Are you Billy?"

"Yes, sir."

"My name is Doctor Bowers, and I am glad to meet you. Tomorrow, you will be placed in Building C, where our women patients are housed. Do you think you are ready for that responsibility?"

"Yes, sir," Daniel said, sticking his chest out. "I will not let you down."

"I will be the judge of that. You will receive a pay increase, but it is small. You will no longer clean unless told. But I want you to get rest tonight and be ready in the morning."

"Yes, sir, and thank you for believing in me."

"Billy, you are thought of very highly in this building. Just continue to do what you are doing, and it will be fine."

The doctor turned and walked away. Daniel felt his plan was working out. He had been there seven months, and finally getting the opportunity to interact with patients. If his mother were a patient, he would get to meet her. And before long, Sally would be arriving and working there as well. Daniel knew he wouldn't sleep that night. He would have to write Sally another letter, using code words so she could share in his happiness.

The following day, Daniel was dressed and ready to be taken to Building C. He had an orderly he had never met come to his locker to meet him.

"Are you Billy?"

"Yes, I am."

"I am Scott, and you will never use my name outside this room. Is that clear?"

"Yes, sir, it is."

"We are not friends. The patients are not your friends. The nurses are not your friends. You will never use names for the staff, and you will only know the patients' names if they tell you. You are young, so many women will want you to be their son. You are not, no matter what they say. You may be asked to escort, watch the recreation room, break up fights, and always protect the nurses."

"I will, sir, thank you, and I will always do what I am told."

"Follow me, let's head out."

Scott took Daniel outside, and they walked toward Building C. Daniel was pretty shocked by how large the complex was. When they got outside Building C, Scott turned to him and handed him one key.

"You must have this key in your pocket at all times. It can never be out of your reach, nor will you give it to anyone, including me."

Daniel took the key and noticed it was very well-worn.

"Put the key in the lock and give it a turn. Let's make sure it works."

Daniel placed the key in the lock, turned it, and heard it disengage. He opened the door and was standing outside another locked door. Daniel did the same with the second door.

It took him a second to realize what he saw when he stepped inside. A black gate attached to a six-foot fence stretched across the walls. He could see inside the area where women were walking around. Some were fully clothed, some were not. Daniel blushed. He could see two nurses in another locked location, surrounded by glass.

"Don't worry, these women are harmless. Some like to take their clothes off, and we try to get them dressed. If they don't listen, we can take them to their rooms. When that happens, you must have another orderly or a nurse. Never be alone with a patient. Do you hear me?"

Daniel nodded yes. The orderly hit a button on the wall outside the gate. They made eye contact with the nurse in the nurses' station. She hit a button, and the door buzzed and disengaged. They walked through the gate. Daniel was now inside Building C. He took a breath and followed the orderly, not wanting to make eye contact with the patients. They went inside the nurses' station when the nurse buzzed them in.

"Nurse Blackburn, this is our new orderly, Billy."

"Nice to meet you, Billy. You look pretty young to be in a place like this."

Daniel stated, "Nurse Blackburn, I just want to do a good job no matter what job I have. I hope that my work ethic will make you happy."

Blackburn stared a hole in him. "Did your mother tell you to say that?"

FAMILY DIRT

Daniel looked down at the ground and said, "No, Nurse Blackburn, both of my parents died when I was a very young boy."

She said nothing. Daniel was hoping this wasn't his mother's nurse. If she was at this hospital, in this building, her nurse would be difficult to work with.

The orderly explained how all of them work as a team. He explained how new patients arrived and what was needed to get the patients settled. He reviewed the schedule and how the day was set up for staff, with everyone having a job to complete to maintain safety. He emphasized that violence was not tolerated and that Daniel should never hit a patient. Daniel would be trained to control a patient, walk a patient, and take a patient down to the ground if necessary. The orderly explained why an alarm would sound and what to do when it did. Daniel would have to stay with the other orderly for six to eight weeks until the orderly felt comfortable, allowing him to present himself as a trained and educated orderly. Daniel could not be out of his sight and had to stay on his hip as he moved through the hospital.

Daniel was happy and paid attention to the file cabinet in the nursing station. He could see that the nurses had patient files out on the desk. He noticed there were numbers on the folders, not patient names. This may be more challenging than he thought to find his mother. But he promised himself that he would see her no matter how long it took. Daniel needed to be friendly and a great worker to keep his job and be ready for Sally when she was discharged from the orphanage. Daniel saved all his money to afford a larger room with two beds and a small kitchen. His plan was to get Sally hired as a nurse's helper. He didn't know if he wanted the staff to know they were related. That might be a disadvantage, and it may be easier if no one knew. He had a few years to think about his master plan and felt that, by that time, things should work out for both of them. He just wanted to settle in and find people he could trust.

Daniel came in every day and followed the orderly around. The orderly did not speak to the patients or go out of his way. Daniel could see others talk to the patients and offer kind words, followed by small comments. He spent his day not only in Building C but also being taken around the entire complex to understand the layout of all the buildings, the yard, where the doctors were housed, and the infirmary. As part of his training, he had to lead the orderly when told which building to go to, testing his memory. Daniel did very well and had a great sense of direction. They were supposed to take a radio with them when out of their building in case of an emergency. The orderly didn't allow Daniel even to hold the radio. There was an unpaid 15-minute lunch break, but Daniel never brought a lunch.

"Why you have no lunch, kid?"

"I eat a big breakfast and dinner, so I ain't that hungry at lunch," Daniel lied. He thought if he commented about needing to save money for his sister, it would make them think he was a wimp. Daniel would sit and draw during lunch to take his mind off food. He tried his best to draw the hospital's buildings, thinking that would help with his memory. He also felt that if his mother were here, he might find a way to sneak her out.

Daniel continued to do his best, keeping his head down and paying attention. He would try to stare without actually staring to remember the women and try to guess their age. He believed his mother was young, but most women looked old. There were so many of them that he felt it would be impossible to find her. He thought he would remember her voice, but only if she sang.

His priority was to get into the files, but he would have to look at every one since no names were printed on the folders.

Daniel wanted to meet the most competent patient on the floor, hoping she could help — but only if she could be trusted. He saw some women playing cards, so he knew a few patients understood how to use their brains. He was trying really hard to listen and remember the women's names in case anyone would accidentally call them out. One woman in particular would stare at him. She seemed like the leader of the card game. She would be too old to be his mother, but something about her made him think she could be the key. He heard the name Barb, so he tried to watch her as best he could without overstepping his bounds. He was warned that he would be reassigned if he broke any rules.

Daniel had settled in Building C and gained the nurses' trust. He worked every day he was allowed and kept saving his paycheck. He would need money to travel to his sister and bring her back. He would take a bus, walk two miles to the orphanage, meet her, and return to the bus stop. He already knew how much the tickets cost and wanted money to buy Sally new shoes or a coat. Once getting her to the room he was renting, he wanted to make sure she could get a job at the hospital. He thought about his plan every waking minute, day and night. He had time to plan it out but would become overwhelmed, thinking it might never work. Sally would be coming home later this year, and he had to find his mom before she arrived so he could tell Sally.

Daniel decided he would make eye contact with Barb and watch the women when they played cards. The other orderlies were starting to trust him more, and once in a while, they allowed him to escort a patient to the doctor's office across campus. He could take a radio and walk with the patient, but only if the patient was elderly or disabled. The staff felt it was too risky to have a young man like Daniel with a grown woman who might be able to overpower him. Daniel grew and started looking more like a young man than a boy. People would guess him to be older than he actually was. Daniel used this to his advantage whenever he could.

Luck would have it; Barb needed to be brought to the doctor for her annual checkup. The orderly who was supposed to escort her that day had just started his lunch. Daniel asked the nurse if he could escort her instead. The nurse said no and that she would call the doctor and reschedule. When the nurse made that call, the doctor told the nurse he needed to see all patients scheduled because he was going on vacation and would be gone for two weeks. The nurse made the decision to let Daniel escort Barb. Daniel knew this was his one chance and the only chance he would get to find his mother.

The nurse called Barb to the cage, where the nurses' station was. The head nurse explained to Barb that the young orderly would escort her to the doctor. The nurse gave Daniel a radio and told him to call if he needed assistance. The walk was less than 100 yards, and they were expected at the doctor's office within ten minutes. The nurse who worked for the doctor got a phone call and told them to expect Daniel and the patient. Daniel knew he would have to act fast.

He stood behind Barb as they went to the gate and waited to be buzzed out. Barb walked, and Daniel followed. As soon as they went outside the building, Daniel put his plan into action.

"Please do not turn around. I need to tell you something, and I pray you do not tell anyone what I am about to tell you."

Barb slowed her walk, and Daniel grew scared.

"Please, I need your help, and I do not trust anyone here. But for some reason, I hope I can trust you. Please nod your head once if I can trust you."

Barb gave a very slight nod and continued to walk. Daniel had only a few minutes left in their walk.

"My mom is here, and I need to find her. She may be in Building C, but I need to check. Her husband left her here, even though I know she did not do what he said she did. I have been in an orphanage with my sister since we were babies."

They were starting to get closer to the door.

"I miss her so much and cry myself to sleep. I have to know what happened and what I can do to find her. Will you find it in your heart to try and help me? I just want to know if she is in your building, but I do not want her to know who I am until I can think about my plan."

Daniel reached for the buzzer on the door.

Barb turned and looked at him, and he saw a tear in her eye.

Daniel mouthed a whisper, "Her name is Lillian."

Barb did not move nor show any emotion. She knew they were on camera, and someone may also be listening. Barb moved her head in a slight nod.

The buzzer sounded, and Barb opened the door. Daniel followed.

Daniel said, under his breath, "Thank you, and I will be forever grateful to you."

Barb started walking to the doctor's office door with Daniel behind her. They passed staff as Barb kept her head down. They stopped at the door when Daniel placed his hand on the doorknob. As he started to open it, Barb whispered, "She is here."

Daniel opened the door and led Barb in. The nurse told him to return to Building C and that another orderly would return the patient when the exam was done. Daniel's heart skipped a beat. He feared that Barb might report him to the doctor for making contact with her and that she might reveal that his mother was here. He had kept it a secret from everyone and hoped she would, too.

Daniel returned to the cage with the nurses and placed the radio on the desk. The head nurse asked Daniel if everything was okay because he looked pale. Daniel explained that he was fine and was just happy to be chosen to escort a patient by himself. The nurse nodded and explained that he would get more opportunities if he kept that attitude.

Daniel sat in the cage, waiting for Barb to return. Even though he was a young man, he understood the magnitude of what could happen. He wouldn't have enough money to bring his sister home if fired. And worst of all, he wouldn't be able to meet his mother now that he was aware she was a patient. While he waited for Barb, he continued to stare at the patients. He had made a mental list of who he thought could be her. He still felt strange saying the name Lillian out loud — almost like it was some rule he had broken by calling a parent by their first name.

He had numbers that the patients were identified by, but no names. That was why he paid attention whenever the nurses had the folders on the desk. He silently repeated the patients' numbers: 505, 817, 392, 613, and 934. Daniel thought the numbers were consequential, that the patients with the smaller numbers were the ones who had been in the hospital the longest. Then he overheard the nurses talking — when a patient dies, the hospital could reuse that number for a new patient. If Daniel couldn't see the patient files, Barb was his only help.

Within thirty minutes, Barb appeared on the floor with an orderly following her. She immediately looked at Daniel. His breathing increased as she made eye contact with him, then turned her head back to the floor. He was scared — something told him that Barb had reported him. He waited in the cage, expecting the doctor to come get him with security in tow.

Barb went over to a patient sitting in a chair, looking outside a window- the same patient who sat there every day, not moving or talking. Barb put her hand on the woman's shoulder, which was against the hospital rules. She leaned down and whispered something to her. The patient didn't move, but she became interested and stiff. Daniel then realized — he had found his mother. Patient 817 was *Lillian*.

Daniel understood that his mother was sick. He had difficulty seeing her appear frail and old when she was a young woman. He would try to gain as much information as possible about patient 817 using Barb and the staff. He needed to be nosy but not cross the line. Daniel wanted everything to be perfect before Sally arrived. That meant approaching his mother within the next few months. Sally would be discharged from the orphanage, and he would be there to pick her up and tell her he had done it — he found their mother.

In the next few weeks, he made it a habit to make eye contact with both Barb and Lillian. His mother seemed indifferent, and he realized it was because she was being taken to the third floor for therapy. When she returned, she seemed unable to show emotion, couldn't talk, and was unsteady. But as the days passed, Lillian regained more of her senses. Daniel was able to sneak words to Barb, who would claim she needed help with the card table or walking Lillian back to her bed. Barb told Daniel that Lillian understood he was there but wouldn't tell anyone because she knew they would move him to another building. They used Barb as the messenger and stayed discreet. Barb explained that Lillian understood words better if they waited at least two weeks after her therapy sessions. Daniel wanted to know why his mother was being taken to the third floor when she wasn't doing anything to harm the other patients or herself. Barb wanted to know the same thing.

Daniel would approach Lillian daily, sometimes helping her walk to her favorite chair. He'd offer to clean the glass window, give her a blanket if she was cold, or move with the nurse when delivering her medications. The nurses thought Daniel was just being kind to a frail patient, and when asked by staff if Daniel was giving patient 817 too much attention, they would say, "Daniel gives every patient that amount of care." Daniel was aware of their comments and assisted every patient or staff member who needed help. He also knew Sally would be less friendly if she came to work at the hospital.

.

As months passed, Lillian would hold Daniel's hand tighter, look for him on her good days, and whisper his name very slowly when he was next to her. Barb could see a twinkle in Lillian's eyes whenever she admired him. Barb knew she needed a plan to get both of them more time together and began trying to get the staff to allow the patients outside for a walk. She argued that it would help them be less stressed and improve their attitudes toward the staff. Barb made her case to the new doctor who had recently been hired by the hospital. She was the first female doctor employed in the state as a psychiatric doctor. This doctor was trained in the importance of sunlight and fresh air. It was spring in the Midwest, and what better time to introduce a new program at the hospital?

The doctor asked Barb to be the patient liaison and work with the nursing staff. Daniel was unaware that Barb had set the wheels in motion so he and Lillian could have quality time together.

Within weeks, Daniel was pushing Lillian in a wheelchair outside to the recreation yard. The yard was just a tiny plot of grass, surrounded by a fence with barbed wire stretched around it. As Daniel moved slowly, pushing his mother, he would start talking about his life. He wanted his stories to sound cheery, keeping any bad experiences out. Daniel knew how important it was to keep Lillian as stress-free as possible. Barb had told him that if there were any incidents with patients, those patients would lose their outside privileges. Daniel would continuously tell Lillian how sorry he was for her being in the mental hospital. He was teaching himself the law and saving money to get her discharged. He told her it would be difficult but hoped to have her court case reviewed. Women did not have many rights, and Daniel understood the mountain ahead of him.

Lillian did not speak; if she did, it was impossible to understand what she was saying. Gibberish, as Barb called it. She blamed the third-floor shock treatment they used on Lillian. Daniel was afraid the treatment was silently killing his mother.

Daniel told Barb and explained to Lillian that he was leaving the following week to bring Sally back to be with the family. He would try to get Sally a job, but he couldn't promise anything. He knew there were no visitors, so Sally would have to get a job if she wanted to see Lillian. Daniel would make sure Sally had a fake name to keep the doctors from knowing they were Lillian's children. He could see the excitement in Lillian's eyes. Her family would finally be together.

1956 – A Daughters Mission

Daniel had his bus ticket and suitcase in hand. He had called the orphanage to confirm when Sally would be permitted to leave. He wanted to make sure Sally would not feel forgotten. The nuns were supposed to tell her that he would be there to meet her.

Daniel walked to the bus station, starting his morning before sunrise. He was so happy that he would get to see his sister, and he knew the hospital was looking for nursing assistants. His dream was for Sally to attend school and eventually become a nurse. He was doing well, and in a few years, he may get the opportunity to be a boss. They would be with their mother, making enough money—not rich, but possibly enough to afford a better room for rent. Some small homes were being built next to the hospital, and Daniel had heard rumors that employees might get the first chance to purchase one. People didn't want to live next to an insane asylum, giving him an opportunity.

It took hours to get to the orphanage. Daniel arrived early. He sat outside the fence, waiting for Sally. The nuns were aware he was there but did not invite him in. Instead, they allowed Sally to walk out early. Daniel had tears in his eyes. Sally looked so grown up, even though she was wearing tattered clothes. The gate opened, and Sally and Daniel stood looking at each other before they embraced. They were both crying with happiness. Daniel opened the suitcase, took a nice, heavy jacket, and draped it around Sally. Sally was overcome with her brother's generosity.

"Let's go. We need to start walking to the bus station. I have your ticket, and I'm taking you home. We have so much to talk about on our walk."

Daniel told Sally how he had planned to find their mother, and he did. He had a great job but had to keep his name a secret. He was spending more time with their mother, but she was ill. He explained that their father had her thrown in jail and that she was taken to a mental institution, even though she was sane. He allowed Sally to ask questions and emphasized how important it would be for her to gain employment at the hospital. Then, they could plan together to get their mother discharged. Daniel promised to help Sally get a job at the hospital but didn't want to force her to do so. He needed Sally's help to get their mother released. Sally told Daniel that whatever he wanted, she would do. It was the first time in her life that she felt happy, knowing someone loved her.

Daniel was taking on more responsibility at the hospital. It was rumored that he would be the next supervisor for his shift. He made sure to stay with the patients in Building C, or he would refuse the promotion. Sally and Daniel stuck to their plan once they arrived home. They agreed that Sally would start school immediately. She would take classes for three months to train as a nursing assistant. Once she passed the exam, she could start nursing school. That would take a year. The state allowed students to work while attending school, and a hospital agreed to sponsor them. Daniel wanted to get Sally hired and have the hospital help pay for her schooling. As long as Sally worked and kept her grades up, she would be a nurse by the end of the following year.

Daniel and Sally saved all their money, spending only on necessities for living. They got along very well. They did not date, and people in their apartment complex thought they were living in sin. They had to explain that they were family and that Sally was attending school to become a nurse. That explanation quelled the rumors. Daniel managed to get Sally hired at the hospital as an office secretary. It wasn't patient care, which made Sally sad because she wouldn't get to meet her mother. It was quicker than for her to wait for a nursing assistant job. Daniel told her that day would come, and she just needed to make the doctors happy. One day, they would hire her as a nurse.

Until then, she would have to find ways to see her mother from a distance. Sally knew when Lillian was taken outside on nice days because they followed the same schedule. It had been a cold spring, so there weren't many visits to the yard. They would sound a horn when patients were allowed outside. Sally would walk over to a window overlooking the yard and watch Daniel push their mother in a wheelchair. Her heart ached every time she saw them, but she understood that her time would come and she would meet her mother. In the meantime, her plan was to get into the patients' files and read as much as she could about why her mother was there and why she was receiving shock treatment.

One afternoon, all the doctors had to leave the facility to attend a meeting at a nearby hospital. They needed to speak with community leaders about the importance of their hospital and what it offered patients. Sally was given the job of filing paperwork in the doctor's office. It was the opportunity Daniel and Sally had been waiting for.

Sally started filing the papers, but the pile didn't include any documents that belonged in the locked patient cabinets. She managed to find the key that unlocked the long bar running through the handles of the filing cabinets. She would have to quickly grab the file and lock it back up if someone came in. She had been told to leave the office door open for security reasons. Sally could feel her heartbeat in her throat. She was scared and didn't want to lose the opportunity her job offered her. She was known as Jill, and if caught, she hoped her true identity would still be hidden. Sally had worked too hard to get caught up in a scandal.

Sally inserted the key into the lock, turned it, and removed the bar over her head. She knew that would be difficult to explain if she were seen. She was looking for patient 817, which was easy to find. She grabbed the file, shut the cabinet, and placed the bar back to make it appear locked. She closed the door halfway and stood behind it, pretending to file paperwork in the unlocked files. Sally read fast. She learned about the attempted murder charge, her father's name, where her mother had hidden from him, and how their father had taken them to an orphanage. She began reading about her mother's treatments, catching the big words that she understood. She wanted to cry but realized someone was walking down the hall, getting closer. She froze, shut the folder, and placed it inside a cabinet. She heard Daniel's voice.

"Jill, are you okay?"

"Yes, Billy, I'm behind the door, just filing some reports for the doctors."

"Would it be okay if I stand here for a few minutes?"

Sally knew that was her cue to hurry and get the information she needed while he was on the lookout.

"Billy, that would be super nice of you so no one slams the door into me. Can you give me just a few minutes?"

"Sure, take a few minutes and let me know when you're clear."

Sally opened the file and read as much as she could for the next few minutes — enough to be satisfied with the information. She quickly lifted the steel bar, returned her mother's file safely, and locked the bar. She opened the door and made sure Daniel saw her wink at him, though he could see the sadness in her face.

That night, Sally told Daniel everything she had learned. Their father had left them with a prostitute, sent them to an orphanage, and had never tried to reach out to them. Their mother had left the state because she thought she had killed their father; she would have never gone otherwise. Their father had tried to find her and never gave up. She was found by a private investigator and taken back to Illinois. The judge had thrown her into the mental hospital, where she could never leave. She received shock treatment after once making a comment that she wanted to die because she had left her children and their father had dumped them in an orphanage. She hadn't known that information until she was arrested. Sally cried as she told Daniel the story. Their mother and their lives had been forever changed due to one man—the same man was living free, without remorse. She told Daniel that their father was Melvin Martin, and he had remarried and was now living in Tennessee. Daniel and Sally promised each other that they would work even harder to get their mother out of the insane asylum and bring her home so they could be a family.

Sally had kept the news that their mother had put her first baby up for adoption—a little girl—but there was no information about who she was or where she lived. Sally didn't know why she kept that hidden from Daniel, but it may be too much for him to grasp.

Eight months had passed since Daniel had waited outside in the cold for his sister to be released from the orphanage. Sally had done everything that was asked of her. She had started working as a clerical secretary, and the hospital had told her she would be hired as a nursing assistant once her training was completed. If Sally showed up for her assigned shift and location, the hospital would sign off on her certification. Once that was accomplished, she enrolled in classes at a nearby nursing school. The hospital would offer her part-time work while attending school and assist her with the cost of the schooling. The State Hospital had found it challenging to hire nurses, and offering to pay for school allowed them to retain nurses. Sally grew up fast, and Daniel was proud that his sister was working with him on his master plan.

Daniel explained to Sally that their mother's health was not improving. He needed Sally to do well in college because he needed to get their mother out of the hospital. He wanted to take a trip to Joliet to speak with the police officer who had arrested her or with the judge who had sent her to the insane asylum. Daniel and Sally promised each other that their mother would be their focus — getting her out of the hospital, legally or illegally.

Sally had done well in nursing school. She would be taking her state exam in the next 30 days. She was worried that once the hospital realized her given name, they would never allow her to visit her mother. Sally could only see Lillian from afar and could not attempt to visit her. Being a nursing assistant for the past year meant she was stuck in areas where she never got the opportunity with the women in Building C. Daniel could see their mother daily, and she had to admit it made her jealous. He would say their mother gave no verbal clues but would have expressive eyes to show she understood when he would tell her about Sally. Sally didn't remember her mother but wanted to take advantage of their remaining time. She was well aware that patients died young at the hospital and that their mother, at only 36 years of age, looked twice that. She found it challenging to be so close to her mother but unable to speak to her.

Daniel had purchased a tiny two-bedroom home next to the hospital so they would always be near their mother. He had hoped that it would help Sally with her anxiety of not being able to be as close to their mother as he was.

Daniel had spent the past year speaking with judges and lawyers to find a way to get Lillian discharged from the hospital. He also traveled to Joliet to talk with the police officer and defense attorney who had handled his mother's case. The county no longer employed the defense attorney, but the police officer remembered Lillian. He explained how she had lived in fear, with her husband beating her and trying to hide her bruises. She had wanted to keep the family together, minus Melvin, and flee when her kids got older. The officer gave Daniel Theresa's name and told him to contact her. She would probably love to see him. He was right. Theresa was excited to see how much he had grown. She told Daniel about the fight that had put his mother in the asylum, and he told her about the abuse in the orphanages, his sister, and their plan to get their mother discharged from the hospital. Theresa explained that she wasn't much help but would do anything possible to see Lillian again.

When Daniel returned home, he looked five years older and wiser. He told Sally he was ready to give up—that the law was not on their side. He wanted to find their father and make him come to the hospital. That would be their best opportunity since he was the victim and the reason she was in the hospital. Their father had beaten their mother, so he was just as guilty as she was. Sally agreed and had his address if he lived in the same home.

Daniel decided to let it drop until Sally got her nursing license. They made an agreement not to talk about their father or mother. Daniel helped Sally study and told her how excited and proud he was that she would be a nurse.

Sally passed her nursing exam and was now a state-licensed nurse. Her license was mailed to Sally Martin. She and Daniel knew that now would be the real test — giving the license to the hospital with a different name than what she used. Daniel's plan was to be in the office when Sally gave her license to the secretary and hope she didn't look at the name before filing the certificate in Sally's file.

The next day, Daniel and Sally planned it perfectly. While Sally was telling the secretary about the test and the different questions on the exam, Daniel came in to ask the secretary about a potential problem with one of his staff. He wanted to know how to handle an orderly being continuously tardy. Whenever the secretary tried to stop Daniel from talking, he kept interrupting.

"Billy, please, I am trying to speak to Jill about her state exam. She is now a nurse."

"Congratulations, Jill, but I need an answer about this orderly because I don't have anyone to replace him if we fire him for excessive tardiness."

"Wait your turn, Billy!"

"I will just file this in my folder. I know exactly where it goes. I've had a lot of practice in this office," Sally replied.

"Oh, thank you. Do you have a copy for your records? If not, you must give it to me so I can make one."

"I already did, and thank you. No need for copies."

"I apologize for butting in like this, Jill, when you are enjoying good news. I am ashamed."

"Don't be, Billy. You stay here and get your answer. I want you to ensure your staff is not short on orderlies."

Before Sally walked out of the office, the secretary stopped her. Sally turned around very slowly, thinking she had been caught.

"Tomorrow, report to Building C to start your training with Nurse Gretchen."

Daniel and Sally showed no excitement. Sally was going to meet their mother.

That night, Daniel and Sally agreed to remain secretive and not let anyone know their mother was a patient. Barb and Lillian knew Sally would eventually graduate from nursing school and hoped to be a nurse on their floor. Lillian's health was starting to worsen, and she had more comatose days than good ones. Daniel would remind Sally that their father was the reason their mother was in such poor care. The hospital was also guilty, but the main suspect was Melvin Martin.

Sally excelled in her training. She was able to make contact with Barb and her mother. She would sit beside her mother and hold her hand as her mother stared out the window. Sally made sure her mother received the best care possible. Any chance she got, she would help her mother eat, walk her to the bathroom, and always have a warm blanket for her. Lillian's electric shock therapy stopped, with doctors stating the treatment had worked and Lillian no longer wanted to harm herself. Sally was so angry with the doctors, knowing she could be a nurse advocate for Lillian but had no rights as a family advocate. Daniel felt the harm had been done, and no care could reverse the damage to their mother's brain.

Both Daniel and Sally cared for their mother while she was a patient. Daniel had run out of any type of assistance to get Lillian discharged. He felt like a failure. He explained to Barb all the obstacles he was facing and how horribly society treated women. Barb told Daniel that he and his sister gave Lillian the best life possible. Barb had never seen Lillian smile, and now she did, with both of her children by her side. It was not the best situation, but they had made the best of it for her, and they needed to be proud of what they had accomplished. Look at them from being in an orphanage as a baby to now. Not many children could have done what they had. Daniel agreed, and he did feel that his mother was slowly getting better.

It happened very quickly. Daniel was in the nursing station with Sally while she was passing out the morning medications. Barb had just sat down at the card table and placed Lillian next to her so they could play the game of War. Barb had taught Lillian the easiest card game she knew to keep Lillian's mind working. It was a beautiful spring day in 1963. A soft rain was falling, and all their spring flowers had bloomed in the recreation yard. Barb had managed to get the doctors to agree to buy bulbs, and a few patients and staff had planted tulips of all different colors. Lillian was proud that she had handed the bulbs to Barb, and Daniel had helped plant them. Lillian whispered to Sally that day was the best day of her life. Every time Lillian looked out the big picture window, she could see the flowers blooming.

Barb and Lillian had been playing cards for thirty minutes when Lillian suddenly appeared to pass out and fell out of her chair. Barb let out a scream and tried to catch Lillian before she hit the floor. Daniel and Sally ran to the table to help their mom. Lillian had stopped breathing. Daniel scooped her up and ran to the gate. Sally opened the gate, and they took off running toward the infirmary. Outside, through the rain, they rushed to the back door and down the stairs to the infirmary. Daniel held Lillian to his chest. Sally had tears in her eyes.

Daniel laid his mother on a bed, yelling for a doctor. Lillian was not moving, nor was she breathing. Lillian died of cardiac arrest with Daniel holding one hand and Sally the other. They had just found their mother, and now she was gone. The world seemed unfair. The three of them had experienced hell in their own lives, only to see each other—and now, their mother was dead at such a young age. Lillian would be buried on the hospital grounds. Daniel and Sally could not claim her as their mother. If that information was uncovered, Sally would lose her nursing license, and Daniel would lose his job. Keeping the secrecy seemed to be their best option.

Lillian was buried under a small headstone with 817 printed on it. Daniel and Sally would pay their respects at the grave in the state hospital's woods. No one cared for the cemetery, nor was it secured. It would not be easy to find if someone needed to know exactly where to look. Sally would bring flowers, Daniel would pull weeds, and the grass would continue to grow over the plots.

1998 – My Broken Branch

Ruth and I finally arrived at my mother's home. My mom never met me in the driveway or acted excited to see me. I had to approach the door and knock like a stranger. Lynn appeared and opened the screen door.

"I was wondering when you would be here. Did you have a good trip?"

"Ruth is in the car."

"Ruth? You brought Ruth!"

My mom quickly opened the door and took off around me, heading straight to the car. I had already been replaced, even though that bar was really low.

"Come to Grandma," she said as she opened the car door.

"Mom, she's wearing a seat belt, and she needs her leash."

My mom shot me a look like I was an overbearing parent.

I hooked her leash on and unhooked her safety belt. I grabbed my bag and Ruth's bag. My mom took Ruth's leash, and off they went into the house. I just stood there. I could hear a laugh from a few houses away. I looked and saw my old neighbor, Art. He laughed and yelled to me, "I see nothing has changed. We still love you! Thank you for finding the little Boyd girl."

I smiled and gave him a wave before trudging toward the house. Ruth and my mom were already in the backyard playing fetch. She always kept some old tennis balls she collected on her walks at the high school. Ruth was having a great time while I stood and watched them play. My mom turned the hose on and sprayed it in the air as Ruth ran back and forth through the water. I always thought it was strange that I was denied a dog all my life, but now she loves my dogs. I was glad this made my mother happy, but I was ready to leave and return to North Carolina.

I could smell the crockpot and knew my mom was making something for dinner. I grew up with a mom who left for work and put food in the crockpot for me to eat when I got home from school or my many practices. I looked around and could see my mom had started packing, with a few boxes already taped and labeled. I went to my old room, which had nothing on display. It had been turned into a makeshift guest room years ago. I put my bag down and pulled Ruth's food and water bowls out. I heard my mom and Ruth come inside the back door.

I came into the kitchen with Ruth's bowl, but my mother had already put water and ice in a bowl for her. Ruth was drinking and slobbering at the same time.

"I put your favorite chili in the crockpot for dinner."

"Oh, thank you. I can smell it, and it does smell good."

"Let me know when you're ready to eat, and we can grab some bowls and sit on the back deck. It's not too cold out, and your hoodie should keep you comfortable."

My mother and I sat on her deck, eating chili and discussing the Boyd case. My mom wanted to ask about my feelings and how difficult it was to be there when she was found. I then realized she didn't know about the shooting, so I decided to wait until tomorrow when we were drinking our coffee on our morning walk.

Ruth and I lay on the bed that night and looked at each other. I called Syd on my cell phone and put her on speaker so Ruth could hear her voice. I told her that my mother hadn't asked about her or even brought her name up once. It was business as usual.

Syd had to smile as she hung up the call. She looked down at Keaton, who was whining.

"I know, she will be home, and so will Ruth."

Syd had worked all day piecing the story together with Lynn's family. She realized the story was crazy. She called Alice and gave her some facts to double-check. Syd was finding it difficult to understand how easy it was to put a person in an insane asylum. She had much more work to do over the next few days and hoped to hear from Kris or Tad. The story was still heading in a direction she didn't like, but she understood that the truth can be challenging to grasp.

The weekend was coming to a close. I spent time with my mother and helped her box up donations while Ruth tried to take things out of the boxes as we put them in. My mom doesn't like throwing things out, so the donation center was getting a box of my old softball trophies. She swears the marble bases could still be used. I only argue with her if it's about political ads, so I give her the lead to do what she chooses.

I brought up her childhood and asked about old pictures she may have. She claimed she found some and threw them in a box labeled "old pictures." I wanted to know if I could take the box home to look through it. To my surprise, she said I could. She thought there were some old pictures of my dad and felt I should have them. Later, I found there were no pictures of her when she was a child. They were of me.

I took some old albums, found an old T-shirt that Ruth loved, and that box of pictures. I packed up the car so I would be ready in the morning. I told her I was stopping to see Trooper Gray and Ruth would have a play day with his hounds. The day before, I explained the shooting situation and toned it down a bit, but I let her know I might be getting a possible award from the Governor.

She wanted to know when I would retire because I was doing a man's job on a woman's wages. My mom didn't know my current salary, but she guessed it. I explained that Syd and

I were laying out our plan. I may be taking a teaching job within the next few years, and Syd was in high demand in the political arena. We just wanted to stay grounded and not look too far ahead. My mother was against that, even though she didn't say anything. She felt every person should have a thirty-year plan at all times. A ten-year plan for us was complex enough to sketch out.

Monday morning could not come soon enough, and it was time to get Ruth on the road. The car was packed, and we were heading to West Virginia to visit the Grays. My mom stood in her driveway as I backed out and headed down the street. I looked in my rear-view mirror, and she was still standing there. Lynn had never done that before, and I found it really odd. I wanted to know if my mother had not been honest with me and if there was more going on with her. Then I realized she would miss Ruth.

I called Syd to let her know we were on our way. Syd was always upbeat, and I felt I needed some positivity in my life after this weekend. When Syd answered, I could tell something seemed wrong.

"Hey, baby, on my way home."

"Okay, are you still planning to visit the Grays?"

"Yeah, I wanted to catch up on some things about the Boyd case and let Ruth see some friends. She was cooped up with my mom, who couldn't keep her hands off her."

"She'll like that. Just call me so I know when to expect you."

"Everything okay? You sound a little down for a Monday morning."

"I didn't get out much this weekend. It rained, and I found my head stuck in the computer. I need a break. I feel like I'm losing my mind. I still have work to do this afternoon, and I hope to get some clarity."

"Let's plan something this weekend and get outside. Can't wait to get home and see you and Keaton."

"I promise to be in a better mood. I need to see you and know you'll be home for a while."

"Plan on it! I'll give you a call when we leave the Grays."

"Love you."

"Love you too."

I looked back at Ruth in the rear-view mirror. "Your mama is sad, and I'm sure my family is bringing the headache." Ruth just stared back at me, showing no emotion.

Hours later, I was pulling into the Grays' home and getting Ruth out for some playtime. It would be a short visit, but worth every second.

Syd spent every waking moment of her weekend putting Lynn's family tree together. It was day three of her Lynn Project, and she still had unfinished business.

Kris's ears must have been burning.

"Good morning, Syd. I got some news for you."

"Hey, Kris, anything exciting?"

"We were able to track down some history on this guy, and I'm going to scan and send you an email with some attachments. We drove over to where he lived; his wife still lives in that house. We went to the library and collected information from the local newspapers about when he was living here, and the day he went missing."

"Did any news clippings talk about his first wife or kids?"

"No, it's almost like he didn't have that family. We also went to some neighborhood bars to hang out and see if anyone was talking about him, missing."

"Good idea, but it's been years."

"This may surprise you; his wife claims he was murdered because he would never have taken off without telling her. They have his missing poster hanging in some of the bars and at the local supermarket, and they're still collecting money to hire an investigator who took up the case."

"What? She's still looking?"

"Oh, yeah. Smith and I didn't bring up his name. We just ate some bar food and listened. Smith pointed at the picture behind the bar and asked about the story. The bartender was very chatty, telling us the community is divided, some thinking he took off with another woman, while others think he was murdered by someone's husband. I guess he was a womanizer, even though his current wife claims he never had an affair with anyone."

"Great information, and I really appreciate it. I've spent all weekend putting this story together, and this guy's disappearance is still a big question mark."

"We leave later this afternoon. We've got someone at the local news who remembered when he went missing, and we're stopping to pick up some of those news clippings. He's going to give us some news videos, so I will mail those to you as soon as we get home."

"Thank you so much. Really trying to understand the last years of this entire family, and that guy was the main reason they were torn apart."

"C'mon, Syd, you know women had no rights. Men did as they chose. And I don't understand why his wife thought he was a saint. No one has said anything good about this guy."

"I hear you, and the story I'm putting together should be a happy one, but I'm finding out just the opposite. I don't think Emily will be happy with the results."

"I'm sure she'll be happy with the time you put into this, and you've closed the loop for her and her mother."

With that, they hung up, leaving Syd with a question that may never be answered.

Syd decided she was not ready to show me any information she had collected. She realized Lynn had a family but didn't know if they were still alive. She didn't want to excite anyone if she couldn't prove where they were or if they were deceased. She was aware of the 817 grave marker, but now that she understood the hospital would reissue patient numbers, anyone could be buried there. The hospital closed in 1973, and she would love to see the hospital since she had read so much about it. She needed to close all loops, and she started running into many dead ends.

FAMILY DIRT

She had a few holes but felt those questions would be answered in a very short time. Kris was sending videotapes from when Melvin Martin went missing, along with newspaper clippings of the event. Alice had a few ends she wanted to shore up. Some dates could not be found, and Syd needed those dates to close the different storylines.

1972 – Mission Completed

Nine years had passed since Lillian died. Daniel and Sally continued working in their respective fields. They had witnessed many changes within their hospital, which was rumored to be closing soon.

Mental illness treatment was taking a different direction, with both positive and negative aspects. They saw fewer patients each month due to changes in Illinois law, which made it much more difficult for people to drop off their loved ones at the front door, claiming they were insane.

Daniel and Sally were both okay with that.

They still lived in the small home next to the hospital. Their neighbors thought they were married and had no clue they were brother and sister. Daniel and Sally had made a pact after their mother died. They had a plan, and both promised to fulfill that destiny no matter what happened in their lives. They worked, saved money, took a few vacations together, and spent their free time reading at local libraries. Daniel loved studying maps and would teach Sally how to read a map, use a compass, tell time by looking at the sun, identify edible plants, and camp safely. Both of them learned how to fish and hunt. They enjoyed nature, no matter what the weather offered.

Eventually, Daniel put the for-sale sign out on their home. A local realtor drove by one afternoon, stopped, and struck a deal with Daniel. The next day, the realtor had the title of the property purchased from Billy Daniels. The realtor had no idea another person was living in the home. When he looked at the property, the house was emptied, with boxes strewn around. He would recant that story to Syd when she called him twenty-six years later. He remembered Billy because he seemed like a very nice guy with impeccable manners.

Sally came home that afternoon after dropping off items at their local Goodwill. When she left, their van was packed full, and now it was empty, only to be filled again for another trip. Daniel gave her the great news: their home would be sold the following day. The realtor purchased the house for his daughter, thinking it would be a great starter home. They loaded the remaining boxes and went to the donation bin, keeping only the items traveling with them. That night, they set up their camping gear and camped inside their home for one last night.

The following day, Daniel went to sign the papers, collect his check, deposit it, and get some cash for their trip. Later that night, they pulled over at a rest stop in Tennessee. The van had no back seats and was large enough for both of them to catch some sleep before heading to their new home — Asheville, North Carolina.

Daniel had already paid cash for a small two-bedroom cabin deep in the mountains. He and Sally have visited the area multiple times over the past few years. This was where they needed to be. They could get lost, not be seen, and blend in with the many visitors who came to the area. They could go virtually unnoticed. Residents kept to themselves, didn't like outsiders, and knew how to live off the land. They loved the area, could have a small garden, had enough land to supply firewood, and could own a dog.

In their first week, they explored the national forests surrounding the area. They studied the trails, found camping sites, and made sure to be seen when visiting the corner stores for supplies. They wanted others to remember their faces, and if asked, they would say they were regulars at the campsites. They used new names—Jeremy and Tracy. No one asked them for their last names, nor did anyone inquire if they were married. In the mountains, no one cared about your business. Daniel and Sally continued visiting the forests surrounding them for the following year. Every night, at their cabin, they would lay their maps out and rehearse their plan from start to finish. They wanted it to be perfect and knew they had to get it right, or their lives would fail.

It was a Friday afternoon in 1973 when Daniel and Sally drove their old van into Clarkesville, Tennessee. They had been there before. They knew the route, the time it would take to arrive, which roads had tollways, which ones didn't, and, most importantly, how to be seen without being seen. They would stop at the same gas stations and convenience stores when they visited. They parked farthest from the bar but still within sight of the parking lot, trying not to do anything unusual. They knew what time the sun would set and rise the following day. They had all their supplies in the van, including loaded guns.

They pulled up in the parking lot and waited for the special parking spot to become vacant. People are creatures of habit. They do the same things over and over. Daniel and Sally were hoping tonight would be no different. It was getting dark, and they could see the bright red pickup truck parked in the back of the lot at Ruby's. It was Friday night, and men got their paychecks and headed to the local titty bar. Sally never understood why men would work so hard all week just to spend their money watching half-naked women dance in front of them. Daniel had been inside Ruby's a few times to check the layout of the building and exits. He claimed it was a dirty bar with an area in the back where men could get private lap dances. He said it was disgusting.

They knew they would have to sit in the van for a few hours. The man they were looking for usually left the bar around 10 p.m. Daniel made sure they made minimal movement while they waited so no one would remember the van. Everything had to be precise and according to the plan. At 10:15, they saw the man exit the bar's back door. He stopped and lit a cigarette, the same thing he always did. He started walking to his truck and put his key in the door. He felt the electric current start at his neck and travel down to his toes. He dropped like a rock. He was picked up by his feet and wrists and thrown into the back of a van that was parked next to his truck. His hands were handcuffed behind him, his ankles tied together with a rope, and a piece of duct tape placed over his mouth. He was then rolled in a tarp, with a rope tied in a knot around the tarp.

Daniel jumped into the van and Sally into the man's truck. The whole ordeal was completed in less than two minutes. Sally followed the van to the Pisgah National Forest in North Carolina. The drive would take them eight hours. The van had containers filled with gas so they wouldn't have to stop. They knew the truck would have a full tank — again, creatures of habit on payday. They wanted to get to the campsite before the sun came up. They would dump the truck in Hendersonville, North Carolina, in a strip mine. There was an overlook where the truck could go off the rock, landing in the water below. The abandoned mine was over thirty feet deep, so they knew the truck would sink. Daniel and Sally had been to the area numerous times and knew how to get in and out without being seen.

Hours later, they made sure they left no evidence in the truck, and Billy put his foot on the gas as he sat in the driver's seat with the door open. He jumped out and watched the truck drive off the rock. He got into the van with Sally, made sure the man was still breathing, and continued their route. Neither of them talked nor listened to the radio.

Six hours later, the van arrived at the campsite, and the sun was just beginning to break the surface. The campsite was deep into the forest, accessible only by a four-wheel-drive vehicle. Campers could stay there for weeks without seeing another soul. The man would remain in the van until late into the night. Daniel and Sally took turns napping at their campsite. One would sit in the van to keep the man quiet when not sleeping. If he got restless, he would receive another electric shock to the side of the neck. The man was beginning to reek of alcohol, sweat, urine, and feces. Daniel and Sally did not love the man, even if he was their father.

At 10 p.m., the time had arrived. Daniel opened the back of the van and pulled out the man still wrapped in the tarp. Daniel put a rope around the man's ankles and got on the four-wheeler, sitting backward while Sally drove it. It was a short trip, just deeper into the woods, to a six-foot hole they had dug weeks prior. They unwrapped the man from the tarp and placed the tarp in a garbage bag. The man had been crying. They noticed the scar above his eyebrow and a bone missing at the bottom of his eye. Daniel and Sally just looked at each other and laughed. Theresa had told them the story, and they were proud of their mother. As the man lay on the ground, still tied up and handcuffed, Daniel sat on his chest.

Daniel began the story he had rehearsed for many years. "I am your son, and she is your daughter. You beat my mother for years. And when she returned the favor, you had her put in an insane asylum." Melvin's eyes grew wide, and he tried to speak as he looked back and forth between Daniel and Sally.

Daniel continued. "Don't worry, you won't be allowed to talk. We don't have time to listen to you. But you will listen to me. Because of you, my sister and I sat in an orphanage for years. We were beaten, and both of us were raped multiple times. We endured that for years. Our only hope was to find you and kill you. Within that time, we found out where our mother was, and we both worked at that hospital for years. We made sure she understood we were her children. She loved us, and we loved her back. Each day we were with her, we hated you more. You were so easy to find—an alcoholic who spent his money on women. Nothing changed with you, but everything changed for us. Your wife may miss your paycheck, but I doubt she will miss you. You have had so many affairs that we stopped counting. And tonight, you will die as you think about what you have done to three people's lives."

Sally reached over and gave Melvin one last electric shock with the taser. Daniel took off the tape and handcuffs, placed them in the garbage bag, took his foot, and pushed Melvin's body into the hole.

Sally and Daniel took the shovels they had left and started filling the hole. When Melvin became conscious, he would have six feet of dirt piled on top of him. He would slowly suffocate. Hours later, Daniel and Sally left the area, taking everything with them, leaving the site with no evidence that a murder had taken place.

Two days later, they packed their campsite, loaded the van, and returned to their cabin. The next day, they had an appointment at the local dog shelter. They were adopting two dogs, and now their lives were complete.

1998 – Trees Fall

The holidays were approaching, and we invited all of Syd's family to our home. We all agreed to be together on Thanksgiving since Christmas was much more difficult for everyone to schedule. It was one of the best plans we ever pulled off. Alex and her husband flew in from Colorado, and Levi from California. The parents came up from Alabama, and we cooked together. It was nonstop eating and football. We played cards and a few board games. Everyone started leaving from day three to day five. I was really sad to see them go. We all got along well, and no one complained about politics. We ruled not to discuss our jobs, but football teams were not off-limits.

The house grew quieter once we got everyone to their flights. Syd and I learned to relax and enjoy just being in the present. We grabbed a bottle of wine and some grapes and headed for the hot tub. The dogs were already asleep for the night. We turned off the lights, leaving an old black-and-white movie on the television. In times like these, I felt I was the luckiest person in the world to find the one who truly gets me.

December arrived quickly, and I had to take a trip back to South Carolina on the Cisco case. Syd was doing her best to finish her Lynn project before Lynn's birthday in January. Syd had explained that it might be a project failure and that I should start thinking of finding a gift for my mom. She also told me it was troubling that Lynn might not welcome the findings. I was okay with that and explained that I would like to know my heritage, and we didn't have to tell Lynn what was found.

Syd had great information and could tell the story of Lynn's legal parents and grandparents. She would also like to say to her that she had a brother and sister if they could be found. She had run into a brick wall concerning them and Lynn's father. Syd knew where Lynn's mother was buried, so she had closure with Lillian. Daniel, Sally, and Melvin had fallen off the face of the earth.

Her leads were coming up like Swiss cheese, and she was unhappy. She had put all the work and hours into this project, only to have the brakes applied with a loud screech. She called Tad, Alice, and Kris, getting their help and observations. Tad did explain that some people want to avoid being found. Look at the characters. Daniel and Sally had lived for years under different names. Even their tax returns and titles to homes or cars were not legal by today's standards. The house Daniel purchased was under the name of Billy Daniels, bought and then sold in 1972. Sally had an Illinois state nursing license, and that was information that could be a good start, even though she was working under an alias. Her Illinois license had expired in 1974, and she never renewed.

Alice had searched every state that allowed her to do so on the internet, then made phone calls to the state licensing agencies. They were of no help when given Sally's name or her alias. Maybe Tad was right — Daniel and Sally wanted to move on with their lives after their mother died. They had no other family, and perhaps they wanted to live their lives finally. Alice still wanted to visit the grounds of the State Hospital and see the grave site. She thought it was best that it ended, and perhaps that was what Lillian would have wanted — let the kids be and move on.

I was in South Carolina for two days when I received a call from Paul. While hiking the Appalachian Trial, a missing hiker could not be located in North Carolina. The hiker was a sixteen-year-old boy who had gotten separated from his church group. The church had an annual week-long trip in December. They did not go at high elevations to keep the group from getting hypothermia. They used their survival skills, built fires for warmth, and ate MREs (Meals Ready to Eat) supplied by the local Army National Guard. It should have been an easy five-day trip. I didn't understand why Paul needed me to go. He felt it would be an easy trip for me and allow me more holiday time off with Christmas approaching. He claimed it had been a long year for me, and this trip should be the last of the traveling — and an easy one.

I finished in South Carolina and headed for the North Carolina-Tennessee border the following morning. I called Syd and told her the news, explaining that it would be a short trip. The camper might get found while I was on my way. Syd told me to make sure I stayed warm. Some lousy weather was approaching that area, but she knew I kept all my gear in my car. I was a gadget freak, so I had every new item introduced by REI. Plus, I was an avid hiker and climber when I was younger. Being deep in the forest made me feel at home. Syd explained she would take the time to finish her project; if she couldn't close some loopholes, it would be okay. I agreed and told her I would call when I arrived in the mountains.

I arrived in Burnsville at the campsite the church group had set up for the week. They had set up north of the forest and would take daily trips down the mountain, returning for dinner. The area had become popular, but usually not this time of year. Families would come in for the holidays, hoping to hike and capture early snowfall for great family photos.

The state had built lean-tos throughout the forest to provide hikers with places to rest or sleep on the trails. A North Carolina crew was finishing up their current project in the forest. With the yearly budget winding down, they wanted to ensure they built as many as promised.

I met with the State Police, who are responsible for the search party. A young man, Milton Riley, had strayed from his group. He needed to stop and adjust his sock, and his hiking partner continued walking, instructing him to follow the path to the Y and veer left. He would be waiting about one hundred fifty yards from the Y. It was believed that Milton may have veered right, leading him deeper into the forest.

I asked the officer if there was any suspicion of foul play, and he said no. He had met the families of both hikers. They were all out searching with the group. Everyone knew each other, and there seemed no ill intent in their communication. I inquired how I could help and was asked to contact the construction crews working throughout the forest. Two groups started each morning from the visitors center, one heading west and the other east. They returned to the visitors center around 5 p.m. when it began to get dark. They had heavy equipment left where they were building the shelters, and Milton might see the equipment and stay there for the night. Alternatively, he might find one of the newly built shelters, which still needed to be added to the map.

I drove to the welcome center and waited for the construction workers to return for the night. I gave them pictures of Milton and relayed the story of what had happened to him, hoping they might come into contact with him. I had a map of the forest and had them circle where the new shelters were being built, where they were currently working, and how many shelters they had left to make. The two groups would only be in the forest for another week, as the work would be completed for the season.

The following day, I put on my hiking gear and started on the trail. Milton would have known to stay on the trail, but sometimes, hikers may see a bear or hear a noise that might make them leave the trail. He should have enough water and snacks for a few days but would soon be thirsty. There was no water supply, and we had not experienced rain. But rain was in the forecast—and lots of it. That was good for Milton but would create havoc for the searchers.

On day four, the rain arrived, pouring all day as the search continued. Hours later, after I had started my hike, I got a call on the radio that the construction crew had found something. I knew better than to ask on the radio what it was. I headed on the trail toward their known location, fighting the wind and rain. I mumbled under my breath that I had a hot tub back at my home.

I found the crew trying to take cover under a makeshift tent. I was surprised they were still there and hadn't been called off for the day. They explained that they needed to stay for four hours to get paid for the entire day, so they stayed and made the best of it. While they were digging, they found a watch. They didn't believe it belonged to the missing hiker. One of the workers handed me the men's watch.

It was not an expensive watch, but definitely a man's. The back of the watch had initials, but it took work to make out the letters. I had the crew show me exactly where the watch was found and how deep they had found it. They told me they usually only dig three feet when building these structures, but they needed to figure out how far they had gone due to the rain. The hole was filling up with rainwater. The operator thought he might have found it around four feet or deeper. I asked him if he would do me a favor and jump in the cab, going deeper to see if he might pull out anything else. I told him to entertain me since we had nothing to do but stand in the rain.

He started the Cat backhoe, put the bucket deeper in the hole, curled it, and started to bring it out. Then he stopped and yelled at me.

'I feel some pressure. I think we have something.'

I told him to cut the engine, grabbed my flashlight from my pack, and looked into the hole. I saw something hanging off the bucket's teeth. It looked like fabric. I told the operator to lock out the bucket. I think he found a body.

I grabbed the radio to call the state trooper when I heard the radio crackle. It was a broadcast message. Milton had been found. He was safe but cold. He had wandered onto the other crew, who was just getting ready to leave. They put a blanket around him and had someone bring a four-wheeler to the site to get him back to the parking lot at the visitors' center. They had an ambulance on the way to retrieve him.

People were all celebrating on the radio, so I couldn't get a word in. Finally, I reached the trooper and told him I needed to see him ASAP at my location. We did find something.

That night, I called home to let Syd know that Milton had been found safe. She was happy for him but knew I wouldn't be heading home. I told her I had to stay for a few days because a body had been found.

"How in the hell did you find a body?"

"I didn't, but a construction crew was building shelters, and they dug just a little deeper than they thought and found a body."

"Wow, that's strange. Any idea who it may be?"

"No, it appears to be a male and may have been buried for years. We don't have much, but we do have a watch."

"Expensive?"

"It's from the New England Watch Company, which has to be an ancient watch since it's not a manufacturer any of us have ever heard of."

"New England? That does seem odd for the mountains of North Carolina."

"Yeah, it appears to have some initials on the back of the watch, but it's very scratched up. It was sent to a jeweler who's pretty good with watches. The troopers think they may get something in a few days."

"When are you coming home? We miss you so much!"

"I should be leaving soon, maybe tomorrow or the next day."

"Great, we can't wait to see you."

"Same here, babe. Love you, and tell the girls I'll see them soon."

The following morning, the rain continued. I went back up the mountain, where they had made a makeshift covering to sift out any dirt that had been taken out of the hole the day before. The forensic pathologist was on the scene, someone I've worked with many times. He was a really nice guy and an excellent professional. He told me they were determined to find something. The skeletal bones were collected and returned to a local hospital's morgue. They were still missing many of the bones but had enough to start laying out the foundation of the human remains. They did know that the body was of an adult male, most likely under six feet tall, and they found no obvious fractures or deformities with the bones collected. The skull did have an apparent break around the right side of the face, but the bucket of the backhoe had done damage before the operator was aware there was a body in the hole.

They found cowboy boots, size 11. The other clothing items were too damaged to make out size, color, etc. The belief was that it was not a hiker since no equipment was found, and the man had cowboy boots on. Hikers would usually choose a different type of boot for hiking. There was no jacket or coat, so they thought the man had likely died during the summer months. No billfold or other personal items were found with the body. Everyone thought that was odd — if a killer had stripped the body of all personal items, why would they leave a watch? Or, if this man had been hiking, why didn't he have any gear, like a backpack? I asked if a bear could have dragged the man or taken his backpack. Experts agreed and told me this case might go unsolved for years. Technology might have to catch up after we are no longer here.

Later that day, I finally got cell service and listened to my message from Paul. The message told me I could cut loose and head home. It was not our case; I just needed to file my supplement report and call it a week. That was the best news I'd heard. I grabbed the laptop, entered the Welcome Center, and banged out a concise report about my findings. I quickly called Syd and told her I was heading home — to get the hot tub ready. With days of rain, I knew my core temperature needed a nice warm break.

It was 11 p.m., and I was finally pulling into my driveway when Paul called me. He explained that only a little had been done with the case since I'd left. The rain was causing havoc with evidence collection and the possible crime scene. They did get a report from the jeweler on the watch, but at this time, there was no information to assist in understanding why the body was there.

I saw Syd standing on the porch, staring at me with a big smile. She saw me on the phone and knew it was most likely a call concerning my job. I hung up the phone as she came walking toward me.

"Glad to be home?"

"You know it! Missed you and those two big hairy labs."

Syd grabbed my bag out of the back of the SUV.

"I know it's getting late, but I made you appetizers and got the hot tub ready."

"You read my mind."

We entered the house, and the girls were impatiently waiting for me. I ran to the back of the house with them chasing me. I threw the ball for a few minutes, giving them the attention they sought. Syd must have had a fire going earlier in the fire pit, and the smell was still strong. Syd was waiting in the hot tub for me with a glass of wine.

Getting into the hot tub made all the stress leave my body. I put my head back and looked at the ceiling fan, going round and round.

"Did they find anything else? Did Paul say they knew who the man was or how long he had been buried?"

"No, they have nothing other than how tall he may have been and his shoe size. We just don't have the technology to figure it out. We will, but the case may not be closed for another twenty years. The man may or may not have been missing and somehow ended up in a bad situation. The area would have been so remote. Someone dumping a body there would have been ridiculous."

"I hope a family gets closure if the puzzle can be solved."

"They do have the watch. The jeweler found out that it was pretty rare. The New England Watch Company went out of business in the 1920s and was eventually bought out by Timex. Paul said the letters engraved on the back of the face are W-E-M. They did a quick search and had no missing men with those initials. If they were initials and not some part of a word. The other idea is that the watch didn't belong to the man, and he was wearing someone else's watch, or the watch was left from the person who dumped the body — if the body was dumped."

"Wait, when did that watch company go out of business?"

I was sitting with my head back, eyes closed. "I think Paul said the watch was manufactured in the early 1920s and was sold throughout the East Coast and Midwest. I had no clue Timex had been buying up smaller watch companies. But, it makes sense."

Syd told me she needed to use the bathroom and would grab the bottle of wine. I could hardly answer her and was starting to fall asleep.

Syd didn't have to use the restroom; she needed to find her magnifying glass. She snuck into the office and grabbed her yellow binder, which she kept hidden. She opened the binder to the great-grandparents tab, rifling through it and stopping at every picture she had collected. She was meticulous about studying every picture from different angles. Magnifying each one by 200% on her laptop, looking for possible clues.

She had a picture of Melvin as a baby, held by his mother, who was sitting in front of her husband, William Elmore Martin. She grabbed the magnifying glass and looked at the watch on his left wrist. She couldn't make out all the words on the face of the dial, but she did see the word *Fidelity*. Syd went to her laptop and searched the internet for the New England Watch Company. Timex was listing watch companies that they had purchased. New England had a page showcasing their vintage line, which was no longer being produced. The site showed a 1922 model from their Fidelity line.

She then realized Melvin had taken his father's watch when he had left home. The body found was Melvin Martin. That's why he had been missing since 1973. Daniel and Sally were now the only two still unaccounted for. Maybe this is why she couldn't find them—they didn't want to be found.

Syd took a deep breath, took the picture from its plastic sheath, and closed the binder. She put the binder back in its hiding place. She crept out to the back of the house, where the wood was still glowing in the firepit. Syd had just been sitting there an hour before, contemplating letting the whole story disappear. She stuck a corner of the picture on a hot ember, and the picture started to catch fire. She put the picture in the pit and stood there, half-naked, watching it burn, leaving no evidence. She quietly went back into the house. The dogs raised their heads but stayed next to the hot tub without a sound.

Syd returned to the hot tub with a bottle of wine and slid into the hot water. I must have dozed off.

"Did I fall asleep while we were talking?"

"No, baby, you're okay. You just need to relax."

"I would hate to think I'm not interested in your questions." I put my head back and closed my eyes, falling asleep again.

"I think we talked about your mom's birthday next month and what you wanted to get her."

"Can we discuss it tomorrow? I'm exhausted."

Syd heard my breathing grow heavy, and she knew that some things were better left unsaid and kept buried.

2024- My Tree Remains Strong

There have been many changes in our lives.

Lynn died six months after moving into her retirement home. Syd and I traveled to Ohio and had a big party with her neighbors. My mom showed happiness for the first time, and I wondered how my life would have been if she had just found acceptance. We had a great time meeting all of her friends, and one man took a liking to my mother. She had a few dates with him and told me she liked having him around. Lynn died of ovarian cancer at the age of 60. While at work, she felt extreme pain, and her director took her to the emergency room. Stage IV, with only weeks to live. She refused chemo. That was my mom.

After my mother died, Syd sat me down and shared the entire story concerning my grandparents, aunt, and uncle. She explained the picture of the watch and her decision not to share it with me. She wasn't sure if the missing person could be my grandfather, but she felt that, if true, it would eventually come out with new DNA science, which had not yet developed. Syd was a sincere person, so I was shocked when she hid the information from me years prior. She was apprehensive and thought it might cause me to question my career and my understanding that I was related to people who could kill. She thought it was ironic that I had chased a case where a small child was buried, only to find out my grandfather had been found under the same circumstances. She didn't want me to lose my confidence when I had to carry on in a volatile world. In 2012, they ran DNA on the bones but never received a match in their databases. The remains still have not been claimed.

Nancy and Mack both passed. Nancy died first from leukemia, and Mack soon followed with cardiac arrest. Syd was miserable. This took a lot out of us. It pays to have a strong relationship when you experience a crisis. Those two were always my parents, and the grief I still carry can have days of remorse. Two fantastic people who understood what family was about, even if not by blood.

Syd and I finally experienced same-sex marriage. We moved to California after Syd got a fantastic offer to work with one of their Senators. I retired early, working part-time at a local college, teaching law enforcement classes. Ruth and Keaton were cremated and brought with us. We mixed their ashes into the soil of a tree we planted at our new home. We now have Summitt and Swift.

We miss North Carolina but love being closer to Syd's brother and sister. We now have nieces and nephews to experience life with—something we never imagined. Life has taken many turns, but surrounding ourselves with good people has made the journey much sweeter.

www.ingramcontent.com/pod-product-compliance
Ingram Content Group UK Ltd.
Pitfield, Milton Keynes, MK11 3LW, UK
UKHW042119050225
454690UK00017B/137/J